A burning fire was created between the two of them, locked in each other's arms. For blissful moments while her mind spun in dreamy colors, Monica enjoyed the sensual ravishing of her mouth. Cord's tongue slowly explored the sweet recesses until she felt she would faint. She was molded against the lean length of him, and one of his hands cupped her breast.

With a tremendous effort she pulled away. "Cord, please, don't do this," Monica pleaded, her hands nevertheless clutching at his shoulders.

"Why not?" he mumbled in a husky voice against the pulse in her neck. Monica could barely think, could barely talk coherently. "I want to make love to you, Monica...."

## ABOUT THE AUTHOR

Sandra Kitt is a librarian for a major museum in New York City, where she and her husband currently reside. Aside from her writing, Sandra also is a free-lance graphic designer and has several pieces used as greeting cards for UNICEF.

# Rites of
# Spring

## SANDRA KITT

## *Harlequin Books*

TORONTO • NEW YORK • LONDON
AMSTERDAM • PARIS • SYDNEY • HAMBURG
STOCKHOLM • ATHENS • TOKYO • MILAN

Published February 1984

First printing December 1983

ISBN 0-373-16043-7

# Chapter One

There was a clap of hands that echoed in the large open room.

"Okay. That's it for today," the voice intoned, as a multitude of sighs and moans escaped a scattered group of people. There was the sound of soft suede, conditioned into a hard surface, tapping gently against the wooden boards of the floor, as eight bodies with firm well developed muscles gathered towels and totes and sweaters and boots and headed for the locker room.

Monica Hamlin stood at the barre in front of a mirror that ran the length of the room, slowly controlling the exhausted breaths of air leaving her lungs. Her long rich auburn hair was pinned into a sleek coil at the back of her head, and a scarf tied around her hairline over her ears stopped the perspiration from running down her face. Nonetheless, her heart-shaped face and the long slender column of her neck and collarbone were shiny with moisture.

Monica gripped the barre she held on to, and clenched her teeth in sudden pain, fighting the urge to cry out in its intensity.

"Monica, dear, are you all right?" the voice approached her from across the room. She took a gulp of air and stood up straight to her full five feet seven inches. She faced the master and smiled wanly, still unable to talk.

Monsieur Denier minced over in a turned-out position shaking his head regrettably.

"My dear, my dear! You cannot do this thing to your body!" he lamented in his French accent. "Discipline and control are everything! We can push our bodies to the limit and sometimes beyond. But no, no, my dear, we can't abuse it!"

"I know Monsieur Denier." Monica finally got out. "I just thought... I'd hoped it was just a one time thing."

"Monica! If the esteemed doctor who is a specialist in these things says no, you cannot move the body this way, then you must not!"

She walked long legged to the wall to retrieve a hand towel and mopped her neck, face, and throat. "He could be wrong. Anyway, I'm to see another specialist this afternoon. Maybe—"

"Maybe's will not do! Is it not better to follow the doctor's advice? Take eighteen months off from the troupe. No touring or performing. No stress on the system."

Monica groaned. "Monsieur! A year and a half... almost two! Do you have any idea what that could mean to my career? My body?"

"That is precisely what I am thinking about—your body! Is it worth risking serious injury because you cannot bear to take the time to see if the joint will improve? You could dance another five years. Or you could end it all, forever, within the next few months!" He lectured her as though she were a disobedient child, and Monica hung her head, chastised.

The considerations were not just her body and her career. Yes, they were very important to her. They were everything to her. But she also needed the money from working.

"Now," Monsieur Denier continued, wagging an indulgent finger under her nose, "you be a good girl, Monica, and do what the doctor tells you!" He tapped her cheek affectionately and turned back to the open studio to have a word with the piano player.

Monica headed toward the lockers. By the time she'd finished dressing and recoiled her hair she was the only one left on the floor. She took a quick look through her appointment book and checked the address for Dr. Jerome Bender, a prominent chiropractor. With her oversize tote on her shoulder, Monica wandered to the fountain in front of the New York State Theatre of Lincoln Center. She walked erect, as all dancers did, controlled by some center line pulling up straight in their bodies that kept their hips forward and feet turned out. They all had an aura of grace that made them instantly recognizable. The women, reed slender, without breasts or hips, small faces and long necks and arms. The men, not usually much taller, but much more muscular in the legs and thighs, sinew standing out cordlike to give beautiful form and a show of strength.

Monica sat on the cement ledge of the fountain in the late morning gloom of an April day. There was a fair brisk spring wind, which she didn't seem to notice chilling her body as she sat deep in thought. She saw the people who were performers and dancers such as herself as they left or arrived for classes or rehearsals.

She was like one of them, but not of them. She was taller than the average female dancer, for one thing, making it somewhat hard to partner her. On pointe, she was almost six feet tall. She'd had to work harder to conform her body to that of a dancer, and she'd started late. But she was a dancer. It was all she really knew. It had sustained her and given purpose to twenty of her twenty-seven years. And now it was all threatened.

Wrapping her voluminous scarf and sweater around

her thin body she headed toward the box office of the State Theatre to get a pass for the evening show. When you didn't dance, or practiced for it, you watched it. Still, watching was better than nothing.

After having purchased a ticket, Monica proceeded to the doctor, now anxious for the tests she must take, and the X rays.

Nearly two hours later, Monica dressed for the third time that day and came back to sit in the comfortable chair in the doctor's office.

Doctor Bender placed the six X ray sheets on a wall display box lit from behind. He studied them silently for several minutes while Monica watched his face for any changing expression. He leaned back in his chair, and swung around to the open folder on the desk to read for several more minutes.

"I hear Cynthia Gregory is superb in *Giselle*," he mumbled, finally breaking the awesome silence as he began to scribble notes.

"Yes, so I've heard. I haven't seen it yet this season, but she's superb in everything!"

"Do I detect a touch of envy?" Dr. Bender asked, still not looking up.

"No, not really. But admiration, yes!"

He put his pen down on the desk and sighed, sitting back once more. "Have you ever danced *Giselle*?"

The fact that he avoided eye contact with her made Monica nervous. "No. I haven't ever performed it. But I have understudied."

"Umm. I've seen the Royal Ballet in London perform that. So charming. Of course, they see it—"

"Dr. B!" Monica's voice pleaded. She wanted an end to the polite professional chatter. She wanted an answer, a diagnosis, and an end to the wondering.

Dr. Jerome Bender, a balding, robust man in his sixties, considered the attractive woman in front of him over the top of his half-framed glasses. He loved his job, loved working with the scores of dancers, and athletes who frequently came to him with complaints of their misused bodies. It was always a wonder to him what the human body could endure, constantly tested as it was by these vigorous people. And he hated telling them the reality, when they came to him hurt and mangled, that their bodies had definite limitations. Most often, it was not a serious affliction, but almost invariably it was the end of a career.

"Monica," he began, "why are you a dancer?"

She looked at him blankly. "Why? Because...because it's what I do best. What I've worked long and hard for."

"Have you ever given any thought to the time when you can't dance anymore?"

He was frightening her. She was sure he didn't mean to. Still she was suddenly very alert. "I don't know." She shrugged. "Not really. I mean, we all say we'll teach the next generation of Joffrey hopefuls, or maybe choreograph—I've often thought of that. Dr. B, are you...are you saying—"

"No, no! I'm not saying anything. Just asking. Genuine curiosity, I assure you. I ask my tennis pros and my football players the same thing. Funny, no one ever asks a doctor what he'll do when he can't practice anymore!"

Monica smiled nervously. Dr. Bender leaned across his desk and clasped his hands together, eyeing her seriously.

"Dancers are so beautiful! They give so much visual pleasure to the people who watch them perform. All the while, rather gracefully, hiding all the pain they are in in order to perform. You can be a teacher or doctor or cab driver until you're sixty-five if you choose. Dancers don't have that option."

Monica winced at the implications. "Are you saying that—"

"What I'm saying, my dear, is that I hope you are prepared, at least in thought, for the time when you can no longer dance. It's never too early to think about it."

He abruptly ended his tête-à-tête with Monica and turned to the X rays on the wall once more. He pointed a finger to the second and third ones.

"According to these, you should never have been a dancer!"

"What—what do you mean?" Monica barely whispered.

"Your body isn't really structured for it. You know yourself not everyone is built to dance ballet. The dance form itself is unnatural. Who in the world ever heard of twirling around on the tips of your toes! Ridiculous!"

Dr. Bender switched off the box lights and, taking off his glasses, got up to walk to a different wall chart. He began a simple lecture to her about hips and pelvic joints, explaining the differences in body builds, why some people will be wider or narrower, why some people are all hip bones and others are smooth and round.

"You have a kind of structure that has been forced into the ballet stance of hips forward, pelvis straight, and then of course, the legs and feet turned out. You're putting too much unnatural stress on the sockets and joints."

"Do I have to give up dance?" was all Monica wanted to know.

"For now, yes," he said, no longer procrastinating. "The condition is not severe yet. And you're lucky in that it's done no damage to the pelvic bone or cavity."

Monica let out a sigh of despair. The doctor, seeing her lovely posture give way so that she seemed to collapse into her chair, suddenly came around to the front of his desk and took her hand and patted it comfortingly.

"It's not as bad as you think, Monica. All is not lost, as they say. I recommend that you not dance for a time. Say... a year or so. Rest the body. If you wish to continue with your daily classes, that's fine. But there are certain things you should not do. I'll give you a list."

Monica looked up at him through a blur of tears she was not able to avoid. "What happens after the year is over?"

"Well, then you try your complete repertoire of exercises and steps. We'll take some more X rays and see how you look. If all goes well, you could dance for another five, maybe eight years! You probably wouldn't want to go much beyond that anyway."

"What—what if after a year nothing has improved?"

Dr. Bender frowned and pursed his lips together. He went back to his chair, sat down, and picked up his pen to continue his notes.

"Well, then," he said as he wrote, "I can think of at least four Joffrey hopefuls for your dance class!"

# Chapter Two

"Hello, Chicken! How are you?"

"Oh, Niki. You promised you wouldn't call me that anymore!"

"I never promised that at all. I said I wouldn't call you that in front of friends. Especially if one's a male!"

The petulant voice on the other end of the line groaned. "I'm too old for baby names!"

"You're never too old for names of love. What's new? How's Mother?" Monica asked.

"Oh, you know Mother. She's on another diet and is seeing a producer. I don't like him very much. He treats me like I'm in the way all the time."

Monica stiffened at this information from her stepsister. "Well, it sounds as though nothing has changed."

"No, not much. Niki, can't I come to you in New York? Aren't I old enough to leave home, yet?"

"At fifteen? No!"

"Monica—"

"In another year and a half you'll be finished with high school."

"I don't care about high school! I want to go to the academy! I want to study dance like you!"

"No, not like me," Monica corrected. "I was never good enough for the academy. But you will be."

"Yeah. But how do I get there?" The voice was pettish again.

Monica chewed her bottom lip and frowned. If she had been able to perform and tour this summer, she could have afforded it. That plus the scholarship Lee was sure to win would have been enough to see her through the three-year program. It would have been tight.

Now Monica knew she'd have to come up with another idea.

"You let me worry about how you'll get there, Chicken. You just practice like hell for those auditions. How are the classes going?"

"Pretty good. They've put me into another advanced toe class."

"That's great, Lee! I guess you must be doing something right."

"Dance is the only thing I can do right!"

That sounded so familiar, Monica thought, she might have been listening to her own voice twelve or thirteen years ago.

"That's not true, love. You do lots of things right."

"Oh, Niki. I miss you so. When are you coming to visit? Will I see you before the auditions? Where are you touring this summer?"

"Not so fast!" Monica chuckled. "I don't think I'll make it to the west coast soon. If we're going to send you off to the academy, I have to earn money, so I have to stay put."

"We're not sure I'll make it yet. I'd be very happy to study in New York," Lee hinted broadly.

"You'll make it. And the minute you start to dance for the judges, they'll know it too!"

Lee Ann sighed over the long distance line. "I really wish you were here. Mother is so—so—"

"Mother is just a perfectionist. That's why she pushes you so hard."

"But she doesn't see, she doesn't understand. I need...I need..." Lee floundered, trying to put her frustration into words. Monica knew what she needed. It was all so familiar. But once Lee got to the academy, it wouldn't matter. And what she missed from home wouldn't seem so important anymore. In the meantime Monica couldn't let her be discouraged.

"Yes, Lee Ann. I know. Believe me. But you're growing up fast. Pretty soon you'll be living your own life."

"But, Niki, growing up takes so long!"

"I know. Everything worthwhile does. Look, Chicken, I've got to go. This call is eating into your trip money. I just wanted to see how you were."

"I love you, Niki."

"I love you too. I'll call you just before your audition. Tell Mother...tell her I said hello. Bye."

Monica sat for long moments after hanging up the phone. Old emotions and memories were always stirred up each time she was in touch with home, but she called because of her love and concern for her stepsister. Lee Ann was the only thing, the only person, that legitimated her connection to the West Coast and home.

Monica Hamlin had no image at all of her natural mother, save the ones her father had shown her throughout her childhood, of a sweet-faced woman with reddish hair and green eyes. To Monica she was a stranger, having been almost four when her mother had died, leaving her with a father too devastated by his loss to have much time or attention for her. He saw to her physical needs, but it seemed beyond him to meet her emotional needs.

When Monica was seven, her father met and married a petite beautiful woman who was a dancer. Eileen filled her father's needs for a wife and companion more than she did Monica's for a mother. Eileen had danced to an adoring following in San Francisco and purred under the love and attention of her husband. She took and accepted much, but gave almost nothing in return.

At seven, Monica was very withdrawn and shy. Eileen decided at once that the cure for that was to study dance, to become involved with something that required discipline and attention and hard work. Monica's father was very grateful for Eileen's attention to the little girl he didn't know what to do with. For Eileen, it was a way of having Monica away and not underfoot all the time.

For Monica, it was a lifeline. She soaked up the dance and the music and the atmosphere like a sponge. She'd slip into another world until the classes were over and it was time to go back home. Monica was the tallest student in any of her classes, always causing the mistress of the studio to tisk and lament on her unfashionable height. She also had more of a feminine figure and had to starve herself into the required look of little flesh on slender bones. But when she had attended her first real ballet performance, she was lost.

Her stepmother, Eileen, suffered a serious injury when Monica was almost eleven, ending her short but successful dance career. Eileen quickly and reluctantly found herself pregnant, and gave birth eventually to Lee Ann. If Monica hoped that a child of her stepmother's very own would soften her selfish, hard edges, she was wrong. The novelty and charm of being a mother wore off rapidly as Eileen struggled frantically to pull her petite frame back to the slender shape she'd had before. At twelve years old, Monica was left to be mother, sister and father to the infant Lee. And this had been her second lifeline, for all the love and emotions and care she so desperately lacked was given to and received from her stepsister.

Monica had never experienced a warm, loving household. Having children was, apparently, something you did as married people. Giving birth was just another body function. She and Lee were probably born out of needs to satisfy an urging, and probably neglected for the same reasons.

Lee Ann was introduced to dance at the age of four, trudging along on plump legs behind her older sister. By the time she was six, it was suspected that here was a natural ballet talent. The only thing Eileen had done for either of her two daughters was to push them in the pursuit of dance. They were both oddly grateful to her for at least that.

Monica sighed deeply and stretched her body. She had to prepare for her afternoon class. She got up and left the privacy of her bedroom, in an apartment she shared with another dancer.

Donna Connors did Broadway musicals, and therefore had a very different schedule and classes than Monica. They'd met in dance class Monica's second year in New York. They had not been tremendous friends, but they got along very well together.

It was the perfect arrangement, for it gave them an apartment overlooking Central Park West they each would not have been able to afford alone.

In the living room, for the first time, Monica saw the note lying half under the base of a fruit bowl on the dining room table. It was from Donna, telling Monica she'd heard of a job opportunity for a period of a year or so that could mean a lot of money. Knowing that Monica would not be able to dance, she thought it would be a good idea to check out the information. She would explain it all that evening.

Monica raised her brows pleased and surprised. Certainly if she could get a part time job that wasn't too unbearable, the next year might not be so bad. Humming to herself she prepared for class.

"I don't know, Donna. It just sounds so strange. Why would he need to see my birth certificate? Or need a record of my health for the last five years? What kind of guinea pig am I going to be?"

"Well, who's to say whether you'll be chosen for a guinea pig? And I honestly don't know any more than what I've told you."

"But who is this person? What does he do?"

Donna sighed, rolling her eyes heavenward. They'd been through this twice already. She began to pull absently on the curls of her short Afro, feeling the hair spring tightly back into place. "I don't know who he is. The man who's the lawyer for my show happened to say a few words to some of the women. If you're interested, I'll give you the name of the lawyer and his number. Then you can call and badger him for more information!"

Monica looked at her roommate, stricken. "Oh, Donna, I'm sorry! I didn't mean to give you the third degree. But it's so mysterious!"

"Well, the lawyer said it could mean a lot of money. Just because you call him for the details doesn't necessarily obligate you. You can always say no and walk away."

"That's true," Monica said, still unsure.

"Or maybe you have some better offer?"

"You know I don't. I don't even know how to begin to look for other work. All I know is dance!"

"I know," Donna said with real sympathy. She was a tall and shapely black woman with a cheerful presence. She moved with so much grace, more than that, self-assurance, that she sometimes made Monica feel like a giraffe. Right now, she was more than grateful to Donna herself for remembering that she needed a job.

"I think what I would do," Donna continued, "is to at least hear what the man had to say. Then it's up to you! Simple!"

Monica gnawed on her lip, peeling the skin off with her teeth. She sat in an armchair and hugged a pillow close to her middle, as though it gave her strength and comfort. "Okay..." she said with real hesitation.

"Good! Now just wait a minute and I'll get the number."

Donna returned, giving her the information, and discreetly left Monica alone to make the call.

A rather abrupt secretary answered the phone and asked Monica why she was calling.

"I—I had some information about a job..."

"Well, I'm his secretary, and there's no job that I know of."

"I believe Mr. Jacobs is acting on someone else's behalf."

There was a moment's silence. "I'll connect you to his line," she said, and the line went momentarily dead. Another abrupt voice got on the line. Monica began again.

"I'm calling about a job. I understand—"

"How did you hear about the proposition?" he interrupted tersely.

"Well, my roommate is one of the dancers in the show that you represent."

"Oh, yes. I see. And what's your name?"

"Monica. Monica Hamlin."

There was a scratching of a pencil, and a page being turned. "Well, Miss Hamlin, the first available date when you can be interviewed will be in three days. Kindly bring your birth certificate and medical records

for the last few years, or some sort of certificate of
health."

"Can you give me some information as to the nature
of this job?"

"No, I'm afraid not. I'm only authorized to make the
appointments. You'll be meeting with another lawyer
who'll give you all the details."

"But couldn't you just—"

"Sorry. I can't."

Monica was uncertain again.

"Miss Hamlin, if you're not sure about this there's
no need—"

"Oh, no! I want to find out more—"

"Then you'll keep the appointment?"

"Yes. I'll be there."

"Fine." He gave her a hotel address and a suite
number and a time to appear.

"Well?" asked Donna from the doorway. Monica
turned to look at her roommate.

"I have an appointment in a few days to be interviewed."

"Great!" Donna exclaimed. Monica smiled but still
felt uneasy deep down inside.

Monica had never been to the New York Hilton Hotel.
The front door this sunny April day was manned by
two liveried men with white gloves and whistles. A
shrill sound constantly pierced the air as the shiny instruments were used to summon cabs for waiting visitors.

With a knot of tension working in her stomach,
Monica entered and approached the information desk.
She wanted to check whether or not her appointment
was indeed registered at the hotel. The desk clerk eyed
her suspiciously, thinking the obvious: that an attractive woman like her was here for an assignation. Re-

sentment filled Monica, but she merely raised her chin stubbornly and waited for the records to be checked.

"I'm sorry," the clerk returned. "Our records do not show a registration for a person by that name."

"But I have an appointment to see him. I was told to go to suite four thirteen."

The clerk began to check another ledger. "I show a Mr. Cortland Temple registered for that room. Are you certain you have the right name?" he asked her, doubting her intentions further.

"I only have the one name. Look, could you please call this room for me?"

The clerk dialed a number, and after only a moment he began to speak.

"Ah, sorry to trouble you, Mr. Temple. There's a young woman who says she has an appointment to meet a Mr. Gordon in your suite.... Oh! Yes, yes, of course. I'll have her come right up. Good-bye." He hung up and had the grace to look embarrassed for his earlier thoughts as he directed her to a bank of elevators. The ride up was quicker than Monica expected and when the doors opened, she momentarily stared at the flowered corridor wall. She stepped onto a narrow hallway, going off in either direction for quite a distance. She stood in indecision, wondering which way to go when a voice to her left called her name. Monica turned around to find a middle-aged man leaning half out of a door beckoning to her. Moving cautiously, she approached the door.

"Are you Miss Hamlin?" He smiled, putting out a hand to shake hers.

"Yes, I am."

"Nice to meet you. I'm Lawrence Gordon. Please come in!"

Monica stepped past him into a huge sitting room, tastefully decorated with two very long sofas, armchairs, a large desk, and a picture window behind the desk running the width and length of the wall. Monica heard the door close behind her and turned back to face Lawrence Gordon. He was a kindly looking man of average height, a bit overweight, dressed conservatively in a dark gray business suit. He was bald, with just a fringe of hair at the back of his head. Monica guessed him to be about sixty years of age. His glasses were perched on his forehead, and he pulled habitually on his gray neatly trimmed mustache.

"Have a seat! Have a seat!" he urged Monica forward, further into the room. "I know you're anxious to hear what this is all about."

Monica allowed herself to be led to an armchair and gently seated.

"Can I offer you something to drink? Coffee...a cocktail?"

"Nothing, thank you." Monica smiled fleetingly, sitting on the edge of her chair. Mr. Gordon sat in an armchair across from her and crossed his legs. He let out a sigh and pulled again on his mustache. He quickly looked Monica over, assessing her.

"Well, why don't we start by you telling me a little about yourself. What you do, where you're from."

"I've lived in New York for almost seven years. I'm originally from California—" She hesitated, not really knowing what to tell him. "Both my natural parents are dead, but I do have a stepmother and sister still on the west coast."

"Are you close to your family?" Lawrence Gordon interrupted. Monica was surprised by the question. She decided to be honest.

"Not particularly. At least, not with my stepmother. I'm very close to my stepsister."

"I see. Please continue."

"I'm a dancer."

"Are you really? How exciting! Have I seen you in anything?" His obvious surprise caused Monica to smile.

"Perhaps. I'm with the New York Corp de Ballet."

"Yes! Yes, of course. I wouldn't know you specifically, but they are a very good troupe!"

"Thank you."

"Are you performing now?"

"No," Monica answered bluntly. "I've been advised by my doctor not to dance for a while, to try and correct a—a condition that I have."

"Oh, a physical disability," he said mysteriously, sounding disappointed.

"Not a disability. If it's not corrected it just means I can't dance anymore. That's all." *That's all!* Monica wanted to scream. *That's everything!*

"Ah," Mr. Gordon said, satisfied with the answer. "So of course you must find, ah, some other kind of work. True?"

"Yes. That's why I'm here."

He uncrossed his legs and cleared his throat. "Yes. I suppose you do want to know about the, ah, the job." He got up and went around to the desk. He put his glasses on and sat down, opening a folder.

"I represent a gentleman, who for the moment will remain anonymous, who wants to put forth a—a business arrangement, to last for a period of twelve to sixteen months. It would provide the, ah, the settlement, or salary"—he smiled at her quickly and returned his gaze to the folder—"of fifty thousand dollars—"

Monica's eyes widened in astonishment at the sum. Mr. Gordon was reading on, unaware of her reaction.

"Mr. Gordon. I'm sorry to interrupt, but you did say fifty thousand—"

"Dollars. Yes, indeed I did."

"But that's a lot of money!"

"Yes, it is. Of course, all expenses and personal needs will be taken care of above and beyond that."

"For what?" Monica asked, no longer able to wait for Mr. Gordon to follow his own line of delivery. He stared at her for quite a long time. Then taking off his glasses and folding his hands in front of him, he responded seriously without his previous jovial demeanor.

"For having a baby."

Monica stared. He couldn't possibly have said that. She heard a short laugh escape her, but Mr. Gordon's eyes never left her face, and he never changed expression.

"For..." Monica prompted, wanting to hear him repeat his words.

He nodded. "... having a baby." A long breath came out of her as she sat back heavily in her chair.

Mr. Gordon cleared his throat once again and put his glasses on.

"Perhaps I should give you a bit of information about my client. It may help you understand why he would propose such a thing." Mr. Gordon sat back in his desk chair and clasped his hands over his ample middle.

"He's a businessman of some talent and standing. He's single and forty years old. He's without, ah, any attachments." Gordon hesitated as though to say more on that, but changed his mind and continued. "He has amassed a bit of an estate—money, stocks, property— that he'd like to leave to an, ah, an heir. He loves children and would dearly love to have one of his own.

"A conventional marriage would not suit his needs, and there are personal reasons why he does not wish a permanent on-going relationship. He's ruled out the question of adoption, although he has considered it seriously. I think... I feel it's a very personal need to satisfy his ego."

Monica stiffened. Another person not giving particular thought to the result of his ego gratification. She began to shake her head negatively and to gather her things. "No," she said. "You can't be serious about this."

"I assure you my client is very serious. It may certainly sound cold blooded, but his intentions are very sincere. I've known this man for quite a number of years, and I am sure of this." Again Mr. Gordon hesitated, obviously preparing in his head how much to tell her.

"I know his history and background, and while you may hold this scheme in abhorrence, I can assure you, he is an honorable man. This is why it's to be a business arrangement. A complete contract with terms will be drawn up. Should you decide to continue with this, and I might add should you be accepted, your own lawyer will be expected to be present when the papers are witnessed and signed."

Monica listened, but was still very shaken by the nature of the information. It would be like selling herself. More than that, selling the baby. She said as much to Lawrence Gordon.

"I suppose that's one way of looking at it. But suppose you became pregnant and decided you couldn't or wouldn't keep the baby. You'd put it up for adoption in exchange for having all of your medical expenses covered."

Monica reluctantly saw the similarity. "But, Mr. Gordon, there are options to getting pregnant, and options to giving birth."

"Yes, yes, of course. But if you felt that way you would then leave, or my client would just continue his search if those options were exercised. He's looking for a willing partner in this, not someone who finds herself with an accident on her hands. He wants the baby to be his. He wants to know something, in advance, about the woman who'll bear his child. That in itself is not unreasonable."

Monica let out a sigh. They were just looking for an attractive someone to carry a baby for nine months and then willingly turn the child over to the father.

"If you have no particular thoughts about motherhood or raising children, then it becomes just a job. Unusual, true, but any other kind of job would also be using you and paying you for that use." Lawrence Gordon saw the doubt in her face, but she was listening. He found himself wanting, inexplicably, this young woman to understand the case presented.

"Take yourself. Think of all the years and pain of classes and training you willing subjected yourself to to prepare for someone else who would use your body to an end and pay you. You do that freely."

"But you're talking about a child, Mr. Gordon."

"Do you hope to be a mother someday, Miss Hamlin?" He switched tactics suddenly. Perhaps getting more personal would help. Monica thought sadly of her own parents and her own childhood of loneliness and solitude.

"Not especially," she answered softly, not looking at him.

"And you have no objections to someone who dearly wants a child and obviously can't have one to do so...with help?"

"No," she said reluctantly.

"Well, then, we're only asking you to help achieve that end. We wish to use your body. In exchange, a fee will be paid you."

Monica was silent, again twisting the handle of her totebag in her nervous hands.

"Perhaps it would help if I tell you that my client will go through a marriage ceremony as part of the legal agreement, to be terminated at the end of the contract. This way you at least have the protection of a name and a husband, so to speak. It will simply end as a no-contest divorce!''

Monica's head came up. ''But what if the woman refuses the divorce? Or changes her mind about the baby? What legal grounds do you have to stand on?''

''All of this has been carefully thought of. There's a provision for all possibilities in the contract.''

''But is it legal?''

Mr. Gordon shifted again. ''It's been carefully worked out to be legal.''

Monica could not help but be impressed with how much consideration had apparently gone into this proposal. She looked thoughtfully at Lawrence Gordon. ''Your client must want a natural child very badly.''

''He does.''

''I don't know, Mr. Gordon. I just don't know!''

He chuckled in appreciation. ''Believe me, Miss Hamlin. Your position is well taken. And I fully understand your hesitation. But you would be taken care of.''

''Do you mind my asking how your other candidates have responded to the proposal?''

''Not at all. It's been pretty broad—from eagerness to comply to absolute disbelief.''

Monica shook her head. ''It's—it's just that I—''

At that moment a door opened behind Monica and closed again. Mr. Gordon stood up and smiled. Monica stopped talking and turned her head to look over her shoulder at the person entering the room. It was a man, whose mere physical presence seemed to shrink the size of the room. He was very tall, at least six foot three, and seemed to be all shoulders and long solidly shaped legs.

Monica was aware of raw, animal strength and virility. She drew in a deep breath. Monica knew beyond a doubt that this was Lawrence Gordon's client.

She stood up from her chair as he moved more into the room. His eyes were on Mr. Gordon, but Monica saw that they were oddly light and clear in color. He had a strong athletic build. Monica noticed two other distinctive things about this man. First, his thick slightly curly hair was almost all iron-gray, but his eyebrows and the tight curl of hair on his chest at the opening of his shirt were black. The second thing she saw was the hard, controlled cast to his features. There was not an ounce of softness in this man. Monica lowered her eyes to the floor. She wondered how he could ever unbend enough to show love and affection to a child dependent on him for those needs.

Lawrence Gordon came forward to shake the giant's hand, and Monica looked up enough to see how large and beautifully shaped the hand was. Gordon made the introductions.

"How do you do, Miss Hamlin," Cortland Temple acknowledged in an incredibly deep voice, but his facial features did not change at all. Yet Monica had the impression that his eyes took in every detail of her appearance. She raised her chin almost defiantly. He shook her hand and her delicate dancer's palm was lost in his. The grip was firm, but not hard. "Please continue." He waved a careless hand to Mr. Gordon, who retook his seat.

Gordon cleared his throat and pulled on his mustache again. "Now, where were we?"

"You were still trying to convince me that this isn't all crazy," Monica supplied, trying to ignore the presence behind her.

Mr. Gordon laughed. "But it is all very serious!"

"Do you really expect to find someone to go along with these plans?"

Lawrence Gordon stole a quick look at the other

man. "Some interest has been expressed. You're not the first person or the last to be interviewed. Are you trying to tell me, Miss Hamlin, that you could not consider such a scheme?"

Monica frowned and thought of her options. There weren't any. And she remembered that the money was not needed for herself. If it were, she'd certainly manage some other way.

There was a lengthy silence while Monica ran myriad thoughts through her head, trying to decide if this was really such an awful arrangement.

"I don't know, Mr. Gordon. I'm just not sure."

"Would you mind if I asked a few questions, Mr. Gordon? Miss Hamlin?" came the voice behind her. Monica said nothing as Cortland came to sit on the edge of the desk facing her. He crossed his long arms over his chest. "Do you find the arrangement distasteful, Miss Hamlin?" he questioned in his deep voice. It was quiet, but controlled. Monica met his icy gaze and refused to be intimidated. She lifted her chin and stared back.

"Not distasteful. But certainly of questionable taste!"

"Have you never heard of this sort of thing before?"

"Not exactly. I'm aware that there's always been a black market in babies. It's not that hard to arrange, although shady."

"Exactly. But we're not proposing to be clandestine about this. We're proposing an up-front, above-board business deal."

Before Monica could respond he asked to see her birth certificate and health records. She hesitated, but Cortland reached to take the documents from her. As he stood to go back by the light of the window he asked, "Is there any insanity or mental illness in your family?"

"Yes!" Monica responded at once, causing the two men to quickly look at her. "Me!" she said caustically.

Cortland Temple said nothing, but Mr. Gordon allowed himself a small smile.

"Why do you have to stop your dancing, Miss Hamlin?" she was asked.

"I—I have a hip disorder associated with dancers. There's no help for it except rest. I'm not supposed to dance for a year and a half."

"And then?"

She shrugged. "And then we'll see. Either the ailment will be improved, or it won't." She looked at him directly. Perhaps he read in her eyes how hard it was to just speculate on the future, because he didn't ask her what happened after that. Cortland seemed to sense what a sensitive, still undealt with question the future was.

He handed the papers back to Monica. "Have you any particular gynecological problems?"

Monica blushed pink. "No, none," she answered.

He nodded to Mr. Gordon and moved in the direction of the door. "Okay, Lawrence," he said, as if giving approval.

"Just a moment," Monica said, stopping them both. She lifted her chin. "I'd like to see *your* medical records!"

Gordon raised his brows and covered his reaction in a discreet cough. Cortland Temple frowned and a muscle tensed in his jaw, but he walked back to the desk and searched for another folder. He passed it to Monica. He sat again on the edge of the desk while she looked it over, feeling both sets of eyes on her. Monica had no desire to read the folder, but she felt the need to exercise some consciousness of her own.

She made quick note of the fact that other than a broken arm at thirteen, Cortland Temple was in excellent health. Monica fingered the folder for a moment, another thought occurring to her. She looked first at Lawrence Gordon, who was in turn intent on her every move. Cortland Temple, on the other hand, showed barely suppressed impatience.

"You don't have to do this," Monica said finally to Cortland. He tilted his head just enough to indicate she was to go on. "I mean, you could just go to a sperm bank. That's a perfectly accepted way of finding a surrogate mother."

A muscle jerked in his jaw.

"If all you want is the child and you're indifferent as to who carries it—"

"Not indifferent, Miss Hamlin. After all, biologically the child will be half hers," he said, raising his brows at the phantom woman who was to take part in his scheme. "I want to know who she is."

Lawrence Gordon came forward then, clearing his throat for attention and fingering his mustache. "Ah, also there is the other fact that women generally go to sperm banks to be injected because they want the baby themselves. It's very unlikely that Mr. Temple will find a satisfactory partner in that way."

Cortland turned back to Monica. There began a small sardonic lift to the corner of his mouth that could not exactly be described as a smile. "And besides, I want the personal contact with the mother of the child..."

Monica closed the folder abruptly and felt the heat of further embarrassment tinge her cheeks.

"... to insure the parenting," Cortland finished, holding out his hand for the folder. Monica passed it to him, avoiding his eyes.

"Does it meet with your approval, Miss Hamlin?" he asked sarcastically. Monica only nodded. "I'm so glad," he said in the same tone. He continued his movements to the door. "You can finish, Mr. Gordon. I have a business appointment to keep. Nice to have met you, Miss Hamlin." The door closed behind him.

Monica and Mr. Gordon talked for another half

hour, and Gordon suggested she think about the proposal for a few days. Monica could always call and let them know her decision. Mr. Temple would be in New York for another week.

Monica promised she'd give Cortland's proposal serious thought, and she promised not to talk about it, although she had no idea whom she'd tell.

She left the Hilton feeling overwhelmed, with the image of Cortland Temple fresh in her mind.

For three days Monica battled with the idea until she was dizzy. She lay awake at night debating the moral side, the ethics, the right or wrong. The one factor that finally swayed her, was the pressing need for the money. Feeling anxiety ridden and not able to delay longer, Monica called the number at the Hilton and told Cortland Temple she wished to be considered in his plan. He turned the phone over to Lawrence Gordon rather brusquely, who told her Mr. Temple had some business matters to see to and would have to make a decision soon. He promised to let her know as soon as possible. Monica thanked him and hung up.

In the mail that afternoon was a letter from her stepsister informing Monica of Lee's audition date for her presentation to representatives of the Royal Ballet, London, England. It was in three weeks. Monica exclaimed in sudden alarm and sat down heavily in a chair. The time was closing in. She had to get the job now. She paced the floor, wondering what she would do if Cortland Temple did not choose her. She knew no one from whom she could borrow that kind of money, and it was too late to consider or attempt a bank loan. Besides, she had nothing to use as collateral.

It was four thirty the following afternoon when the call came through. Mr. Gordon's jovial voice informed her that Cortland Temple would like to enter into a

business agreement with her and would like to meet
with her and an attorney as soon as possible to draw up
the contract and necessary papers.

Monica agreed somewhat breathlessly to all the arrangements. She got off the phone feeling as though
she'd been swept through the center of a storm. She
had not yet begun to consider the extent of things to be
seen to before the deal was started. She got in touch
with the lawyer and gave him the meeting date.

On the appointed day, Monica took extra care of her
appearance. She decided on a lightweight spring suit
and heels. She met her lawyer in front of the hotel and
together they proceeded to suite four thirteen. It was
Cortland Temple who answered the knock on the door
and, nodding hello, led Monica to a chair drawn up
around the low coffee table.

Lawrence Gordon was busy shuffling papers and
looked up only long enough to smile at Monica's presence. Cortland Temple wasted no time.

"Gentlemen, Miss Hamlin, there's quite a bit to
cover before we actually sign the papers so I suggest we
begin at once. I've arranged for us to have lunch here
should these proceedings run past noon." Nodding to
Mr. Gordon to continue, he took a seat almost directly
opposite Monica, which she found very disconcerting.
Once or twice she found his gray eyes fixed on her in
open observation. Monica had to admit to herself that
he chose and wore clothes well. She could not avoid
looking in his direction and confirmed today her earlier
impression of a strong face with a square jaw and wide
full mouth. It was rather grimly closed at the moment,
and she wondered how his face would change if he
smiled. He chose that moment to look at her directly
and her gaze shifted guiltily.

If Monica's lawyer was surprised at the proposal, he

was composed and professional enough to hide it. But when he was given a copy of the contract to go over, a low whistle escaped him as he read the terms. He drew Monica aside to ask if she understood what the deal was about. He also asked her if she wanted time to reconsider. Monica looked at Cortland Temple's taut body, thought of her sister, and knew there was no time left.

She assured him it was what she wanted to do. That left only details to be worked out. An account would be opened in Monica's name with one thousand dollars. An additional ten thousand would be added when she became pregnant. At the mention of her expected condition the men visibly squirmed, except for Cortland, who merely looked briefly at Monica and allowed a muscle to twitch in his jaw.

Fourteen thousand would be added at the baby's birth, and the rest when the contract was terminated. As was also agreed to previously, they would go through a civil wedding ceremony for the sake of appearances. That was scheduled for a week's time. Monica was told to bring one witness. She was then told she could continue living, basically, her own life in her own apartment if she wished, so long as Cortland Temple could keep tabs on her condition and progress.

Thankfully, no one mentioned when or where the consummation of the marriage would take place, but suddenly it was the foremost thing on Monica's mind.

While the two lawyers continued to talk and room service prepared to serve lunch, Monica wandered over to the window overlooking Manhattan. She watched fascinated as thousands of people scurried below her, going about their day-to-day lives. She wondered absently how many of them had ever embarked on schemes such as the one she was agreeing to.

"Having second thoughts, Miss Hamlin?" Monica

turned at the deep voice behind her and looked up into the face of Cortland Temple. This was the closest she'd been to him and it surprised her to see again what a giant of a man he was. Monica smiled openly at him.

"You must start calling me Monica. We can't be married in a week and have you call me Miss Hamlin!" But he didn't return her smile and continued to stand rigidly in front of her. Monica sighed inwardly and turned back to the window. "No. I haven't changed my mind."

"Is there anything I can supply you with for next week? Perhaps I should give you—"

Monica whirled on him. "No! There's nothing more I need, really. I would think you've done enough already," she added.

"Is that a criticism?"

"Not at all. Merely a fact."

"Would you prefer if it were all different, perhaps?"

Monica again turned to the window. "I think we both would prefer if it could be different," she answered softly. When there was no further comment she knew he'd moved away.

They had lunch and allowed a period to ask and answer last-minute questions. Both lawyers said they'd make themselves available for helping with other problems until after the ceremony a week hence. Finally, the lawyers seemed satisfied. Reams of paper were signed, witnessed, and notarized.

As she was leaving, however, Monica felt compelled to ask one more question. "Mr. Temple, aren't you the least bit curious as to how I'll use the money?"

He quirked a black brow at her and smiled tightly. "My friends call me Cord." Monica flushed. "It must be highly personal for you to enter into such an agreement. I'm sure if you wanted me to know, you would tell me. But I am also not particularly interested in knowing." He then held the door open until she had passed through, saying he would see her in a week at the county clerk's office on Center Street.

Monica moved in a daze. She hoped fervently that Lee Ann wanted to study in London, and that her dance teachers over the last ten years had not misjudged her talents. She hoped she was not making a dreadful mistake.

It was a travesty that the day of Monica's wedding the sun shone brilliantly in a clear blue sky, and it was May first. Somewhere ancient rites were being performed with ribbons and children and songs around a pole in celebration. But for Monica it was just the beginning of a long performance, this time offstage.

She elected to wear a simple ecru silk dress belonging to Donna, since she'd refused to miss any more dance classes in preparation for this farce, as she called it, and had waited until the last moment for everything. The dress had a high button stand-up collar, which only served to emphasize her long graceful neck. The sleeves were sheer and very full to the wrist. Her hair, as always, was neatly but softly twisted into a bun, today more on top of her head than at her neck.

Monica had been forced out of desperation to tell Donna of the arrangement, eliciting from her roommate a gasp of pure surprise. But seeing Monica's chin jutting out stubbornly, Donna declined questioning her about the wisdom of her decision. Donna agreed to act as witness for the civil ceremony because she was curious about the man who could persuade her friend to take on such a chore. She didn't realize at the time that it had nothing to do with the man himself, but Monica's love for her sister.

It was Donna who saw to it that Monica had a small bouquet of flowers to hold. She also offered to make herself scarce from the apartment for Cortland and Monica later that afternoon. And it was Donna who remembered to bring Monica's birth certificate and proof that she'd had the necessary blood tests. Monica gave all the outward appearance of someone in control of the situation. But inside she was numb. If Donna had not been there to nudge her and push her, she might never have shown up at the judge's chambers on Center Street.

As Cortland Temple stood calmly talking to Lawrence Gordon, Monica and Donna slowly approached. At the sound of their footsteps Cortland turned around and carefully appraised the woman, a stranger, who in another half hour would be legally declared his wife. She was very pale but seemed calm and, he had to admit, beautifully dressed. Accompanying Monica was a very attractive black woman, also stylishly dressed, who he assumed to be Monica's witness.

Cortland excused himself to Gordon and faced the two women. On closer examination, Monica seemed to be stiff and aloof when he took her arm to lead her into the judge's chambers. He could feel her tremble. Cord frowned. He hoped she wasn't going to faint.

But she didn't. She went through the entire brief ceremony, if a little glassy eyed, at least with a clear firm voice and her head up. Cord bent to give the traditional kiss but Monica moved her head, and he only just grazed her pale cheek.

Donna quietly congratulated them, but soon escaped, anxious to leave from the tension and awkwardness of the occasion. She kissed Monica on the cheek and promised in a whisper to call her in a few days. Donna wasn't sure Monica had heard her.

Lawrence Gordon suggested getting a drink somewhere. That would allow everyone time to relax and catch their breaths. Monica almost let out a hysterical giggle. She would never be able to relax again. The unusual bridal party got into a cab and headed for Tavern on the Green in Central Park.

Monica sat somewhat crammed in between Gordon and Cord. She was made very aware of Cord's powerfully muscled thigh pressed next to hers. She was so close to him she could have rested her head on his shoulder. She stared straight ahead trying hard not to touch too much of her new husband.

For his part, Cord was at first concerned, but now only mildly amused, by his wife's attitude. He thought if he'd taken that moment to touch her she would have screamed. As it was he couldn't help feeling a bit contemptuous of the fix she'd gotten into, even though the offer had started with him and was serving his ends.

Monica did little talking while they had their drinks, absently peering through the restaurant window to the profusion of spring flowers in its enclosed garden. She responded to the two men only when spoken to. Cord tried not to show his impatience with her, concentrating his attention on the talk with Gordon.

Finally, Lawrence sensed it was time he left the newlyweds alone. The two men rose and shook hands. Mr. Gordon, pulling on his mustache, took Monica's hand in his and squeezed it, smiling in his friendly manner. "Good luck, my dear. I hope this works out for you." Monica smiled weakly, as they both knew there was only one way it was supposed to work out. Cord sat back down and turned to Monica.

"Look, I know it's been a trying afternoon...for both of us," he began in his deep voice. "I think we should have something to eat. Drinks on an empty stomach are not good for you."

Monica nodded gratefully. "I don't really like to drink very much," she volunteered.

"Good!" he responded bracingly and passed her a menu. Monica knew she could never swallow more than a salad right now, and that was all she ordered. Cord ordered soup, stuffed veal, vegetables, and a bottle of wine. He quirked a brow at her, looking at the hollow cheeks. "You're much too thin, you know. You should eat more."

Monica immediately became defensive, her nerves already raw. "Dancers are supposed to be thin."

"But you won't be dancing."

"That's no reason to let my body go!"

"You will gain weight, you know," he said in amusement, causing Monica to go red. The sudden coloring was much better than the pale drawn look she'd had all afternoon.

Monica picked at her salad the way she'd nursed her drink earlier. She was almost revolted that Cord could think of eating so much food under the circumstances. They spoke little during the meal.

"What will you do during the days ahead?" he suddenly asked, sipping at his wine. Monica looked up in surprise, but there was real curiosity in his gray eyes. She couldn't help but notice once again how ruggedly handsome he was. The dark gray suit he wore made his hair look silver.

"I'd—I'd like to keep my apartment, first of all. I thought I'd continue to take my daily classes. The chiropractor for the ballet troupe devised some special exercises for me for my hips. I might try to find classes to teach...." her voice trailed off, and suddenly she felt close to tears.

Cord frowned at her, considering this attractive stranger with burnished hair and so much poise and grace. He saw her as if for the first time as a person. She was very strong, he could see that. And she'd have to be to face the possibility of losing her career. But she was also vulnerable. Despite what he'd said to her a week ago, he was curious as to why she agreed to this arrangement.

"Why don't we leave?" he said softly.

Monica's amber eyes flew wide open to his face. "Where to?" she asked, bewildered.

A grim expression settled on Cord's face. "My hotel . . . your apartment . . ."

"Oh!" she said, realizing how naive she sounded. "My apartment, then." Whatever was going to happen next she didn't want to take place in the impersonal atmosphere of a hotel room.

"Fine. I'll just get the check."

They walked the five block distance to her apartment in silence. Once there, Cord walked casually into the living room and scanned with interest the inexpensively but warmly furnished space.

"It's comfortable here," he commented quietly.

"Thank you."

"Where is your roommate? Donna, was it?"

"Yes, Donna. She . . . she's away for a few days."

"I see." He turned now to face Monica and she was suddenly frightened of his look, of his alert eyes seeing too much, exposing too much. They seemed to have the power to reach right into a person's soul.

Cord slowly walked toward her and Monica's heart began to race. Her eyes never left his. His male presence was very powerful and Monica was acutely aware of him. "Monica," he began with surprising gentleness, but it didn't reach his eyes, "we both know what has to happen."

She nodded as though in a trance and turned to walk into her room. Cord was right behind her, and he closed the bedroom door. With her back toward him and feeling somewhat in a daze, Monica began to unbutton the dress and remove it, placing it on the bench

at the foot of her bed. She could hear Cord silently
removing his own clothes. Quickly he was pulling back
the blanket and climbing into her bed. She didn't want
to be left there, his eyes on her naked back watching
her, but there was only one other place to go.

Cautiously she climbed into the other side of the
bed. It was a peculiar feeling. Monica had never slept
with a man in this bed, in this room. She felt now as
never before that Cord was invading every part of her
life and existence. Her arm and leg touched his and she
found his limbs cool.

Cord reached out a large hand and gently turned her
to face him. She instinctively placed both hands on his
chest as though to brace herself. The thick curly hair on
his broad chest was crisp and springy under her fingers.
Cord drew her slowly against his hard body and she was
shocked at the firm feel of him. Their closeness
trapped her hands between them, her face almost
against his shoulder. Monica remained stiff but Cord
slowly began to stroke her shoulder and slender back.
He pressed her hip and buttocks, pulling the lower part
of her body closer to him. Monica could not help a soft
gasp as she felt him full, aroused and taut against her
middle.

Cord did not kiss her at all. He did not caress to pleasure either her or himself. He only stroked her to relax
her and therefore make it easy to accomplish the act.
His hand was slow beneath her thigh, continually pressing her against him. Monica continued to lie unyielding, practically holding her breath. She could not help
but be aware of him, of the warm air of his breath
against her hair. She began to relax and finally softened
against him. Little eddies, swirling sensations that she
had never felt before, began in her stomach.

Cord carefully rolled Monica onto her back. He was
careful not to let his entire weight settle on her, but he

brought them together, intimately, Monica's arms still caught between them. She concentrated on moving the way he indicated, rhythmically, slowly. Nothing was said and there was very little sound. Cord moved suddenly hard against her. Then he let out a sigh and lifted himself away ending his embrace. Monica felt an odd dizziness and she trembled.

The two of them were silent for quite a long time, so Monica was surprised when Cord turned to her a second time. There were strange, new feelings this time that she was not ready to deal with, and she kept herself removed and aloof. She was just a body, performing a function.

She must have fallen to sleep because the next thing she was aware of was the door opening. She started violently awake, drawing the sheet up to her chin for protection. Cord was standing fully dressed in the doorway against a soft light from the living room.

"I'm going back to the hotel," he said, all gentleness gone from him once more. "It's been a long day. I suggest you get some rest."

Monica said nothing.

"I have to take care of some business tomorrow, but I'll be here at six o'clock. We'll go for dinner if you wish."

"Fine," she managed to get out, a cold chill shaking her body. He continued to look at her, but he was only a silhouette to Monica and she could not see his expression. Cord finally said good night and quietly let himself out of the apartment.

# Chapter Three

True to the arrangement, Monica received a savings passbook in her name with the first entry of one thousand dollars stamped at the beginning of a clean white column. It came to put the final touch on a two-week period of emotional turmoil. Nothing much had changed in her day-to-day life. Yet, everything had changed. Faithfully each afternoon was spent in the dance studio repeating by rote the exercises and forms she'd known since childhood.

Monica felt almost no pain and it gave her hope. She now believed the doctors that rest was very likely the only cure. Monica left the studio each afternoon exhilarated and it kept her going.

At night, at least for the first week, the exhilaration invariably gave way to tension in anticipation of the other function she was to perform. Every night for a week Cord had come to her, to lie with her and use her body to achieve his desired result. The first night she'd been too unsure to do, think, or feel anything much. But by the second night a fear had gripped her, a realization of the full meaning of a man and woman being together in this dark, intimate embrace.

Monica would cross her arms over her naked breasts, hands clenched tightly. She would barely breathe, afraid of giving herself away and being fully noticed.

She lay stiffly in Cord's arms, biting her bottom lip, once drawing blood.

Their third night together the tension had driven her to the very edge of hysteria. For the third night, Cord had to force her arms apart and put them more comfortably around his neck. But Monica didn't want to be more comfortable.

Shortly after Cord had begun to stroke her, she'd started to silently cry. He became aware of the quaking of her body, but said nothing. Cord continued his movements until his release. Monica continued to cry, rolling onto her side until she was again asleep. She did not awaken when he again let himself out of the apartment.

A week of this was about all either could stand. After another sterile night together, with Monica stiff, tense, and in tears, Cord impatiently flung himself from the bed.

"Dammit, Monica. Why are you crying? Am I hurting you? Are you in pain?" His harsh tone only added to her misery and she silently shook her head no to all his questions.

Muttering a further oath under his breath, Cord dressed hurriedly and left without saying another word. He called the next day to say he had to fly to Texas on business and wasn't sure when he'd be back. His voice, as always, was controlled, formal, and removed. He further instructed her that if there were any problems she was to contact Lawrence Gordon, and he gave her the number of a New York law firm.

Monica was relieved for the sudden departure, hoping the time to herself would allow for a chance to pull herself together.

Monica and Donna had always liked each other, but it was a friendship founded on mutual interests. Having Donna to talk to lessened her strain and also helped glean some insights into the mysterious workings of male–female relationships. At an early age, Donna had been married and divorced, and now Monica absorbed everything her friend imparted to her "like a sponge."

Cord had been gone a week and Monica had again begun to feel safe in his absence. She'd taken a part-time job in the box office at the Metropolitan Opera—not because she needed the money now, but because it helped to fill the now long hours of the approaching summer days. She'd attended the last two performances of her own troupe before they began a two month tour of Europe.

Monica stood in the wings chatting and joking with the costumed dancers. She experienced the indescribable frustration of someone watching dances being performed that she knew she could do as well. She fought against tears, feeling that it was all so unfair, feeling childishly contrite.

"Monica, love, we're truly sorry you won't be joining us," Monsieur Denier cooed to her. "But think of this time as a prolonged vacation. No strict master admonishing you for a poor jeté, or making you do a barre over and over again, *n'est-ce pas?*"

Monica smiled wanly knowing that she would gladly put up with the scolds, the exhaustion, the bleeding feet, and the repetition for any assurance that it was not gone forever from her life.

Peter, a tall Dane who'd partnered Monica during the last season, gave her a brotherly hug and wished her well. But it was the sad-eyed director of the troupe who nearly caused Monica to lose her control.

"Ah, my sea nymph," he whispered, making reference to her being the only dancer he'd ever managed from the West Coast. "She is beached for a time. This is true?" He cupped her face in his cold bony hands and planted a warm fatherly kiss on her forehead. Patung her shoulder in comfort, he let out a sigh of empathy.

"Once again Mother Nature only shows us she is not to be bested. Our *Coppélia* will not be the same without you, Monica."

She smiled, grateful for this confession. "I'm sure Patty will not disappoint you."

"Ah, well, I'm sure she will not disappoint me either, my dear. But I do not expect the great heights! However, she will do."

There was a hurried offstage summons for the director. Monica decided it was also a good time for her to leave; she didn't want to be there for the final curtain and the inevitable gathering for celebration as the spring season drew to a close. She remembered too well the euphoria and made a quiet, graceful exit.

On Sunday after the troupe left, she and Donna went for a walk in Central Park, before Donna had to report for her matinee performance. Monica loved New York best in the spring, when the trees grew full and lush and served as a touch of color and backdrop to an otherwise gray city of concrete. She watched a young father keep a patient but watchful eye on an energetic three-year-old while pushing a carriage containing an infant. The scene fascinated her as she watched him speak softly, lovingly, to the little boy scampering around, or watched the way he tucked the coverlet more securely over the sleeping baby.

Monica tried to envision her father doing these things for her as a child, and the image completely evaded her. She frowned as the image of her father changed to that of a tall, unsmiling, untender Cord Temple. She knew nothing about him, except that he wanted a child. Oddly, that allowed her to fantasize and see a suddenly lighthearted Cord, gently tending to a miniature of himself. Monica blinked rapidly back to reality when she saw the toddler of her imagination with gray curly hair.

"So...how is married life agreeing with you?" Donna asked.

Monica nearly laughed out loud "what marriage?" but instead she shrugged. "I'm not sure what I should have expected under the circumstances. Suddenly, there is a stranger I'm bound to."

"You haven't seen him lately?" Donna asked delicately. Monica blushed.

"He's away on business. I don't know when he'll be back. I know so little about him," she admitted, embarrassed.

"I have no idea what kind of work he does, where he lives, nothing of his family—" A thought suddenly hit her. "Oh, Donna! He could be insane...or a murderer!"

Donna chuckled without humor. "Well, he can't be any more crazy than you!" When Monica looked uncomfortable, she was immediately sorry for her thoughtless remark.

"I'm sorry, Monica. It was insensitive of me to say that."

"But true," Monica sighed. They stopped and sat on a bench.

Donna chuckled deep in her throat and flashed Monica a wide smile. "I don't know what I expected either when I got married." Donna's eyes got distant as she obviously relived the occasion. "I loved David something awful! I just wanted to be with him. I thought we'd get married and...play house," she said with irony. "I'd go on and dance, and he'd do whatever he was doing. But you can't have a marriage and have separate lives. It just doesn't work that way. Believe me, marriage takes work! And sacrifices! I guess we were too young," Donna sighed. "All hot and bothered and not much else!"

Monica frowned. "What do you mean, hot and bothered?"

"You know. Wanting to make love all the time. But you can't spend your life in bed. Lord knows we tried! David and I had a great sex life." Monica blushed in embarrassment hearing this private admission, but she was fascinated.

"He really knew how to turn me on! He was the best lover."

"I guess you really... enjoyed that." Monica made it a statement.

"Honey, I loved it!" Donna exclaimed. "Don't you enjoy it?"

Monica felt trapped. How could she answer without sounding childish? "My situation is very different. I don't have a marriage. I have a business arrangement. I'm not supposed to enjoy this."

"But really, how can you not? There's that gorgeous man with that sexy gray hair making love to you, and you don't feel anything?" Monica was spared the need to answer when Donna laughed and launched into another opinion.

"Honey, you'd have to be dead from the neck down not to feel something! Either that or he doesn't know what he's doing." She laughed again. Donna stole a look at Monica and saw that she was sitting stiffly and silently beside her. She knew Monica to be sensitive and bright and straightforward. So it puzzled her still that she would be drawn into such a questionable arrangement. Donna thought to herself it had to be a pretty important reason.

"Monica," she began, "are you sure you want to do this? I mean, give up a child?" she asked seriously.

Monica smiled grimly and shrugged. "People have

children all the time they don't really want. It's a body function. A reflex. You bring forth a child into the world and then it's on its own. If each of us is lucky there will be love, like in your family, Donna. And if we're not, we manage nonetheless, like in mine." She sounded hard and resolved. It surprised Donna.

"Cord Temple wants a child," Monica continued. "I'm simply going to give him one."

"Not simply! For a fee! Don't you realize that you're selling your baby?"

Monica jumped up, agitated, startling Donna who watched her with parted mouth in wonder.

"No, not *my* baby. It will be Cord Temple's baby. It's business, purely business." But she felt dizzy and confused and her voice suddenly shook. She wasn't doing this for herself. She had a very good reason. At least she hoped it was a good enough reason.

"Monica, I'm sorry I—"

"It has to be the right thing! I don't have any choice! None!"

Donna spoke to her quietly, trying to calm her down. She caught Monica's eye, holding her gaze. "Yes, we always have choices."

Monica turned away from her and slowly began to walk aimlessly along a footpath. Donna walked behind her, and when she caught up to Monica and linked her arm to hers, Donna squeezed it against her side. Monica looked at her and smiled.

"I didn't mean to judge you," Donna apologized. "I'm just concerned. And I don't want to see you hurt, that's all."

"I know, Donna. I didn't mean to snap. But not dancing, not going on tour, worrying about my sister...I have so much on my mind!"

"Then you don't need criticism. You need support and understanding."

Monica smiled again. "Thanks," she whispered.

There was a compatible silence as they walked, listening to the joyous squeals of children at play and the admonishing voices of frantic parents, or the masculine voices of men playing soccer or touch football. It was so peaceful, so normal, but Monica felt very much as though she were on the outside of it all looking in. All of these people seemed to be participating in full lives, and they seemed happy. She wasn't sure she knew what happiness was outside of her dance, and right now she didn't even have that.

"I guess we should head back. I have to get to the theater," Donna said.

"Let's then.. You don't want to be late."

"How would you like to come and see the show?" Donna asked suddenly.

"I can't tonight. I'm putting in some time at the Met. Some other time."

"Okay." Donna shrugged "Look, Monica..." she began and then hesitated. "I don't know what I can do to help. But I'm here. If you ever need me... I'm here."

Monica was touched. She felt her throat constrict and tears sting her eyes. She gave Donna what she hoped was a brave smile. "Thanks, Donna. I may take you up on that offer."

Monica stayed at the Met until eleven o'clock, then slowly made her way home. It was a lovely spring night and she felt lulled by the warm air. The New York dance season was over, and most troupes were gone on their European summer tours. Even Donna would take a vacation in July away from her show.

By next week Monica had no doubts that she would be in the midst of getting Lee off to England, and that was the most important thing to her right now. Lee deserved to have the chance to succeed.

Monica sighed and hugged her body as she entered

her building. Once Lee was settled, she would finish this...this thing she was to do, which was making the Royal Academy possible. Afterward she would take several months to get back into shape and restore her body to performance level. Then, hopefully, next summer she would again be on tour. But as hard as Monica tried to avoid it, she couldn't help a final abstract thought as to what Cord Temple was doing at that moment.

Cord's head was pressed firmly into the back cushion of his seat. He showed all the indications of a weary traveler taking advantage of the long plane flight to get some rest. But he was not asleep. His long legs were stretched out as far as the seat in front of him would allow, and he was slouched, one elbow on the armrest with his hand supporting his cheek and chin. Sunlight through the narrow window streaked across his iron-colored hair, giving an odd impression of dazzling silver, or a halo. Cord would have laughed at that image—he was no angel.

Through languid, half-closed eyes, he watched an attractive raven-haired stewardess in her efficient well-trained movements, as she saw to the needs of the passengers. He couldn't take his eyes off of her, so he pretended he wasn't looking. Yes, she was pretty, but that was not why he stared. She reminded him rather painfully of someone he used to know.

When Cord had first boarded the plane and saw her, he had had to stop and grip a seat back to steady himself. The stewardess had turned to face him and, seeing his distress, immediately came to his side.

"Sir! Are you all right?"

Cord closed his eyes momentarily and drew a ragged breath. The stewardess took his arm and involuntarily he stiffened and slowly pulled away.

"I'm fine," he managed. "I just need to sit if you don't mind."

"Of course," she said solicitously. And taking his ticket, quickly guided him to his first-class seat. Cord could see, once she spoke and was near, that she was not Natalie. But still, the moment had been devastating. It had been a long time—almost fifteen years since he'd seen Natalie. He should have known instantly that the pert woman performing her tasks in front of him could never have been Natalie. She would never stoop to such a menial chore as stewardessing. Cord couldn't consciously remember the last time he'd been so badly shaken. No...no, that was a lie. He could remember the moment very well. It was the day he was to have been married....

It had been just past his twenty-fifth birthday. He'd finished his degree in architecture, had several offers of jobs to choose from in two major U.S. cities, and the person he loved most was about to become his wife.

Natalie was petite and stunningly beautiful. She didn't just make heads turn, people stopped in their tracks to watch her motions.

Her hair was jet black with streaking highlights of blue. Her eyes a delicate violet so that they threatened to drown a person in their depths.

Natalie Kingman was the only child of the head of Cord's architectural college. He'd met her when Dr. Kingman had invited a very select number of top students to his home to see its controversial form and design. Kingman had been noted as a protégé of Frank Lloyd Wright's and had many of the same criticisms as Wright thrown at him, but that had not stopped Kingman from being one of the most respected and sought-after young architects of his generation.

Cord had been stopped cold on the doorstep when

Natalie opened the door to admit him, looking up at him beguilingly with her wonderful eyes.

Cord knew she was fully aware of her effect on people and realized that Natalie was no doubt used to being fawned over. From the first moment he knew he wanted her totally for himself.

Natalie was terribly spoiled like a queen bee holding court solely for her own purposes and means. If Cord was to have her—and he meant to—he'd have to make her come to him.

By the end of that afternoon he had cultivated just enough interest in Natalie to make her curious to know more about this giant of a man with the silver hair and pale eyes. For months they played a cat-and-mouse game of enticement, teasing each other until she gave in and came to him in haughty frustration.

"Cortland Temple, what kind of man are you anyway? Do you want me or don't you? Have you no idea how to treat a lady?" She went on and on while Cord watched her in amusement and love. She had a temper, as he would fully discover, and she did want things her own way. When she finally ran out of breath, he'd held her gently and kissed her into acquiescence.

"Call me Cord," he whispered against her soft cheek, holding her to him. "And yes, I want you."

Natalie became very ambitious for Cord, pushing him forward, encouraging him. Cord didn't want or need to be pushed, but he humored her, basking in her attention. Yet their relationship was by no means smooth. Natalie also had it within herself to be petulant, impatient, and impossible and she exasperated Cord more often than not with her willful ways. But all she had to do was turn her violet eyes to him and he'd give in. He knew that he would have to take better control sooner or later.

Natalie saw Cord's future brighter than he himself did. She made plans for promoting and pushing him to the forefront of his field, using her considerable charm and her father's connections. It was not what Cord wanted but until he finished school it was okay for her to play her games. Except that for Natalie, they were not games. She was deadly earnest about being the wife of the best-known architect in America.

The young couple planned a conventional June wedding with all the trimmings, to take place right after Cord's graduation. He would have been perfectly happy with a small chapel ceremony and just a few friends but Natalie wanted the full regalia or nothing. Once more Cord gave in.

It had rained steadily the whole morning of the wedding, perhaps a prophecy of things to come. Cord's best man, Matthew Bell, had been late and had to drive back to his dorm room because he'd forgotten the ring. Then Cord couldn't locate the license, resulting in a frantic upheaval of his room until the misplaced paper was discovered being used as a bookmark in one of his texts. The caterers had phoned to say it would be impossible to hold the reception outdoors because of the weather, and asked if he had any suggestions. Cord was about to say cancel the damn reception, he just wanted to get married and get the hell away from everyone. As it turned out, the wedding was canceled anyway. Cord was given a hastily scribbled note on cloud-blue tissue-thin stationery that begged his forgiveness for what she was about to do, but Natalie found that she was madly in love with Jeffrey Alan Burke, and they were going to elope.

"Please understand, darling..." she'd written. "But I've decided that Jeffrey and I are very much more suited to each other. Yours faithfully, Natalie."

Yours faithfully....

It had taken Matthew and the father of the bride to keep Cord under control.

Well after midnight Matthew finally left Cord alone, his dishevelled form stretched cockeyed across his bed, clothes and papers flung everywhere as though a storm had passed through. Matthew had taken a quick shower, made the other phone calls that had been necessary to cancel the day, made yet another pot of coffee, and gone back to sit vigil over his broken friend. It would be nearly four months before a hard, sullen, silent, and older Cord would resume his life.

In fifteen years Cord had never again seriously considered or gotten involved with another woman. He'd had his affairs purely for the sake of his physical needs, and then gone back to his own inclusive world. But Cord had never ever given up wanting a child. Natalie had made it very clear that she thought children tiresome, which was not too surprising in someone still so much a child herself. Cord had thought he'd change her mind after they were married.

Natalie had been right about one thing. She and Jeffrey Alan Burke were much better suited. He was now a senator... and she was a senator's wife. So much more valuable than being the mere wife of a humble architect.

He was very sorry that all those memories had been stirred up. It was going to take him several days to work them out of his system again.

Cord let his eyes close the remaining distance, feeling the strain pull at his eye muscles. He wanted about three days of nonstop sleep. And then he would get back in touch with Monica Hamlin. No... Monica Hamlin Temple. The irony of it struck him in the stomach—marriage, which at one time had held such a sacred and important meaning for him, should now be used as a simple expedient, legal means to an end.

Monica was a very pretty woman, Cord thought, although entirely too thin for his tastes. He wondered how her lovely face would look filled out a bit. He especially remembered her rather sensuous mouth, well shaped and soft looking, but he viewed her rather clinically, from afar, not at all as a man would normally look at a woman.

Monica was very much taller than Natalie and seemed more fragile, but Cord knew she wasn't. Under that delicate body was a very contained, controlled person. Purposeful, but in a different way than Natalie ever was.

It was very evident to Cord from their first night together that Monica was inexperienced. He had been oddly pleased by that. And the feel of her body against his own had been another surprise—despite her thinness, she had been very soft. She'd felt so light in his arms that he was sure he could easily have crushed her under his weight. Cord did not want her in his life. But she—or someone like her—could give him what he desperately wanted.

So, he would do his part, if she would do hers. He didn't care what thoughts she had about relinquishing the child, as long as she did. He didn't care what she did for the nine months when she became pregnant, as long as she was healthy and took care of herself. He didn't care what became of her afterward, or what she did with the money, although he cynically thought that people would obviously go to great extremes for the right price. In that respect, Monica Hamlin Temple was no better or worse than Natalie Kingman had been.

Monica left the studio in a hurry, flying out of the door. Strands of burnished hair escaped her usually neat knot, but she'd been in too much of a hurry after class to fix it properly. She burst into the apartment and dumped her bags, keys, and scarf to the floor as she headed to the phone.

Nervously handling the receiver, she dialed her step-mother's home in California. It rang only once, and then a very excited Lee Ann was on the other end, virtually screaming in her excitement.

"Niki, Niki, I won! I'm in! They liked me, Niki. Oh, God, I was so nervous. But you should have been there! You would have been so proud of me. Oh, and there were hundreds of guys and girls there, but I won!" Suddenly a horrible thought struck her. "Oh! Monica, it is you, isn't it?"

Monica started laughing joyously at her sister's enthusiasm. "Yes, Chicken, it's me! I called as soon as I could. Oh, Lee Ann, I'm so proud of you. Tell me all about it."

"Where do I begin?" But she didn't lack for words despite her momentary confusion. "Well, I didn't get a wink of sleep last night. And you know Mother— checking to see that my leotard was clean so I wouldn't embarrass her."

Monica smiled in understanding. She sat back in her chair and listened with pleasure to the details.

"... I was about the thirtieth dancer. Boy, do they torture you! First they made everyone do the barre routines and then a pas de deux, which is weird with people you've never danced with before. Anyway, they called me to stay for part two and I knew I had one foot in the door!"

"Were you pleased with your performance?"

"No! I was awful! I felt like I had the arms of a gorilla and the feet the size of a kangaroo! And the judges seemed so unfriendly. The principal judge didn't have a smile bone in her whole body!"

Monica laughed. "I'm sure that's not true. But after all, Chicken, this is serious stuff. So you're in. Are you happy?"

"Happy! Niki, I'm practically out of my mind!"

"What happens now?"

"Well, school is out, thank goodness. If we accept the position at the academy we have to be there by June first. I have to get my school to send transcripts and stuff. It's not going to be all dance, unfortunately."

"At least you won't be an illiterate ballerina."

Lee giggled like the little girl she still was. "Oh, Niki, I'm so happy. Can I go?"

Monica's smile slowly faded as she remembered her promise to her sister. She reminded herself it was worthwhile. With a catch in her throat she assured Lee Ann that it would be possible.

"Is Mother helping you at all?" Monica asked.

"She said she'd pay for my plane ticket and give me money for new clothes—but we're really counting on you."

Monica raised her brows and smiled ruefully. "Don't worry. You'll be in London on June first with everything you need. Now listen. I—I have a job. I'll send you regular checks to pay for the room and board. Make up a list of what you need and I'll get a check off to you to get you started. It will be easier for me to keep in touch with you, so be sure to write me your address and the number for the school."

"Oh, Monica," Lee began in a sob, surprising her sister, "you are the best sister."

"Oh, come on, Chicken. Don't cry. You've worked so hard for this and you deserve it. You're going to be a great dancer."

"But you shouldn't have to pay for it all."

"Who else should I do it for if not for my favorite person in all the world? Now enough. You have lots to do."

Monica could hear her sister sniffling over the phone and heard her blow her nose to get control of herself. "Was Mother there, Lee? Was she happy?"

"Oh, yes. And she was good. She didn't criticize when I flubbed one routine. She just winked at me and told me to go on!"

Well, that was good, Monica thought. Her stepmother had her moments, few and far apart though they were. Monica cleared her throat and her voice became strained.

"Look, Lee. I'd love to talk but I must say a few words to Mother and get off the phone. Now, don't forget to let me know how your plans are going."

"I won't, Niki. I'll talk to you soon. Here she is..."

Monica had not spoken to her stepmother in months. And when her distinct, husky voice came on the line, a chill went through her, reminding her of how remote Eileen could be.

"Hello, Monica dear. How've you been?" Eileen Hamlin began politely.

"Fine, Mother. And yourself?" There was a dramatic sigh, and Monica braced herself to listen to a variety of ills that made her stepmother's life so trying. She was not disappointed. But Monica had little patience or understanding for Eileen today. Monica interrupted the older woman's dialogue to change the subject. Monica had never been in the habit of speaking intimately with Eileen and she found herself embarrassed for a way to start.

"Mother, would you mind very much if—if I asked you a—a personal question?"

There was a noticeable pause. "Well... I don't really know, Monica," she said suspiciously. "I guess it depends...."

Monica took a deep breath and the direct approach. "I—I want to know, what was it like when you were pregnant with Lee Ann?"

After the long silence there was a husky surprised laugh on the other end.

"Why, Monica! You're not—"

"No! Oh, no!" Monica said a bit too forcefully.

"Oh, I just wondered. Why, your poor father would turn in his grave if he thought— Well, never mind. Why do you wish to know?"

"I have a friend. She's just married and is thinking about having a—a baby. She has no...real family and I thought I could pass along some information," she ended lamely.

"What was it like? My dear, it was awful!"

Monica was confused. She hadn't expected that reaction.

"I was sick as a dog for months! And then of course I gained weight. In five months I looked like a cow! Those maternity outfits were so ugly, and I was so uncomfortable. If I wasn't so afraid of what your father would do I swear I would have considered abortion!"

Monica was shocked.

"And of course labor was a total nightmare. The pain was just unbelievable."

"But after Lee Ann was born, after you saw her, how did you feel then?"

"Oh, I thought she was cute and all that, but who would have imagined that such a small sweet thing like that could cause such trouble!"

"But you're happy now, aren't you? You have a daughter that's almost a young woman herself!"

"Oh, yes," Eileen said languidly. "Lee is a dear..." and she let the sentence trail off.

Monica licked her now dry lips. She had only one more question.

"Eileen, why did you become pregnant?"

There was another pause and then a sigh.

"Oh, at the time I thought it might be fun. And of course your father wanted another child. He was so hoping for a boy. However, I made it quite clear that I had made my one and only contribution to the cause. As a matter of fact, while in the hospital with Lee, I had the doctors— Well, anyway," she laughed nervously, "I decided then and there not to have any more children."

Monica sat listening in depressed silence.

"Are you still there?" her stepmother asked into the long quiet.

"Yes, I'm here."

"Well, dear, I hope that helps you. I would tell your friend to think about having a baby very carefully. Believe me, motherhood is *not* for every woman!"

## Chapter Four

It was Friday and Cord had spent three days meeting with Lawrence Gordon to take care of some business. He had been back in New York nearly a full week and had given Monica no thought except to ask Gordon if any of the one thousand dollars had been drawn on yet. The answer was no. Cord shrugged indifferently and went back to his paperwork.

It was almost five o'clock when he finally decided to call Monica. The phone rang for seven uninterrupted tones, before he finally gave up in annoyance. It had never entered his mind that she wouldn't be home. But then, he knew nothing about her and hadn't seriously thought of what her life was beyond the points where it touched on his. Even now it was only in his own personal frustration that he wondered where the hell she was—and with whom.

A black cloud settled upon him, spoiling the rested look he'd finally achieved this week. He took a walk, meandering north along Fifth Avenue. He was completely unattracted to the stores and displays and the street activities that New York was known for, including the lovely ladies in their summer wear.

Cord himself made an attractive masculine picture in a lightweight summer suit, the sleeves of his sky-blue shirt folded back from his wrists to expose muscular forearms. He walked with one hand in his trouser pocket, the other hooked in the collar of his jacket, slung over his shoulder. Cord was not a man used to having his time wasted. Not being able to see Monica had upset the schedule he'd planned for the evening. He didn't relish the unstructured time he now found himself with.

Cord wandered north to Central Park South and aimlessly followed a path into the interior of the park. He shortly found himself near the pond for small model boats. Sitting on a bench occupied by one elderly woman, he absently watched several youngsters at play with a radio-controlled boat. He knew that if he had a son, this was just the sort of thing they'd do together.

Cord turned his head to see the elderly woman, talking in the direction of a young boy of six or seven as he struggled with a scale P.T. boat almost as large as the boy himself. Cord turned his attention to the youngster, who was trying to get the small craft to turn a certain way by reaching out with his arm to push the boat. He was precariously balanced and obviously not the least concerned that he could topple into the pond at any moment. The woman was on her feet, already moving to grab the boy by the arm.

Cord stood up and waved the woman back to her seat. "I'll get him," he said, and in two long strides had reached the youngster.

"I think if you let it drift for a minute, the current will bring it back to you. Then you can set it where you want," Cord offered in a quiet, unassuming voice. The boy followed the suggestion until the boat drifted to within his easy reach.

The little boy finally, shyly, looked up at Cord over his shoulder and smiled. "Thanks. Are you a sailor too?" he asked in a small voice.

"I used to be," Cord answered easily. "But you're much better at this than I was."

A wide grin replaced the shy smile, and the boy turned happily back to his boat. Cord turned and walked back to the bench and the woman.

"Thank you so much!" she said sincerely.

"He's doing fine now."

She hesitated before asking. "Do you have children?"

Cord shook his head, watching the youngster walk around the edge of the pond as he followed the movement of the boat. "No, I don't. Not yet," he amended.

The woman sighed heavily. "It can be very hard being a parent. Children require a lot of time and attention...and love."

Cord frowned. "He doesn't seem so hard to take care of."

She hesitated. "Well, his parents are always so busy. You know how it is. And I'm no company for a little boy!"

Cord couldn't help feeling resentment toward the parents of one small lonely boy. His eyes followed the child at play with the boat. "He'll be okay," Cord said with assurance to the woman.

"Thanks again!" the woman said to Cord's retreating back as he walked back the way he'd come.

The small encounter had done nothing for his frame of mind. He found himself getting more and more angry at Monica. Cord had his solitary dinner and at ten o'clock he again tried calling Monica but again there was no answer. The weekend suddenly loomed ahead of him, unavoidable and empty. But he was determined not to let it remain that way. Making quick mental plans for the next day, he settled himself to get a good night's sleep.

Monica had been surprised when the phone rang at ten o'clock that Saturday morning and Cord was on the other end. She'd almost forgotten. She'd been rather euphoric the last few days as she knew her sister was leaving for Europe. Lee Ann had a stopover of a few hours at Kennedy before her long flight overseas and Monica had promised she'd be there to see her off, not knowing for sure when she'd next see her sister. Friday had been happily spent with her, as excitement made Lee Ann hyperactive with excess energy.

Monica was still filled with that warm feeling when Cord had called. She felt generous. She wanted to share some of her happiness.

"I've been trying to reach you," he said in a none too generous tone.

"I'm sorry." Monica fairly bubbled. "I had to take someone to the airport," she improvised. "I didn't expect you to call . . . it's been weeks!"

"It hasn't been that long," Cord said still feeling disagreeable. He wondered abstractedly what had caused her sudden personality change. "I thought I'd come over."

Monica's heart lurched at the thought of his presence in the apartment again with her. A memory came back to her of several weeks ago, and she suddenly couldn't catch her breath properly. She knew she could not avoid him, but she had to put him off for a bit. She had to have time.

"We could spend the day together," she responded, with a marked drop in manner of a moment ago.

Cord frowned. He wondered if she disliked his company that much. "What do you have in mind?"

"I—I don't know, but I'll think of something by the time you get here."

"All right," he agreed, not much mollified. "I'll be over in an hour."

Monica hung up and was surprised to find her hand shaking a bit. She walked slowly back to her room and noticed the still unmade bed. It spurred her into sudden action as she made it neatly and set the room to rights.

Donna yawned her way into the kitchen from her own room ten minutes later in search of a reviving cup of coffee.

"Did I hear the phone?" she asked in a sleepy voice.

"Yes," Monica called out already beginning to pull clothes onto her thin body. She chose a soft silk dress with tiny flowers printed on it. It hugged her torso, gently emphasizing her firm breasts and tiny waist, and swung free from her hips to swirl lightly with each movement of her long legs. She put on a pair of low-heeled summer sandals and combed her hair into its usual knot. She made a very attractive picture, her rising apprehension adding natural color to her usually pale skin.

"Donna," she moaned, joining her in the kitchen, "he's coming over. What are we going to do all day?"

"He who?" Donna asked nonsensically, still not fully awake.

"Cord!"

"Oh...well, if I'd only been married a month, I know where I'd want to spend my time!" She chuckled wickedly.

Monica groaned in frustration. Donna watched her and sighed. She ran a hand absently through her tiny corkscrew curls and leaned toward Monica.

"Look, hon," she began lightly, "you're not going to a slaughter. You knew what this was all about."

Monica blushed, looking a bit ashamed. It was true. As Cord had said to her that night of their wedding, she knew what had to happen. "You're right, of course. This is my doing. I've made my bed, now I must lie in it."

Donna quirked a brow. "That's better. If you can pun about it, then how bad can it be?"

"It was unintentional, I assure you!" Monica answered bitterly.

"Look. Play it loose. Part of the problem is you two don't know a thing about each other. Who is this man anyway, and why does he want to father a child? What is he really like? You need to find out; after all, there are too many distractions between the sheets of a bed for that kind of discovery."

Monica knew Donna was right. Perhaps under different circumstances there would have been a chance for that. As it was, it didn't seem to matter to Cord what kind of person she was beyond her capability to become pregnant and carry a child to term, and even Monica had no assurance that she could do either. What a chance they were both taking!

"I suggest going for a walk. Maybe have lunch somewhere where you can talk and not glare at each other," Donna offered. "If you like I'll leave passes for the matinee at the box office for you. See my show, I'm terrific in it, you know!"

Monica smiled.

"By evening, then you'll be in more of a mood for... whatever happens."

Monica thought about it. She gave Donna a very grateful look.

"You can thank me by not making yourself a nervous wreck everytime he calls," Donna said softly. "We don't know if he's worth that much feeling yet." Donna stood up. "Well, I have to shower and get to the theater. I'm so tired! I can't wait until vacation next month."

Monica thought over what Donna had said. Then she got a shawl and her straw shoulder bag and left the apartment to meet Cord in front of the building. Fifteen minutes later he pulled up in a cab and gracefully stepped out. Only a slight surprise showed in his gray eyes as he saw her standing there smiling shyly at him. As Cord walked slowly up to her, Monica admired the lean virile presence of him. He noticed how attractive and cool she looked in her summer dress.

Monica spoke before Cord had a chance to. "I thought it would be nice to spend some time outdoors. It's too nice a day to be inside. Do you mind?" she asked, looking up at him charmingly. Cord was not fooled by her smile and recognized at once that she was merely stretching for more time. But he only shrugged and said, "Where would you like to go?"

"I like walking in the park. Can we do that for a while?"

"All right," Cord answered, taking her arm and turning in the direction of Central Park. They crossed the street and followed a path, but Cord did not know this section of the park. He wondered fleetingly if it was anywhere near the boat pond, thinking of the small boy he had seen the day before.

"How was your business trip?" she ventured to break the silence. Cord was surprised at her asking.

"It went well. I accomplished what I had to do."

"I don't doubt it," Monica mused under her breath. When Cord threw a quick glance in her direction she only smiled at him. He hadn't really seen her smile before, or perhaps he just never noticed. He was surprised at the transformation. He found himself staring for a second. She had dimples he had never noticed.

"What kind of work do you do?" she asked next.

"What is this—twenty questions?" he asked disagreeably.

"No."

"Then why does it matter?"

"It doesn't. I just wanted to know," Monica admitted.

Cord's brow went up slightly. "Why doesn't it matter?" he couldn't help asking.

"Why? Because...because it's only important that you like what you do!"

"I'm an architect," he said after allowing a pause.

"How interesting!" Cord smiled in amusement to himself. He experienced the oddest feeling of having just been put in his place. "Do you like being an architect?"

"Yes," he answered, this time without hesitation.

"Then that's really wonderful." Cord had no comment to that.

"What sort of buildings do you design?"

"The usual kinds," he said sarcastically making her feel like it was a dumb question. He was still unaccountably annoyed about Friday, but he finally reasoned that there really was no way she could have known he would call. Cord relented.

"Mostly corporate buildings. But I've done a few small schools, private homes, a church..." And an orphanage, which he didn't add.

"A church," Monica breathed. "A church has such special requirements. Did you find it a challenge?"

"As a matter of fact, I did. Not having spent a lot of time in any, I found I knew nothing. It needed a lot of reading and research and visits to churches."

Monica was smiling at him, somewhat pleased with herself that she'd hit on something he would talk about. But she was also listening with interest. Cord continued.

"I found that I actually became involved in their structure. I once spent two weeks visiting cathedrals and abbeys throughout Europe in order to get a better sense of their history. It's very different from the houses of worship here in the States where the buildings are historically very new."

"It sounds very exciting. And fun," Monica commented.

Cord quirked a dark brow at her. "I don't know if it was fun exactly. But it was enlightening."

Monica winced. They looked suddenly at each other and grinned. "I know...no pun intended!" For the moment she found herself dazzled by his smile and thought how much younger it made him look. They walked for a moment, much more relaxed with one another.

"And I suppose you enjoy being a dancer," Cord commented.

Monica said nothing for a second and a soft light sparkled in her amber eyes. "Enjoy it," she repeated. And whispered almost fervently, "It's my life!"

Cord was silenced, not being able to think of a thing to say after that.

They found themselves in the children's zoo. Cord had never seen so many little kids and pregnant women and strollers in one place before. He watched the women with a sudden new and total interest. He and Monica finally circled around and came back to the west side of the park, ending up at Tavern on the Green again.

Cord suggested they stop there for lunch. Monica experienced a moment of dread as she remembered the last time she'd been here, and why. Cord displayed no such sentiments until they'd ordered. When the wine had been poured he touched his glass to hers and raised his in a toast that was both joyless and empty.

"Happy Anniversary!"

"What?" Monica asked, stunned.

"Don't you remember? One month ago, almost to the day." He said it in rather a brittle and hard voice that sent a shiver through Monica. Cord noticed, but only looked at her grimly, as though it were all her fault.

"Yes, I remember," she whispered bitterly and took a gulp of wine, enjoying the sudden warmth spreading through her. She sat in angry silence. She didn't need to be reminded that there was hardly cause for celebration—of any kind.

He looked at Monica impatiently, as he saw her stiffen and withdraw from him. But he also recognized that his comment had been mean and unnecessary. And he liked it better when she smiled. "What do you have planned for this afternoon?" It was asked in such a way that Monica blushed, for she knew he realized what it was she'd been doing up to now.

"Oh, I thought we might go see the show Donna performs in. It's supposed to be quite good. She said she'd leave tickets for us."

"That sounds fine...and safe," he said with meaning, and Monica wanted to throw something at him.

Cord had never been to a Broadway play and did enjoy the performance. He and Monica left the theater and stepped back into a day still brilliant with sunshine. But Monica knew her free time was over. She looked at Cord, who in turn was looking at her rather coldly. Monica forced herself to smile at him. Cord took her hand and helped her into a cab and they went back to her apartment on Central Park West.

## Chapter Five

There was a rustling behind Monica and she turned her head to look toward the bed. The room was almost dark and mostly in shadows, but Monica knew exactly where everything was. Nothing was hidden. Cord's long form was easily discernible under the light bedspread. She knew the covers to be somewhere around his waist, leaving his hard chest exposed. She knew his left arm to be thrown back over his head, partially obscuring his forehead and temple, the other arm to be stretched out to the side a bit, where she would have lain.

Monica hugged her knee, feeling warmth flowing through her. She was still experiencing, still remembering, what had happened here just a few hours ago. She watched Cord's chest rise and fall with the steady breathing of sleep. She remembered the feel of his muscles under her roaming hands, the feel of the curling hair of his chest and head under and around her fingers, the feel of the entire length and weight of his body pressed completely on her much smaller frame. She couldn't help remembering...and she didn't want to ever forget.

It was six o'clock when they'd returned to her apartment. She'd offered Cord a drink and poured herself fruit juice. She'd put a Chopin recording on the stereo and they'd sat next to each other in a silence that was strained. Monica began to panic and Cord was aware of it.

Cord remembered their last encounter with anger, especially Monica's tears, and the way she'd curled into herself after he'd released her and rolled away. He'd been impatient then, and he was beginning to feel impatient now. She behaved as though he were intolerable to be near, to have him touch her. He put his glass down on the coffee table so sharply that Monica jumped, swinging wide amber eyes to his suddenly icy gray ones. His hair curled freely over his well-shaped head, and Monica had the absurd thought that he would have made a great and commanding Roman orator.

Cord stood up and reached out his large hand to her. Monica took it, almost hypnotized by the sense of authority and power that emanated from him. He turned and led the way to her room, again closing the door behind them. Turning back to her, he gently placed his hands on her shoulders, then frowned when he felt the tremble begin in her body. She refused to meet his eyes now.

Cord moved his hands slowly down her bare arms. There were goose bumps on her skin. At her wrists he let her go and put his hands on her waist. He was surprised to find how small it was, that his hands could reach around her with no trouble. His fingers brushed a string or a tie. Grabbing it, Cord pulled and her summer dress loosened around her. Monica moved for the first time, putting her hands on his to stop his movements.

Her breathing was suddenly shallow and difficult.

"No," she murmured in a pleading voice. Cord looked sharply at her, but he shrugged and stepped back.

"Suit yourself," he said indifferently. He turned away and began to undress. She might be hesitant, but he had every intention of getting her into bed before very much longer.

There was still sun coming into the room, and Monica realized that he'd be able to see her completely now, and she him. It was so silly. What was there to hide after having been so intimate with him? But he was still as a stranger to her, and that's what she hid from.

Cord pulled the coverlet down and stretched out naked on the cool sheets. Keeping her back to him, Monica finished undressing and self-consciously moved to the bed. Cord chuckled grimly.

"You practice dance in almost nothing. You wear almost nothing when you dance on stage. Every nuance of your body is open to an audience of hundreds of strangers. Why are you so modest now?

"You don't need to hide," Cord said in a low voice to her. "You have a beautiful body."

But this did not make her feel any easier and she didn't respond, just lay next to him stiffly as she'd done in the past. When she made no attempt to move closer, Cord turned angrily to her.

"Dammit, Monica," he said threateningly, as though to warn her he'd had enough of her play at shyness. But her lips were parted softly and looked full and pliant. Cord watched in fascination, suddenly forgetting his irritation. He slowly bent forward, watching her mouth, her parted lips, and he gently kissed her. He pulled back. It had been sweet. He leaned over and kissed her again, teasing the corners and the full curves. Then he stopped the teasing and completely covered her mouth with his own, kissing her fully and deeply, pulling her entire body against him.

Monica fought her growing feelings as the instant

contact of his mouth sent shivers through her. With an almost painful moan she responded to the lips over hers.

Cord had never kissed her before and he enjoyed the feel of her. He could also feel her body quake as he began to caress her, feel her hesitation, but the kiss was real. Suddenly, he looked questioningly at her. She trembled all over. Her hands clutched the bed linens, her eyes closed against him, but her mouth remained parted, as if she waited.

"My God!" Cord murmured in realization, watching the flush in her cheeks. "You've never fully—" But he got no further as Monica turned her head away and quietly began to cry.

But this time Cord was not angry or impatient with her. She wasn't crying because she was hurt or thought he was going to hurt her. She wasn't crying out of fear of him, or because he repulsed her. She cried out of her own wanting and needing. Cord now recognized that in her inexperience she had never been able to judge what she should feel or how she should respond. He'd aroused her, made her totally aware of him and his sexuality, and she didn't know what she should do with all the new feelings. She had never been touched or explored quite as he had done, awakening her body to exquisite feeling that left her shaken.

Now Cord realized that Monica had never known the complete physical release and pleasure that was possible between a man and woman. Perhaps she'd always believed one had to be in love to feel such total consumption. And if that was true, what was she to do with blood coursing rapidly through her veins as her heart pounded, or with skin so sensitive to the touch she felt as though she'd been burned?

He looked in total wonder at Monica's profile. He gently took her chin in his hand and turned her face back to his. She kept her eyes squeezed closed, too ashamed by her own conflicting emotions to look into his eyes. Her face was streaked with tears. There was a softening of Cord's features, the dark ominous brows not so imposing or the gray eyes so icy, nor the full mouth so stern. But Monica's eyes were closed and she did not see.

Cord took her gently into his arms and lay on his side with her. Now he was gentle with another purpose in mind. He kissed the salty tears from her cheeks and eyes, and Monica's opened in surprise. Cord began to stroke her, caress her, and make love to her expertly. He trailed kisses down her throat and neck while his hands cupped her full breasts and thumbs teased pink tips into erection. Monica's breathing was rapid, but she lay unyielding. Cord took his time. He took her arms and put them around his neck, and drew her close to nuzzle the space between her neck and shoulder.

Monica could feel the whole room spinning around her as all her senses came alive and she felt herself slipping into pure feeling. Cord ran a hand sensuously down her back and under her thigh and her body jerked, her hips rising up to his. Cord's lips moved to her ear and the warm air of his breath made her tremble yet again.

"Let go, Monica," he whispered softly to her, sending a shiver through her. A low moan escaped her. "Let go," he coaxed again, even softer, his hands still caressing and stimulating her.

"I . . . can't!" she gasped, her fingers working convulsively through the curly hair on his neck.

"Yes, you can." And his mouth moved to kiss her. Her lips were already parted for him and when his tongue moved between her teeth to deepen the caress she relaxed completely against him. Cord made no move to satisfy himself, only reading her movements and sounds. He never released her mouth, as if by concentrating on the kiss he could coax her body into responding on its own. He wasn't sure how long it took, but suddenly he heard her moan, and her back arched as she pressed closer to his taut middle.

Something reverberated through her body, rocking it, spiraling it beyond her control. Some kind of explosion that filled her with a languid, liquid warmth, making her breathless and unbelievably weak. But Cord only held her while this thing happened to her, and after what seemed forever, her body settled itself back to something normal. She buried her face in Cord's shoulder and held on, trying to catch her breath.

The strain was more than Cord would admit to, but he held her more comfortably against him, and holding her this way they both fell to sleep.

Two hours later Monica woke surprised to find herself pressed against Cord's chest. She quietly moved away and got out of bed and stood looking at him in wonder and something like tenderness. She stood that way for a long time before making her way to the window to sit hugging herself and staring into the dark.

And now she turned again to watch Cord. His gentleness had surprised her. That, combined with steady persistence and her own highly stimulated condition, had served to release her at last. He'd known exactly what he was doing, and she couldn't help wondering how many women he'd been with over the years to gain his expertise.

"Monica" came the husky deep voice from the dark. "Come here." It was said softly, but it was a command. She only hesitated a second before uncurling herself from the windowseat and walked slowly toward the bed in the shadows. She stopped within a foot of him and wrapped her arms around her naked breasts. Cord's hand reached out to her. "Come here," he whispered

seductively, and the richness of his voice drew her onto
the bed and next to him. Cord clasped her around her
ribcage and pulled her on top of him. Monica drew in a
breath at finding him already hard against her.

An old habit began to take hold of her, but Cord ran
his hand down her back to her buttocks, pressing her to
him. The other hand brought her face down to his so
that he could kiss her in a leisurely, lazy fashion. When
he released her mouth, Monica found that she was already beginning to succumb to his nearness and touch.

"There's no need—" She tried to pull away, but
Cord interrupted in a voice that said her objections
would be brushed aside.

"There's every need. The lesson isn't over yet." He
wrapped his arms around her and rolled to reverse their
positions. Monica wasn't sure she wanted to experience
that losing of herself again, but she knew she was to
have no say in the matter.

Cord took over again, building up her desire and
need until she wiggled and arched under him. This
time Cord settled between her legs bringing them together. He moved slowly on her until he felt her peak-
ing and began to move to finish as well. He drew back
and away trying to catch his breath. Monica didn't cry,
but when he saw her begin to curl up again, Cord
turned her back into his arms.

"Monica," he began firmly, "there's no need to be
embarrassed. This is supposed to feel good, you know."
He stopped himself from adding that with someone you
cared for it was the most joyous thing to share. It was
enough that they'd finally gotten this far.

Cord stayed the night. Monica was very shy with him
in the light of day, but he behaved as though nothing
unusual had passed between them, and his usual cold
mask dropped back into place. He showered, dressed,
and looked clean, virile, and back in command as he

entered the kitchen where Monica was making orange juice. She had a flowered kimono tied over a pair of black trousers. Her hair was loosely knotted, a few wispy strands feathering around her face. Her skin was still a bit flushed, and her lips looked well kissed as Cord knew they had been the night before.

"I don't know why I'm so ravenous this morning." She laughed nervously. Cord raised a mocking brow at her. He'd made love to her yet a third time and knew exactly why he was hungry. He sat at the table and she poured orange juice and coffee for him.

All the while her hands were busy with breakfast, her mind and body and every nerve were aware that there was something different between them. Clothing seemed superfluous. Cord now knew her more thoroughly than anyone ever had. He had touched and kissed every inch of her body last night, bringing her to experience exquisite sensations. It had been mysterious, delicious, and frightening, and Monica knew she would never be the same again.

Cord told her of his plans for the week, including a cocktail party he was giving for some of his clients, which he wanted her to attend. It was important that he begin to make her existence and their relationship known to others or the termination of their agreement in a year would seem peculiar to those who hadn't known they'd been married. Cord said he'd pick her up on Thursday evening to bring her to the town house where he was staying, and Monica agreed to his plans.

"That was a good breakfast," Cord said, pushing his plate away. "I haven't had breakfast cooked for me since—" Monica's head came up sharply. But whatever it was he was about to reveal was cut off. He tensed a muscle and absently sipped at his coffee. His eyes strayed over Monica and she sat stiffly under his penetrating gaze. She wondered if he was remembering her naked in his arms, and indeed that was exactly what he was thinking. Cord finished his coffee and stood up suddenly.

Monica was curious as to when she'd see him again, but she was too ashamed by her interest to ask. "I might be over Tuesday," he casually said, bending to kiss her.

Perversely, she became angry at the information and raised her chin stubbornly. How dare he decide when they'd see each other.

"Sorry. I have something planned on Tuesday," she lied to him.

"Then you'll have to cancel. As I said, I *might* come over!" His tone made it clear that he was calling the shots. But Monica persisted.

"My life doesn't revolve around just you, you know!"

"For the next nine months or so, it better!" Cord said with meaning and Monica blushed. Without saying another word, he left. Monica closed the door behind him none too quietly.

But Cord knew that he would be back on Tuesday. He'd thoroughly enjoyed the feel of her now responding body under his, knowing he was responsible. He intended that it should happen again soon.

Donna put aside her magazine gingerly, trying not to smudge her newly applied nailpolish. She held her ten fingers out in front of her and gently blew air across the tops to hasten the drying process. She glanced across at Monica who, curled up in another chair, was reading intently a letter from her sister Lee Ann.

"How's she doing?" Donna asked.

"What? Oh. Apparently very well." Monica mused, shaking her head. "She loves Europe, thinks the women stiff and unfriendly, but the men sexy."

Donna laughed. "How old did you say she was?"

"I'm beginning to think she's not old enough!" A frown wrinkled Monica's forehead.

"Don't be too concerned," Donna advised gently. "She had to spread those wings sometime. It sounds like she's just having a good time. Aren't you glad? What if she were homesick and hated it there?"

Monica looked wide eyed at Donna, never having thought of that.

"Wouldn't that throw a rather large and untimely monkey wrench in your situation?"

"I—I still think it was worth the risk to find out that's not so. Lee is going to be a great dancer!"

"I just hope she appreciates how it's been made possible," Donna commented caustically.

Monica went pale and folded the letter away. She uncurled her legs from her chair and went to change a record on the stereo.

"She's never to know."

"How do you intend to do that?"

"Donna, you're the only one who knows what I'm doing. The only one in the whole world besides myself, Cord, and the lawyers. Lee Ann is not to find out from me or you."

"Monica, you know I'd never divulge that kind of secret. Besides, it's none of my business."

Monica sighed and smiled ruefully. "Yes, it is. You're the only person who might understand and who's been supportive. I can't forget that."

"Well, when this is all over, you can quickly begin to put the whole thing out of your mind and go back to your own life."

"When I have the baby," Monica repeated vaguely. "If I get pregnant."

Donna chuckled knowingly. "You've been with Cord almost this whole month. I would think there's every possibility."

Monica turned away. Yes, she'd been with Cord the

whole month. And each night had been the same, this wonderful feeling of floating free. She had openly defied him that Tuesday making sure she wasn't home when he came by. He had not said anything to her about it, but had taken revenge that Thursday evening, after the cocktail party, allowing her no sleep at all. Regardless, Monica allowed passion and desire to consume her so that she responded to his very nearness. It had been both breathtaking and heady, but that was all they shared. By day he became Cortland Temple, businessman, and she, Monica Hamlin Temple who still knew almost nothing about him except that he was hard and determined and arrogant, but capable of warmth, as she was witness to at night.

Donna frowned at Monica's sudden silence. "You haven't heard from him this week, have you?"

"No, but then Cord's busy. And very unpredictable. He never tells me his plans, or very much else for that matter. It's hard not knowing what to expect." She shrugged.

"Look," Donna said to her, "I'm going home for a week before catching up with the road troupe in Washington. Why don't you spend it with me? Mama would love to see you, and it will be better than being here alone."

"But what if Cord should call?" Monica asked. Donna shrugged.

"It won't hurt him not to find you for a day or two. Besides, I think you've been too tense. You're looking thinner. Mama will put a few pounds on you!"

Monica laughed. "Probably lots more than a few pounds!"

"So, you'll come?"

"Of course. I'd love to."

Lawrence Gordon allowed himself an exhausted sigh and leaned back in his chair. He put his glasses on the top of his head and wearily glanced at the man standing with his hands thrust into his pants pockets, and whose proud iron-gray head was facing out the window in front of him.

The shelter that Cortland Temple had thought up, designed, and sold to the people of this town was complete. This had been a dream, a pet project that had become somewhat of a purpose, a guiding light for Cord ever since he was a youngster. Other than that time over Natalie, this was the one thing Cord believed in. A youth shelter for homeless kids that was built and operated like a home, not like an institution.

Cord had grown up in the latter, and it had done well by him. But he would have preferred a big house with many rooms and floors and a rambling kitchen where there was the constant smell of good cooking and baking, brothers and sisters—and a dog. And parents, of course, who were kind and loving and always there. But his life had not been that way.

He should have been exuberant, that he'd come back to the city of his youth and to which he now had given something back. Yet, he felt oddly depressed and let down. The youth shelter was everything he wanted it to be, but he felt now, looking at the lines, which were somehow a cross between the contemporary and the old, that there should never be a need for these buildings. Every child born of two people deserved two people to love him and take care of him. Cord suddenly swung away from the window.

"Is there anything else, Cord?" Lawrence Gordon asked him.

"No. I think not. Let's just get these papers together and sign the one that says the property has been inspected and now officially belongs to the city."

Gordon gathered papers and folders while Cord neatly rolled the blueprints. "What do you want to do about dinner?'' Gordon asked, stuffing materials into his briefcase. Cord looked at his watch and shook his head.

"I think I'll forgo dinner, Larry. There's an eight o'clock flight back to New York and I'd just as soon make it."

"Where will you be staying this time?"

"With the Clarks. They have that town house on Madison—"

"I'll never understand why you don't get an apartment in New York. You can't enjoy practically living out of a suitcase."

"No, I don't. But I'm never in New York for very long. Now that the summer's here I'm anxious to get up to Randolph for a few months, work on some other projects and designs."

Gordon stopped his movements to look at Cord speculatively. Keeping his voice nondescript he asked. "How's that young lady you married two months ago?" He could almost feel Cord's icy eyes on his back.

"Why do you ask?"

Gordon finally swung around to face Cord, his kind face set in an innocent expression of curiosity. "I just wondered how she was doing. How the, er, arrangement was working out."

Cord took the time to straighten his tie and put on his jacket, making it obvious he didn't want to talk about it, but he answered the question.

"I was with her just before this trip. These things take time. Even I realize that."

Gordon shrugged, pulling on his mustache. "She seemed a nice young woman. Smart, pretty. I liked her."

"What's to like?" Cord asked impatiently. "She's suitable. She's doing what she's supposed to. And she's being paid rather well for it, I might add!"

Lawrence Gordon was not surprised at this attitude.

In the ten years he'd known and worked with Cortland Temple, he'd always known him to be a rigid man. Not cruel, but unforgiving. Gordon was not sure what he'd expected to happen once Cord was set on this marriage with the sole purpose of fathering a child. Maybe he'd hoped that having someone else to be responsible for would soften him, or give him something else besides the hard work and solitary existence. Gordon couldn't imagine anyone living a whole life that way. Nor could he imagine anyone more in need of something else than Cord. But it was obvious that Cord had not become responsible for this woman—he'd simply made her available to himself.

"What does she do when you're away?"

Cord shook his head absently. "I've no idea. Classes, I suppose."

"She hasn't drawn on the thousand dollars yet. I wonder how she's supporting herself."

"I really couldn't say," Cord continued indifferently taking a final look around to make sure he'd forgotten nothing. "Are you flying back with me tonight?"

"No. I've got to talk to the inspectors in the morning. I'll try for a flight in the afternoon."

"Fine. I appreciate you're dropping everything to come down here with me, Larry."

"No problem...no problem." Gordon waved offhandedly. A wicked gleam came to his eyes, however, as Cord reached the door of the agency office where their business was conducted. "Give my regards to Mrs. Temple."

He missed the scathing look Cord threw at him as he left the room, but Gordon was fully aware of his displeasure in the slamming of the door.

Cord had been successful in keeping his own anger in check during the whole two weeks concluding this business, but he had not forgotten he could not reach

Monica by phone for two days before he'd left for Texas. It infuriated him when she wasn't around to take his calls. And it did nothing for him that on top of this nonsense he kept getting flashes of her as she looked in a silky print summer dress one Saturday afternoon. At the oddest moment he'd suddenly remember the feel of her slim body beneath his as she responded to his lovemaking for the first time, or the softness of her sensual mouth when he kissed her.

Cord muttered an oath violently beneath his breath. Damn Lawrence Gordon for his meddlesome tongue. He slammed out of the front door of the office complex, completely startling workers leaving for the day. But he never saw them. He was trying to picture what Monica would look like with all her hair loose and down around her.

It must have been a record hot day for Paterson, New Jersey. The air was still and thick, and Monica felt suspended in it. Around her were the sounds of many voices in family conversations. Among them every now and then was the soothing motherly voice of Mildred Connors, Donna's mother, as she admonished or scolded one of her various children or their offspring. She was a tiny woman but there had never been any doubt as to who headed and nurtured the members of this group.

A slight smile curved Monica's mouth as she sat back against a garden lounge chair, her eyes closed. She let the garden sounds murmur and buzz through her head and stayed still. They'd tried to get her to eat something a while ago, but Monica wasn't up to eating. Ever since she'd arrived with Donna almost a week ago, Mama Connors had, predictably, been trying to get food into her.

"Lord, I know you girls are always worried about

your weight and how you look, but a few pounds wouldn't hurt you a bit,'' she'd scolded Monica, telling her she looked much too thin. Donna also felt that Monica had lost weight and was looking gaunt and pale.

Monica turned her head in the direction of the voice that had just called her name. Slowly opening her eyes, she watched the petite form of Mama Connors approach her with a plate in one hand and a glass in the other.

"Now you sit up and eat this! I won't take no for an answer this time!" she told Monica, her forehead wrinkling in a frown. "You'll feel better with something in your stomach. I know what I'm talking about!"

"But, Mama," Monica groaned, calling her by the name everyone else used, "I feel so much better when I don't eat too much!"

"Now there you're wrong. You feel bad because your stomach is empty. And I bet it's worse when you get up in the morning!"

Monica looked at her in surprise. "As a matter of fact, yes!"

Mama smiled knowingly and pushed the plate toward Monica. "Believe me. I know plenty about what's ailing you. Here. This is just a tiny bit of salad, and here's some iced tea. Now you eat all of it!"

Mildred Connors would not give an inch as she stood, hands folded in front of her waiting for Monica to begin eating. After the first tentative bit, she nodded her head sagely at Monica and murmured, "That's better."

Monica continued to force herself to eat, and actually began to feel less hollow inside. Monica moved her legs and made room for Mrs. Connors to sit down.

"You know," she said softly stroking Monica's arm, "in a few more weeks you'll feel much better. Your body just needs time to adjust itself."

"Adjust to what?" Monica asked confused.

Mama Connors raised her brows. "Why, to the baby, of course!"

Monica stopped eating and stared at the woman in front of her. It took Mama Connors only a second to assess the situation. Taking Monica's hand, she held the cold fingers in her small warm brown ones. "You didn't realize, did you?" she asked.

Completely numb, Monica just shook her head. Mama looked down at the hand she held and touched the thin delicate band on the ring finger. "Donna didn't mention you'd gotten married. When?"

"Almost three months ago."

Mama chuckled softly, shaking her head. "Well, my guess is you're almost two months pregnant." She frowned. "You haven't quarreled so soon, have you? Where is your husband?"

"He—he's just away on business." Monica suddenly panicked, hoping Mama Connors wouldn't ask, because she had no idea where.

"Well, I've brought five healthy beautiful children into this world, I know what the signs are. I knew from looking at you the first day you arrived."

"What do I do?" Monica asked.

"Besides finding a doctor, there's not a lot to do! Nature will take care of just about everything!" Monica frowned and Mildred Connors had an uneasy feeling.

"You do want this baby, don't you? Hadn't you and your husband planned on it?"

"Yes."

"Then I reckon you're just still surprised. Won't your husband be pleased when he hears!"

"Yes! He certainly will be,' Monica readily agreed.

"I'd always hoped that Donna would have a baby. But I suppose it's just as well since the marriage didn't last. It's hard raising a child alone!"

Monica tightened her jaw. She was sure that Cord had considered all of that. And it was his problem.

Monica allowed herself no thoughts as to how the child would be raised. She wasn't going to think about it. Lee Ann had been her child. Monica had lavished all her love and attention on her sister as though she were her own baby. She knew exactly what it was to worry and care and hope.

Mildred Connor's voice interrupted her thoughts. "When is your husband due back?"

Monica flushed, and fidgeted uneasily on the lounge chair. "I'm not sure. He—he's so busy, he sometimes forgets to let me know what's going on!"

Again Mama Connors frowned, thinking that young people these days had such different ideas on how to conduct a marriage. "Well, as soon as he gets home, you should let him know about your condition. I know he'll be happy. Summers in New York can get pretty unbearable. It's worse if you're pregnant. Perhaps you can get away for a while."

"Perhaps," Monica murmured.

"Well, you just rest now."

Monica smiled gratefully at her and Mama Connors moved back to the other group of people in the garden. Monica sat back once again in her lounge chair and unconsciously rested a hand over her stomach. It was flat and firm under the cotton top she wore, the way it had always been. But it was done. She was going to have Cord's baby. She hadn't connected her nausea and loss of weight to the possibility of a baby. Yet she had to admit she didn't know what to expect. She lay now with eyes closed to see if she could tell any difference in herself, and couldn't.

Four days later back in New York, she received an irate cold phone call from Cord.

"Where the hell have you been? I've been trying to reach you for a week!"

"I was away."

"We're going to have to come to some understanding. When I'm in the city I expect you here as well!"

"Cord—"

"I don't like wasting my time. I hung around for days waiting for you to show up!"

"Cord—"

"Well, I couldn't wait any longer, I had to leave again—"

"Cord, please!" Monica said plaintively.

"Yes, what is it?" he snapped at her.

Monica took a deep breath suddenly, for no accountable reason, ashamed to tell him her news.

"Dammit, Monica, are you there?"

"Cord," she began again, "I'm pregnant!" and it came out barely as a whisper. There followed a small silence, while Monica waited, holding her breath, for him to speak.

"My God!" was his dismayed response.

Monica didn't know what to do with herself, what to expect. She couldn't bring herself to call Eileen again and was too embarrassed by her ignorance to talk to Donna's mother. But she wanted to know what changes to expect. Donna had left with her summer stock group for a six week tour and was no longer available to talk to.

After Cord's initial display of surprise, he had gotten angry with her. If she hadn't been off somewhere unreachable, he might have been there in person to hear the news. Neither had any idea what else he could have done, but at least he would have been there. At the time, Monica was just as happy that he wasn't in New York. But after a week and a half of practical solitude, she would have been happy for even Cord's tall cool unruffled presence.

Trying to take a class today had been a mistake, she thought, as she tried to catch her breath. Monica moved off the dance floor and unconsciously rested an arm across her abdomen. She stood and watched the rest of the class perform the routine, dismayed that she'd been unable to finish even half.

Monsieur Denier waved the class on to the next section, instructing the piano player to pick up the tempo. He then minced his way across the floor to Monica, clucking as he approached and shaking his head in admonishment.

"My dear Monica, what is this you are doing? It is not movement! It is not dance! What has happened?"

Monica stood straight and wiped the back of her hand across her wet brow. She managed a weak smile. "I'm sorry, Monsieur. I just...just seem to be so tired lately."

"You foolish girl! Of course we get tired...and the heat! It is miserable, *non*?"

"Yes, it is."

"Then you should not be here. What are you trying to do? Get heat prostration? Besides the doctor has said you must wait, am I not correct? So"—he began to lead her toward the dressing room—"you will go and shower and go home...and do not come back until spring!"

"Oh, but Monsieur," Monica began, panic stricken, "I must—"

"You must do nothing but take better care of yourself, *oui*? Next spring we will make a dancer of you again, *mignon*!" and with one final gentle push, he sent her through the door to the dressing room.

Feeling weepy and sorry for herself, Monica did as she was told. She showered and changed and walked

out of the dance studio on Broadway for what was probably the last time until the next spring. She contem-
plated her immediate future, not at all remembering
that this had been settled for her, as she headed home.
Once there, Monica kicked off her clogs, sat with her
feet up eating a container of yogurt and reading a newly
arrived letter from Lee Ann.

Her sister was apparently adjusting very well to Europe and having a grand time. The dance clases were
torturous, but already she was showing improvement
and receiving praise. No easy task so early on.

Monica sighed and put the letter away, feeling both
satisfaction and despair. Satisfaction that Lee Ann's life
had suddenly blossomed and opened up to such wonderful possibilities. Despair that her own seemed to
have come to a virtual standstill. She was deep in a fit
of sudden depression when the doorbell rang. She
moved listlessly in her bare feet to answer and was
more than a little surprised to find Cord standing there,
filling her doorframe with his size. He wore tan
brushed cotton jeans and an open-neck shirt, making
her instantly aware of the dark curls on his chest at the
opening. A pair of dark glasses completely concealed
his eyes and their expression from her, but he removed
them now, placing them in the pocket of his shirt. He
looked, as usual, in control and remarkably at ease
standing in front of her.

"Hello, Monica," Cord said, stepping into the apartment. He noticed her nervous movements, but something else as well. She looked unusually pale and
drawn, and thinner than he'd remembered. It flashed
through his mind that perhaps she'd lied to him about
being pregnant. "How have you been?" he asked
evenly, making Monica smile to herself ruefully. He
might have been asking the time of day for all the concern there was in his voice

"I've been better," she remarked sarcastically, leading the way to the living room. "Would you like something to drink?" When he merely nodded she went to the kitchen and came back with two glasses of iced tea. Cord continued to watch her intently as she handed him his glass and took a seat on the sofa some distance from him. He quirked a brow in amusement but said nothing. Monica realized that there would be no need now to spend any more time in the bedroom with him or to experience the effect he had on her there. But she also recognized a regret, having only just learned what that intimacy could mean.

"How are you feeling?" Cord asked her again.

Monica, feeling piqued by his cool front, snapped, "What do you care?"

Cord looked first surprised at her sudden outburst, and then his mouth tightened as he said stiffly, "Don't be foolish. Of course I care!"

Monica went a little limp and her sudden anger died just as quickly. "I'm sorry. Of course you do. After all, the child is what you want, isn't it?" she asked. How could she tell him she felt alone and more than a little afraid? This was just a job, but one she'd never performed before. She wasn't sure what she was feeling. How could she explain that without her dance she felt as though she had no purpose and no focus in life?

What would she have then to take its place?

Monica ran her hand up her neck, pushing the damp loose wisps of hair back into the bun. She closed her eyes momentarily, not seeing the close scrutiny with which Cord watched her every move. "It's—it's been very hot. I've been feeling like a wilted leaf of lettuce!"

"Have you been ill?"

"Well, yes. I've been nauseous. And very tired. It was much worse a few weeks ago."

"And what has the doctor advised?"

"The doctor?" she asked, looking at him blankly.

"Of course! You've been to a doctor, haven't you?"

"No, I—" Monica began in confusion. "I haven't gone."

"Obviously not!" Cord said with impatience. "Just what have you been doing to yourself?" he asked with such contempt in his voice that Monica felt her defenses rising. She lifted her chin stubbornly. "I—I've been busy. I have my classes in the afternoons—"

"Monica! Don't tell me you've been dancing. In your condition?"

"Well, why not?" Monica shouted defensively. "It's what I do! And my classes are all I have right now."

"There *is* something else," Cord said through clenched teeth, jumping to his feet and striding over to stand gigantic and imposing in front of her. "You have a developing infant that you are going to carry to a full, healthy term. Is that understood? I won't stand your taking stupid chances. From now on, dancing is out!" He turned away from her and thrust his hands deep into his pants pockets.

"You have no right," Monica continued to shout, standing now in her own anger to confront him.

"I have every right!" He whipped around to her. "Let's not forget why we're here, shall we? It's my child you're carrying and I won't have it jeopardized."

Monica's fist clenched and unclenched at her side, while warm blood rushed to her face.

"You've shown nothing but complete irresponsibility so far. Not going to a doctor, continuing to dance. One would think you didn't know any better!" He came so close to the mark that tears of frustration welled up in her. She wanted to hit him, to slap that superior smug attitude off his face.

"Stop yelling at me!" Her voice quavered. "I'm not a child to be scolded!"

"Then stop acting like one!" he said uncompromisingly. You look terrible. What have you been eating? Yogurt?" he asked scathingly and pointed to the half-eaten container on the coffee table.

"I know how to take care of my body."

"A dancer's body, perhaps. But not a body carrying a baby. A growing fetus needs a little more than yogurt and fruit juice! Go and get dressed. I'm taking you to see a doctor."

"That's not necessary. I'll go in a few days."

"You'll go now, even if I have to carry you!"

They stared at each other, Cord's jaw muscles tensing in determination and Monica's face flushed and mutinous.

Turning on her heels in further frustration, she stormed off to her room and slammed the door. She emerged fifteen minutes later in a two-piece skirt outfit and her hair freshly combed. Without further words they left the apartment.

Cord gave the cab driver an address on Park Avenue. "While you were changing I took the liberty of calling a gynecologist I know." Monica was curious as to how Cord knew one, but she remained stony and silent through the rest of the short ride.

The doctor's waiting room was large and bright and was filled with women in various stages of their pregnancies and a number of toddlers, happily crawling on the floor.

Cord talked briefly to the nurse/receptionist and led Monica to a seat near the door. He was the only male in the waiting room, and while a few women threw curious, amused looks his way, Cord didn't seem in the least disturbed.

Monica found herself listening to a conversation of two women next to her, as they exchanged stories about having babies. One commented that this was her second child. She suddenly giggled and lowered her voice whispering, "You know, you may think me odd, but I love being pregnant!" Monica turned to look at them openly, envying if nothing else their good humor.

One woman came out of an inner office. It was clear that she could deliver any day now. She moved her awkwardly shaped body, nonetheless, with a certain pride and grace that Monica watched in awe.

She felt something damp and wiggly touch her leg, and she looked down to find a small round face with bright black button eyes looking at her curiously. He, or she—Monica couldn't tell which—climbed up her leg to clutch a hold of her skirt and try to stand on unsteady limbs. Monica reached out to touch the youngster gently on its soft cheek. The infant gurgled and transferred its clutching hands to Cord's pant leg. Monica looked at Cord and was utterly surprised and shocked to find him contemplating the baby with gentle amusement and a smile. Monica was even more surprised when he reached and lifted the tiny form to his thigh, holding it gently and supporting its back. The baby looked openmouthed at this giant who held him and suddenly gurgled in pleasure and laughed. He waved his hands freely in the air, finally drawing his mother's attention. The woman came to relieve Cord of his burden.

"I'm sorry!" she exclaimed. "I'm afraid he's creased your pants."

"Don't worry about it. How old is he?"

"Ten months old...and into everything as you can see! I suppose you'll soon have your own son clutching at you. When it's your own, you don't mind as much!" she said candidly and turned away with the cooing baby. Monica stared at Cord, and when he finally met her eyes she saw him raise a brow and shift uncomfortably in his seat, hastily looking away from her steady gaze. But Monica inwardly knew that he had thoroughly enjoyed holding that baby.

Dr. Molly Kaplan called Cord into the cheerful interior of her office while Monica dressed in the examining room. Her lined and weathered face was the only indication of her age as she stood tall and still slender with a full head of brunette hair. She smiled at Cord and gave him a warm friendly kiss on the cheek.

"Congratulations!" she beamed.

"Thank you," he said evenly, giving nothing away.

"On everything, apparently. I didn't know you'd married." She lowered her voice to a whisper and winked at him. "Your bride is lovely! A little too thin, but that's to be expected right now with morning sickness." Dr. Kaplan sat behind her desk and Cord sat in the chair facing her. She continued to beam at him eyeing him curiously. She shook her head from side to side.

"It must have been one whirlwind affair. Did you simply sweep her off her feet?"

"You might say so," Cord answered mysteriously.

"Well, I'm delighted to be of service to you at last! You did such a wonderful job on our summer house, the least I can do is make sure you and Monica have a healthy beautiful baby."

"Thanks, Molly," Cord said again, but he began to squirm under the weighty knowledge of the true nature of his relationship to Monica.

"I must admit, Cord, I never thought to see this day. You never struck me as the marrying kind, much less the image of a father!"

He raised his brows slightly at her and smiled grimly. "I guess then I'm living proof that there's hope even for the worst of us!"

Molly Kaplan blushed. "I'm sorry, Cord. I didn't mean it quite that way."

"I know you didn't. Just what did you mean?"

She shrugged. "I guess I've always felt that this is just what you needed. I just wasn't sure it would ever happen. You surprised me!"

"Why is it that women always think the answer to any man's problems is a wife and children?"

"Not every man, but some are more obvious than others!" She put her glasses on and leaned over an open folder on her desk. "Well, let's talk about Monica and the baby, shall we? She's about six weeks pregnant." Molly looked at Cord over the top of her glasses. "I must say you used your honeymoon well."

Cord stiffened in annoyance at the inference. After all, it wasn't that kind of marriage. But Molly wasn't to know that.

"She's lost some weight due to morning sickness as I said before, but that should end in a few more weeks and then she'll begin to gain—"

At that moment Monica slowly opened the door and came into the office. Cord immediately stood and indicated she should sit in his chair.

She was pale except for two bright spots of color high on her cheeks. Monica was quiet and somewhat aloof and Molly wondered why, but she smiled reassuringly at her.

"There's no need to worry, my dear. Everything is fine. I have a list of foods you should eat and some recommended exercises. Cord tells me you're a dancer."

"Yes, I am."

"Well, of course you realize dancing is out, but those tedious barre exercises will be very good for you. Just don't overdo it." Monica looked up suddenly and smiled, relaxing in front of this amazing friendly woman.

Dr. Kaplan passed two small capsule bottles across

the desk to Monica. "These are some vitamins and some iron pills. Make sure you take them regularly. You have a small, narrow frame, so you shouldn't gain more than twenty pounds during the nine months. You can expect to feel tired, some tenderness, as well as an increase in the size of your breasts. Certain body functions will occur more frequently," she continued on and on, and Monica was mortified that Cord stood behind her listening. Dr. Kaplan sat back in her chair.

"Summer is an uncomfortable time to be expecting, so don't go rushing around in the heat. You should come in once a month for a check-up—"

"We'll have to work something else out, Molly," Cord interrupted. "I'm taking Monica out of the city until the baby is born."

Surprised, Monica sat up straight and turned with a protest ready on her lips. It died there as Cord placed a restraining hand on her shoulder and squeezed to silence her.

Cord continued. "I think it would be better if Monica didn't have to worry about the heat at all."

"That's okay," Molly said carefully, aware of the tension between them. "I don't anticipate any complications. Just relax and enjoy the experience!" She smiled at them both.

"I have a question," Monica said suddenly, when Cord would have opened the door to leave.

"Yes?"

"When will the—the baby be due?" Cord and Molly looked at each other, having forgotten about this. Molly laughed softly.

"Well, I'm glad one of us remembered that's the most important date!" Molly fingered through her notes, and then beamed at Monica. "How's February fourteenth?"

## Chapter Six

The Green Mountains of central Vermont seemed like a tufted carpeting stretching up and down the creviced hillsides. For a time the car paralleled the Connecticut River on its journey north, showing sparkling waters, and all during the trip that day, scores of people were seen fishing off its shores.

Monica was charmed. She had never known cozy communities and neighborhoods centered unto themselves. There had always been concrete and cement and glass, pollution, and mass transit. She could not even drive a car. She began to realize that the world was much more diverse and complicated, and New York was not the center of it all.

Monica had been sullen as Cord finished loading the station wagon, and on a brilliant day with New Yorkers typically rushing from here to there, he'd pulled the car onto Route 95 out of the city.

Monica had not wanted to leave New York, but Cord had made it very clear that she had no choice in the matter. After only three days in which to pack what she wanted with her through the next few months and notifying several services that she'd be away, she was en route—but she didn't know where.

Once they'd left the perimeters of the city and Cord

had fallen into a pattern with his driving, Monica turned to him. "Where *are* you taking me?" she asked curiously.

He gave Monica a brief cold look before focusing on the road again. "I'm taking you somewhere I can keep an eye on you until this is over."

She shuddered at his indifferent tone. "But where?"

"I have a house in Vermont," he replied brusquely, his brows knitting together.

"Vermont!" Monica exclaimed. "Why that's—that's so far away!"

"Far away from what?"

"From everything! Why are you doing this? I only know New York. What will I do in Vermont for six months?"

"Calm down!" Cord snapped at her, causing Monica to blink and draw back from him. She regarded his stony profile for a moment, watching the muscles in his jaw tense and relax, watching the breeze from the window ruffle up his curly gray hair. Suddenly, the anger and indignation went out of her. She didn't want to fight with him anymore. She was tired. Monica felt now like a child who'd just been told she will obey, no questions asked. All her life someone else had always thought they'd known what was best for her. Her father believing that his grief at losing his wife was more than hers at losing a mother and now needing him. Her stepmother substituting dance in her life instead of love and attention. And now Cord, whom she knew no more about than she did three months ago. He should have had the least hold on her, but oddly, it was the most binding, the most personal and intimate.

"I'm sorry," he said roughly. Monica looked at him in surprise, her amber eyes wide with an appeal. She had to trust him, now more than ever.

"I'm sorry that this"—he lifted his shoulders expressively—"this seems to be going so poorly. I think it's more than either of us anticipated."

"Yes," Monica agreed softly, understanding perhaps a little how he felt. This was all new to him as well. His anxieties were not the same as hers, but he did have them. Donna was right. They didn't know each other. If they were to get through the upcoming months there had to be some common ground for them to work on. Monica flushed red to realize that the only thing between them was this baby. It was to be his, but only after she'd delivered. Until then, it was something wholly within herself. In that, he could not participate.

"I know nothing of taking care of pregnant women," Cord stated boldly, not embarrassed by the implications, but then, Monica was finding that there was almost nothing that embarrassed him.

"It's okay. I know nothing about being pregnant," she said. Cord smiled briefly, his eyes still on the road.

"I'm just concerned that everything goes well. We'll have to cooperate from here on in. Agreed?"

Monica hesitated. "Agreed. On one condition."

Cord stiffened again. "What's the condition?" he asked, unable to keep the suspicion out of his voice.

Monica turned to look at him seriously. "Only that you not demand or order me. I respond much better to please and thank you."

Cord had not expected that. He looked at her, but all he encountered was a pair of bright eyes looking at him earnestly. He nodded and turned back to his driving. "Fair enough," he said calmly.

"Now," Monica began again, "where are we going...please?"

Cord quirked a brow and grinned for a moment, and he found himself giving in to her.

"We're going to Randolph. It's a fair-sized town in

central Vermont. I own an old house four miles outside of the town."

"Is that where you're from? Vermont?"

"No, I'm not from Vermont," he answered shortly.

Monica could see that for whatever reason that had been the wrong question to ask him. "Tell me about the house."

Cord shrugged. "You'll see it soon enough. It's just a house. It's got eight rooms on two levels. Two years ago I added a new bath and an extra room on the first floor, and a storage shed. I was hoping to flagstone an area as a walkway this summer."

"Is there a garden?" she asked.

"A garden? I haven't grown one. I'm never up there early enough in the year to turn the soil and plant seeds. But there's plenty of room for one. And there are wild flowers."

Monica sat back and relaxed, prepared now to enjoy the rest of the trip. They drove a few hours, Cord pointing out the towns and cities to her. They stopped for lunch and Monica was surprised to find herself feeling suddenly very sleepy, and against the soothing rhythm of the car she made a valiant attempt to stay awake. But it was all beyond her. She just closed her eyes for a moment to rest, listening to Cord's deep resonant voice fading farther and farther away.

Cord was still explaining about what Vermonters were like when he turned to Monica and found her fast asleep. Cord smiled slightly in amusement. Molly warned him that Monica might feel tired often for a while. She'd also stressed the need to be patient with her. Having a baby was a total unique experience. Men— husbands— had to be extra understanding and gentle. Molly's information had caused a grim despair to settle over Cord. He didn't know if he could be gentle.

As he went back to concentrating on his driving, he

found himself thinking of Natalie. Her husband had finally become governor, and he'd heard that there were children, which had really surprised him; two boys. They could have been his sons. They should have been his. He was angered and frightened to realize that a memory still had the ability to hurt. When would it all go away? When would he be left alone to put the memory and its pain into proper perspective?

He should have hated Natalie for what she'd done. And for a long time he had. But when the hate had burned itself out, he still found he couldn't forget her. He'd loved her so much. She'd been everything he'd wanted, and their future had promised so much. Cord gritted his teeth and put both hands on the wheel of the car to bring it under control. He was appalled to see he was driving close to eighty miles an hour.

Cord fought for calm and took a deep breath. Well, Natalie was not in his life now. There was only this lovely, fiery-tempered stranger next to him, an odd mixture of vulnerability and determination. There had been a few moments when he wasn't sure if he should shake her in exasperation with her stubbornness and temper, or hold her in her moments of uncertainty and confusion.

When he'd called her two weeks ago only to be told she was pregnant, a cold hard reality had taken hold. It was happening. And she, this young woman he didn't know very well, was all a part of it. *Why, in God's name, was she doing this*? Cord thought, bewildered.

Cord moved in his seat, trying to stretch and unbend his back muscles. He looked at his watch and saw there was another hour of driving to be done. There was a movement on his leg, warm and fleeting, and he looked down to see the slim curve of Monica's fingers over the side of his thigh. Cord quickly glanced at her and saw she was still sleeping. A muscle tightened in Cord's arm and traveled to his neck and jaw. There was no need for him to ever physically go near her again or to share her bed since it was clear that she was to have his child. But with horrifying clarity he knew he wanted her again. Not out of tenderness or love, but out of pure desire and need. Cord muttered an oath under his breath and ran his free hand roughly through his hair. He didn't want to need her. But she was here . . . and he did.

Cord let Monica sleep for another twenty minutes and finally woke her up. He'd become too aware of her hand on his leg. Monica twisted sensuously and stretched her seemingly feline body. Cord could sense and feel, rather than see the motion and he felt his desire rise.

Monica opened her eyes and turned her gaze out the window to the unfolding Vermont landscape. Her fascination and delight grew with each new mile.

"We're almost there," Cord said.

"It's beautiful country!" she breathed.

"Yes, it is."

Monica turned to look at him curiously. "Why Vermont, Cord? What made you want to buy a house there?"

"I didn't really want to. If I hadn't bought the land and house, it would have gone to a developer who had a shopping mall in store for the area. The people in Randolph didn't want that to happen, but couldn't come up with enough money to make a better offer."

"And you did?"

"Well, sort of. The man who owned it was retiring to Florida with his wife. He was a contractor I'd worked with over the years. He wanted to preserve the land and the inherent nature of the area around his property. We made an agreement. He'd accept less money for the land and house, if I promised to leave it basically just as it is. Any improvements he has to agree to."

"But it is still yours. You agreed to his plan?"

"Why not?" Cord shrugged. "I didn't want to see a.

shopping mall there either. And I knew I wouldn't be spending that much time there myself so it was easy to agree to leave things the same. It's very comfortable in the summer. It never gets too hot, that's why I thought it would be good for you. But the winters can be pretty cold."

He didn't add any plans for the winter, and Monica wondered if he'd bring her back to New York when the temperature dropped. She was silent for a while and turned her eyes back to the window. "What are the people like?"

"Quiet. Conservative. Cautious. They don't think much of outsiders, people who aren't from Vermont. But they're polite and willing to assist you if you need it."

Cord turned off an exit and onto a two-lane road. Almost immediately he made another turn onto a graveled road that dipped and curved for almost a quarter of a mile, turning left sharply and exposing to Monica's questioning eyes a background hill covered with dense trees and foliage. Along the right side of the road leading right up to the hills were large maple trees; on the left, bushes of wild raspberries and an old wooden structure like a barn. On the other side beyond the maple trees was a clearing of mowed grass sloping gently downward. In the center of it, partially shaded by the maple trees and backed by the mountainous hillside was a white farmhouse with green shutters and a red door.

Cord pulled the wagon up to the side rear of the house and stopped, turning off the ignition. He turned to study Monica's awed expression.

"Well, we're here," he said.

Monica wanted to laugh, but she didn't because the sound got caught somewhere in her chest. She knew they weren't merely *here*...they were where she'd always wanted to be.

There were three bedrooms on the second level and a large bath. There were two large first-floor rooms separated by the kitchen, which had a fireplace, and the sitting room, also containing a fireplace. There was another bath near the kitchen. Cord led her to and deposited her bags in the large room on the other side of the sitting room. He then conducted her on a quick tour of the house to show her where everything was. Monica was aware that he did not display any of the pride that most people would show when opening their homes to outside eyes. The house was a pure delight, and Monica did not understand Cord's not seeing this.

"There's a housekeeper who comes twice a week to clean and change linens. Sometimes she cooks meals and leaves them for me."

"I can cook!" Monica informed him.

Cord frowned. "There's no need for you to do that. I don't intend that you should have to take care of this," he said, indicating the house. "Or me."

Monica stood stubbornly in front of him. "You mean it wasn't part of the agreement, don't you?" She had the satisfaction of seeing him speechless for a moment. "Look, there isn't going to be anything for me to do all day long. I won't mind cooking and things like that."

Cord looked at her determination and decided it wasn't worth another argument with her. If she wanted to play house, let her. At least he'd know what she was up to.

"Okay," he agreed shortly and turned away into the room off the kitchen. It was large and spacious with only a king-size bed taking up one wall, a desk with chair, and another easy chair near a window. "This is my room," he said unnecessarily, "I'll be near enough if—if anything happens."

"What about the housekeeper? What will she think

when she finds me here and sees that we have—that you and I—"

"Mrs. Gavener knows about you." Monica frowned, wondering how much she knew. "Before I came down to New York to get you I had her prepare that room on the other side. I told her I thought you'd be more comfortable considering your condition."

"You've thought of everything," Monica said absently, smoothing a hand over her stomach. Cord ignored her comment.

"I also felt it would be good to have another woman near..." And he left the thought to hang in the air. Monica said nothing, but turned back into the large kitchen. She ran her hand gently over the marble countertop and listened to the soft creaking of the old wood floor under her feet. Cord was right behind her.

"And what will you do all day?" she asked him.

Cord folded his arms across his chest and leaned a shoulder against a cabinet. "I'd only planned on being here a month or so. But now I think it may be the rest of the year."

"You don't have to do that for me," Monica said earnestly to him.

Cord raised a brow, his mouth slightly curved in a smile. "I'm not."

Monica blushed and turned away from him.

"A few of the local bigshots had been after me in the past to design a new library, and the head of the school board wants to build a new house. I think I'll take on both jobs. It will keep me busy until—"

"What's that house over there?" she interrupted, not wanting to hear any more. Cord came slowly up behind her to look over her shoulder and out the kitchen window.

"That's an old sugar mill," Cord answered. Monica could feel the warmth of his body, he stood so close.

And his warm breath stirred the hairs next to her ear. She moved hastily away, finding it suddenly, hard to catch her breath. Cord's eyes followed her, puzzled by her sudden fidgeting.

"And what is it used for?"

"The last owner used to process maple syrup there. It hasn't been used in a number of years." As he talked he turned away from the window and walked to the door beyond which the car was parked.

With one hand on the knob he looked back at Monica framed in the kitchen doorway. Her hair was a bit disheveled from napping in the car, and her soft cotton skirt and top hugged the slender curves of her body. He pulled his cold gray eyes up the length of her body to her soft full lips and her amber eyes, which were watchful.

In the five years that he'd owned the house, he'd never brought a woman here. Perhaps bringing Monica here was not a good idea. But it was too late for second thoughts.

"I'll just bring in the rest of your things," he said and quickly left, leaving Monica looking at his retreating form with questions in her eyes. She also recognized, but for different reasons than Cord's at the moment, that it was not going to be easy being here alone with him.

The house that Monica grew up in was always unfriendly and cold. She'd never had a sense of warm sunshine or freedom that would have allowed her to run giggling and squealing, as children do, through the one-story structure. She remembered her father as being somber and silent, always. She had no recollection of him laughing in abandon or smiling, except maybe for a while when Eileen first came. She had no memory of ever coming close to her father, of climbing onto his lap for comfort or love or warmth. They were there together, yet essentially were strangers to each other.

As Monica grew older, she had no true idea of what it was that brought a man and a woman together to become man and wife. Why did it happen? Did it really serve a purpose? The contrast of her childhood home and her present surroundings, however, became crystal clear.

Cord's house was warm. The people living in tentative congeniality may have been behaving cautiously and cool, but the rooms and furnishings and sunlight coming through the front door into the rooms exuded cheerful welcome.

Cord began to surreptitiously ask how she was feeling. But his offhand cosseting was not being protective of her—it was concern for the welfare of the baby. They did not focus their individual attentions on each other beyond this consideration. Cord had his daily architectural work and Monica had the house. It was the only thing in her life besides Lee Ann that she'd loved the moment she'd laid eyes on it.

Monica was introduced to Olivia Gavener, a small wiry lady of indeterminate age and incredible boundless energy. She showed Monica how things really worked and explained the odd idiosyncrasies of the old house. Livy, as she insisted on being called, also expressed blatant curiosity about her, and who she was to have finally brought Cord to marriage and imminent parenthood. But Monica would not satisfy her questions, only smiling politely and remaining silent, as Livy and Monica quickly became friends.

Cord and Monica coexisted in the house, but nothing more than that. He got up for work early, leaving her to her own devices. She'd sometimes prepare dinner if he was home, but when they sat together, it was mostly in silence or with polite, safe conversation. Now and then Monica would find Cord's steady gray eyes on her and she'd squirm under the unreadable expression. She'd sometimes go for days without seeing him at all, but at night she'd hear him moving around his large room on the other side of the house. At these moments she'd remember the evening of her sexual awakening in his arms, by his touch, and she'd get hot and breathless with the memory. She was shocked to realize that she wanted him to do that again. But Monica fought the feelings and kept them down, knowing her desire was futile and out of place.

Her body began to change. She put on weight, and her stomach rounded. Monica was afraid of the change, not being familiar or comfortable with it. If she'd been less ignorant about the physical aspects of being pregnant, the adjustment would have been easier. But she fought this as well, only knowing that a dancer must be taut and slender in body.

Few of her clothes fit, and only her loosest garments were comfortable. She knew she'd have to purchase some of those awful commercial maternity tops and she dreaded it. Livy came to the rescue when she told her there was a recreation center in the town that ran an exchange of toddler clothing and maternity wear. One afternoon Livy picked her up in a Land-Rover and drove her the four miles into town to the center. A day camp was in session for the summer, and there was the noise and commotion of young children all over the place. Livy led Monica to the front office, and against the wall, hanging neatly on a clothes rack, were tops and dresses and pants for the expectant mother. Monica thumbed through them and picked out the least obvious-looking constructions in her size. She knew she'd still have to supplement this wardrobe somehow.

With her arms loaded, they retraced their steps

through the building. Faintly Monica heard the piano strains of Erik Satie, and instinctively turned to the direction of the music. She peeped curiously into a room where a dance class was being conducted. A young woman was conducting barre exercises against a mirrored wall for a student body of eight young girls, about ten to thirteen years old.

The instructor at the head of the room was adequate, but she did not have, in Monica's quick eyes, what it takes to fire a child's imagination to dance.

"I see you found the dance room. We attempt to teach the children dance, but don't judge us harshly. This isn't New York!"

"Oh, I wouldn't judge you at all!" Monica was quick to assure Livy. "And they have to start somewhere."

"Come, let me introduce you to Lynn. I believe she studied in New York." Livy had Monica's arm and walked her briskly over to the petite dark-haired woman, interrupting the class.

"Lynn, I'm sorry to break in like this unannounced, but I want you to meet a fellow dancer. This is Monica Temple. Monica, Lynn Martin."

"Hi, Monica." The woman smiled shyly.

"Monica dances with the New York Ballet Corp."

"How exciting!" Lynn seemed very much impressed. "Are you here on vacation?"

Monica blushed and shifted the clothes in her arms. "No, I have to—I mean, I'm here to—"

"Monica's going to have a baby," Livy finished for her. Lynn smiled ruefully and sighed.

"Congratulations. But at least you had the chance to dance before starting a family. I no sooner finished school when I got married and came back home to have two kids!"

"Oh I plan to go back to dancing in the spring," Monica informed her without thinking.

"I see," Lynn intoned, probably not seeing at all. "Well, I guess once it's in your blood it's hard to get rid of it, right?"

"I do miss it already," Monica said, looking at the studio and the youngsters eyeing her curiously.

"I should have known you danced," Lynn continued.

"Why?" Monica asked.

"Because you still walk with a turn out. The kids call it a duck walk." There were a few snickers of laughter from the group.

"Will you dance for us?" came a high tiny voice from the center of the room. The three women turned to see the smallest girl sitting on the floor pulling idly on the strings of her ballet practice shoes, while she also collected dust from the floor on her pink leotard.

"Honey, I don't think Mrs. Temple will be able—"

"Oh, no! I'd love to!" Monica countered.

Lynn frowned. "Mrs. Temple, really, under the circumstances I think—"

"It's okay. Really. I can still move freely, and I know lots of dance routines that aren't too tiring."

"Ooooooh! Can she, Mrs. Martin?" the little girl piped. Lynn still looked doubtful.

"Look," Monica suggested, "I can do a five-minute routine for the class if you like."

"Will you wear a tutu?" the little girl asked excitedly. Monica smiled at her. Her tutu would be uncomfortably tight now.

"I promise to wear something almost like a tutu."

"This is very kind of you. Are you quite sure your doctor would approve?"

Monica hadn't been to see a doctor since she arrived in Vermont. "I promise to tell him when I see him," she fibbed, satisfying both Livy and Lynn Martin.

"Is next week okay for me to come?" Monica asked.

"Next week is fine. As a matter of fact, feel free to stop by anytime you like. I could use an assistant sometimes!" Lynn laughed jokingly, but the suggestion was readily picked up by Monica, who knew she'd very much like to come here again.

"Thank you for bringing me, Livy," Monica said once they were back in the Rover and headed out of town.

"It was no trouble at all. I won't be able to take you all the time. If you learn the route you can drive yourself."

"Oh," Monica said softly, causing Olivia to look at her.

"You don't drive?"

"No, I never learned!"

"Well, you'd better have Cord show you how to run this thing pretty quick."

Monica looked doubtful. "I don't think I should trouble Cord with teaching me to drive."

"Of course you should!" Livy said brusquely. "That's what husbands are for!" Monica giggled, a sudden vision of an impatient Cord growling over her attempts to manage a vehicle flashing through her mind.

"It's very easy, and just takes a little practice and patience."

Monica groaned. If she had to expect patience from Cord she was already in trouble.

That evening while Cord sat in a deep chair with his long legs stretched out in front of him, frowning over a contract, Monica moved restlessly around the room, trying to find a way to broach the subject of her learning how to drive. She picked up a book and put it down. She shifted an arrangement of dried flowers and shifted it back again. She walked to the windows and looked into the inky blackness, unable to detect a single shape in the night. She turned back, only to find Cord frowning at her in speculation. Monica raised her chin stubbornly, already prepared for a fight.

Cord put his head back against his chair and regarded her further through half-closed eyes.

"Okay. What is it?" he asked. "You're about to ask me for something."

Monica stared wide eyed at him, a little piqued that he would guess some of her thoughts.

"Come on, tell me," he said patiently.

"I—I just wanted to ask—"

"Yes?"

"If you'd teach me to drive." There was dead silence while Cord continued to look at her in a lazy way. "Don't worry," Monica added flippantly. "I'm not planning on running away!"

"I didn't think you were," Cord answered smoothly. "Why do you want to learn?"

"Because then I can drive into town and shop. Or visit Livy. I get lonely sometimes being here all day. I'm not used to that." She waited for his decision, feeling like a subject before the king, asking for a pardon or reprieve. After another moment Cord sat forward again and returned his eyes to the contract before him.

"All right. We'll begin Saturday." he answered.

"Oh! Thank you, Cord!" Monica breathed. But he only grunted in reply.

Much to Monica's surprise and secret pleasure, Cord was remarkably patient with her in showing her how to drive a standard vehicle. Monica learned the rudiments quickly and responded to his easy coaxing voice. She also found herself uncomfortably aware of his hard body next to her own. He sat close with one arm behind her along the top of the seat. She could feel the heat of him through the fabric of her jeans and top where it came into contact with his. She felt heady and breathless. Every time he put his hand over hers to correct its hold on the steering wheel or lean over her to point something out, she went rigid.

They drove dozens of times up and down the gravel road leading to the highway. Her steering got straighter and more consistent with each trip. It was only when he touched her that her mind went blank and the Rover would swerve crazily.

"Easy!" Cord warned her firmly, pulling the wheel back to align the tires forward again. "You have to pay attention at all times! I want you to practice on this road for a few days. Next week I'll see if you can drive us into town without killing us both!" He grinned lopsided at her, his eyes regarding her warmly for the first time that Monica could consciously remember. She looked away from his gaze, feeling shy.

"I promise I won't," she answered him. "Thank you for taking the time. That wasn't so bad at all."

"No," Cord answered, his eyes sweeping over her flushed face and slightly disheveled hair. "It wasn't bad at all." His fingers along the seat back brushed gently over her shoulders, and the feeling that went through her was warm.

Cord was bending toward her, his eyes on her mouth. "Monica, I—" But he got no further as a car horn began to honk loudly and persistently in front of them. Cord moved away from her, and they looked out the front glass to see a blue sports car in their path. A head poked out the driver's side.

"Hey! One of us is going the wrong way!"

A scowl settled on Cord's face and he got out of the Rover to walk around to the driver's side, forcing Monica to take his vacated seat. Cord silently started the vehicle and backed it all the way up the road and stopped next to the house. The blue sports car followed slowly.

Monica and Cord were already out of the Rover when a solidly built man, some inches shorter than Cord, got out of the small car. He had a wide merry grin on his pleasant boyish face as he looked at them.

"Well, well! You sly old dog, keeping secrets?" he asked in high good humor. Cord frowned, but the corner of his mouth lifted reluctantly in a return grin.

"What brings you here?" Cord asked bluntly without a welcome, but the other man continued to smile as he now openly surveyed Monica several times from head to foot.

"Go on. Tell me you don't remember asking me to come a week ago."

"Oh, yeah," Cord said disagreeably.

"I understood you had a state job and a very complicated contract." Yet, while he talked, his conversation directed to Cord, he never took his eyes off of Monica. When Cord still didn't introduce them or even acknowledge her, the stranger came right up to her and put out a large beefy hand. "Hello, I'm Matthew Bell. No doubt Cortland here has told you nothing about me!"

"No, he hasn't" was all Monica could think to say, both amused and bewildered. Matthew waited expectantly.

Finally, Cord sighed. "Matthew, I'd like you to meet Monica."

"Well, hello, Monica." Matthew grinned, almost leering at her.

"Monica is my . . . wife."

"I can't begin to tell you how surprised I am to find you married!" Matthew smiled at Cord before sweeping his eyes around to Monica.

"Since you've seen fit to tell me all evening, I'm beginning to get the idea," Cord answered sarcastically.

Matthew laughed, totally unoffended. He looked at Monica and quirked a brow. "It would take a pretty special person to get you settled. I guess Monica's pretty special." He said it seriously, even though he smiled. Monica felt very uncomfortable being discussed in this manner. As Matthew finished his observation, Monica jumped up from the table so suddenly the water glasses swayed.

"I'll—I'll get the coffee," she said unsteadily and walked to the other side of the kitchen. Busying herself with cups and saucers, she could still hear the murmur of their voices at the table behind her.

Cord had not been particularly cordial during the evening. But Monica suddenly realized that the brooding, cold front that Cord put on was in part just that. Matthew Bell, a long standing friend, knew this and knew how to conduct a friendship around it. Monica hoped that perhaps she could also learn to read Cord better.

She came back to the table and poured the coffee, and retook her seat. Matthew leaned forward resting his elbows on the table, circling his large hands around the delicate cup.

"So, tell me how you and Cord met."

Monica's stomach lurched and she glanced in alarm at Cord. He was relaxed in his chair, regarding Matthew with some amused tolerance for his bold questions.

"I'm not known for my tact." Matthew chuckled. "So you might as well tell me!"

Monica blanched.

Cord reached out an arm and rested it on the back of Monica's chair. It was a possessive move, but also an oddly calming one for Monica. "Monica and I met in New York last spring. We were married at the beginning of May."

Monica let out a sigh. It had been so simple. And

he'd spoken the truth, although the details were sadly lacking. Matthew raised a brow at Cord.

"It must have been love at first sight. I didn't know you were susceptible," Matthew said testily.

"I'm full of surprises," Cord responded in a lazy fashion.

Matthew turned back to Monica. "And what do you do in New York that caused Cord to notice you out of so many New York types?"

"She was prettier than most New York types," Cord put in at once. Monica couldn't tell whether to take his comment seriously or not.

"I'm a dancer, Mr. Bell."

"Please. Cord and I go back a long way. Call me Matt. Are you a good dancer?"

"A very good dancer," Monica answered proudly.

"Maybe you'll dance for me some evening."

"Maybe," she answered in a slightly provocative voice. She turned to Cord. "I know you and Mr. Be— Matt have business to discuss, so I'll clean up and say good-night." She stood and Matthew also came to his feet. Cord slowly followed suit.

"Please sit down. I'll just check that your room has everything you need." She smiled at Matt and left the table. As she headed toward the stairs she heard Matt say to Cord, "I don't know how you did it, but she's really something!" Monica quickly started up the stairs, not wanting to hear Cord's reply or see his reaction to that statement. The answer, she found, was very important to her. But she was, nonetheless, afraid to really know.

Matthew Bell stayed nearly two weeks, his days spent with Cord out in the field somewhere, where the new town library was being built. In the evenings after they'd eaten he provided cheerful entertainment in the form of amusing anecdotes about his law profession and his practice. He behaved with flirtatious gallantry toward Monica, which she found harmless and fun. Cord at times seemed not to notice, and at other times, especially as they went into the second week together, frowned in apparent disapproval. But he never said anything.

Matt helped her with the dishes in the evening, and it became a hilarious game between them as he pretended clumsiness with the beautiful flowered china. Monica always said good-night first leaving the two friends to finish the evening alone, a little embarrassed that Matt would discover she and Cord did not share the same room.

Cord saw to it that Monica applied for, and received a driver's permit. During the day while he and Matt were away, she practiced her driving of the Land-Rover until finally Cord was satisfied with her progress and took her for the official road test. Her license was granted on the first try. For Monica it was a major accomplishment.

Finally Matthew left, promising Cord he'd return in September for the next phase of the contract negotiations. Just as carefree as he arrived did he depart, giving Monica more than just a casual kiss good-bye and winking wickedly at a silent Cord. He waved good-bye and his blue sports car gunned off down the rough road.

Monica's days fell into a pattern. Three afternoons a week she'd go to the town recreation center and help to teach the ballet class. Enrollment had almost tripled since her impromptu performance, and she found herself with a following of devoted young girls all of whom wanted to be dancers like herself. A number of adolescent boys took to hanging around the studio, obviously interested, and Monica buffaloed a number of them into the class by casually explaining how the male dancers had the hardest and most strenuous role because they had to be strong enough to lift their female partners. When the boys boasted that anyone could do that, Monica dared them to demonstrate. The strength was there but they were dismally uncoordinated. The girls laughed at their efforts.

Monica promised that if they came to class she'd show them how to do the leaps and jumps. They were hooked. The classes progressed well, and she enjoyed them tremendously.

Monica also took to exploring the area around the house. She'd come back with pockets filled with wild raspberries. Or once she wandered through the old sugar mill and was surprised to find that while the outside looked like it was ready to collapse, the inside was large and open with an upper loft, and in pretty good shape. There was an old sled, and on a peg near the front door she found a heavy wool cape in need of only a good cleaning to be serviceable. She took it with her back to the house.

She wrote letters regularly to Lee Ann and called her once long distance to Europe just to say hello. She also called Donna to let her know she was in Vermont, pregnant and well, and that she didn't know when she'd get back to New York.

Monica often visited with Olivia Gavener, and Olivia helped her to sew a number of loose caftans to disguise her thickening figure. Monica no longer paid much attention to her increased weight. Logically she knew it had to happen as part of the process her body was adjusting to in order to perform well in this task. She did not think about being pregnant beyond that.

If Matt Bell had not come, perhaps she would have gone on for the next few months doing and managing as she had, but he had been cheerful and injected some fun into the chilly Vermont evenings. She missed his presence. And perhaps if Matt had not come, she would have dealt well enough with Cord. But after Matt left she was more painfully aware of her husband than ever.

Monica found herself watching Cord's profile when he wasn't aware, the high cheekbones, the full shape of his wide mouth, the straight line of his nose, and his hair, which looked so soft and curly under its gray coloring. She flushed with the fantasy of lying once more in his arms, against his manly chest, as she had weeks ago. There would be a delicious flow of warmth through her stomach and below, and she'd have to get up and walk around the room to calm herself, often drawing Cord's puzzled gaze to her movements.

It would have disturbed Monica even more if she knew that Cord was also very uncomfortable in her presence. He was aware of changes in her that she wasn't aware of herself. Her face had filled out a bit, making her high cheeks round and not so prominent. There was a healthy tan and glow to her skin, and she was less angular and scrawny, more feminine curves. Her hair had picked up reddish streaks in the sunlight, and even though she still always wore it in a twisted bun, it was looser, softer looking, and filled with a fragrance of outdoors and fresh flowers that filled his nostrils. Monica assailed and affected all his senses, and he wasn't sure he liked it . . . or wanted it.

Their mutual indifference to each other earlier had been so much easier than this new tense atmosphere. It made them stiff and cautious with one another, neither of them recognizing in the other a common malady.

After a particularly whimsical day with Livy and being at the center, Monica had no patience for the silent moodiness of Cord's presence. She put down the book she'd been trying to read and got up to put a record on the seldom used stereo. It was an Erik Satie recording, the same music she heard that first day at the center that had led her to the dance studio. It was a soft piano piece with a slow, rhythmic cadence. Monica sat back in her chair and let the music sweep around her, but she sat staring at Cord.

"No wonder your hair is gray," Monica said aloud in sudden revelation.

Cord looked blankly at her. "What?"

Realizing that she'd spoken her thoughts out loud, Monica nevertheless repeated her statement. "I said, no wonder your hair is gray. All you do is work and frown over papers all the time."

Resting his elbows on the chair arm, Cord clasped his hands on his chest and stared at her. He didn't say anything and Monica rushed on.

"If that's all you do, you'll be old before your time. Don't you ever think of anything else besides work?"

Cord quirked a brow answering dryly, "There are, occasionally, other things on my mind." And his eyes roamed her body, making her uncomfortable. "For your information my hair has always been gray."

"Really?" Monica asked in surprise.

"Well, since I was sixteen. It all happened within a year."

"Really?"

"You're repeating yourself." Cord mused. Monica blushed and went to turn the record over.

"Does it run in the family?"

Cord was silent, and Monica turned to see some unreadable emotion in his eyes. A muscle jerked in his neck and jawline.

"I wouldn't know. I have no family."

"You had family at some time. Everyone has some sort of family."

"I didn't. I grew up in an orphanage. That was my family," he answered tersely.

With that one burst of information Monica understood perfectly why a baby would be so important to him. It would give him family, give him a continuance, perhaps affirm his own existence. She turned away from the look in his eyes and tactfully let the subject drop.

"You must have more than just your work," she said.

"Do you?" he countered.

"My dance can be joyful. It's what I do best. And it makes me happy."

"Don't you want more? A husband and family someday?"

"No!" she said harshly. Cord looked at her alertly. "Dancers are very selfish people. They have to be. They put all their time into themselves." She had a vision of Eileen going off to dance and leaving her alone as a child.

"Then how can you be doing this?" Cord asked her coldly. Monica's hand brushed over her stomach.

"It...it's just a body function. You don't love a body. You love and respect what it can do, how it performs." She began to tremble.

"And I suppose this is just another performance for you?" Cord laughed mirthlessly. Tears blurred Monica's vision.

"Yes!" she shouted. A bleakness took over Cord's features now. "You could have chosen someone you loved and cared for. Someone you wanted to be your wife. But you didn't! You chose someone who could just perform well. Well, here I am. You should be happy about it!"

Cord had no answer to her outburst. She was more than half right. Then why did he feel so lousy about it, and so angry?

"Why did you choose me, Cord?" Monica asked

with sudden morbid curiosity. "There must have been dozens of responses to your offer. Why me?"

He looked at her critically, searchingly, but there was no warmth in him. "You were the only one I could see taking to bed," he said evenly.

The blood drained from Monica's face. Her hands clenched as she went stiff with anger. She felt used and cheap, and degraded. She hated him for making her feel that way. Monica slowly began to shake her head from side to side. "Someone must have beaten you badly once." And she quickly left the room.

Cord heard the door slam to her room. He looked grimly after her retreating form and then went to remove the record from the stereo. Monica had struck, unknowingly, a sensitive nerve. She had evoked in Cord all the most painful moments of his life. He pushed both hands in exasperation through his hair and squeezed the tense muscles on the back of his neck.

Monica and Cord did not talk to one another for three full days. The silence between them was unbearable. It rained for the entire time as though their feelings and attitudes were a barometer for the weather.

Monica played her records and danced ballet in her head, and when she couldn't stand the inactivity any longer she pushed all the furniture to the walls in the sitting room and on the wonderful solid parquet floors practiced some light routines. She wore her tights and swathed her incredibly long legs in layers of wool warmers and wore a loose shirt once belonging to Cord that she'd rescued from a pile of discarded clothes.

She got so involved in the choreography that she didn't notice Cord until she'd spun out of four consecutive pirouettes and ended up facing his stormy features in the doorway. He was drenched to the skin and his gray hair looked black and tight now that it was all wet. Monica gasped in surprise when she saw him.

"Are you out of your mind?" Cord raged at her through clenched teeth.

"I—I was only—"

"You know damned well you shouldn't be dancing like that. What if you fell, hurt yourself?" Monica could not deny that he was right, but she felt her defenses rising at his tone of voice and became angry.

"Why do you care? Your concern is not for me. It's all for the baby!" She flounced over to the stereo in her peculiar dancer's walk, in her ridiculous get-up. Cord's mouth quivered in sudden amusement as he looked at her and recognized his old shirt. Monica jerked the stereo arm so suddenly she sent an ear-piercing scratch across the surface of the record.

"See what you made me do!" she accused and burst into tears. It surprised them both. She sobbed and pushed past him to flee once more to the safety of her room. But this time Cord was right behind her.

"Monica..." he began, trying to catch up to her as she ran through the kitchen. She cried harder realizing Cord was between her and her bedroom. Not caring now, Monica continued through the kitchen into Cord's room and tried to close the door.

"Go away!" she screamed at him as he tried to push the door open.

"Monica—"

"I hate you! And I hate this place! I won't stay here!" Cord got into the room and while she ranted and raved he slowly got hold of her arms and began to pull her toward him. Monica strained against him, both hands braced on his unmovable chest. The space at Monica's elbows got smaller and the distance closed, trapping her arms between them.

"You can find someone else to have your baby!" she cried, illogically adding, "and I hope it's a girl!"

"No, you don't hate me," Cord said very low, and then he was murmuring to her trying to calm her down. Monica couldn't understand what he was saying, but, she was very susceptible to gentleness and coaxing right now, and she succumbed to his voice. Cord brushed his mouth gently against her temple.

"You are going to have my baby," he said softly, seductively. "And I don't care if it's a girl or boy." But Monica did not hear him. She'd stopped struggling and her mouth parted as she became fully aware of the close proximity of their bodies, her clothes now becoming wet from his.

Their heads moved back to look at one another. Monica's eyes stared ahead at the open neck front of his wet shirt, the skin and tight curls there glistening with moisture. Slowly her eyes moved up his throat where a vein pulsed in his neck. She continued upward until she was looking at his chin, and then his wide sensuous mouth, suddenly imagining his hard mouth settling on hers. She continued to watch his mouth and Cord whispered her name urgently, and she felt his warm breath mix with her own.

Cord's arms began to tighten even more, and she did not resist, still fascinated with the sight of his lips. Cord's head began to descend and Monica closed her eyes slowly in anticipation. His mouth just caressed hers at first, and then his tongue flicked out, brushing across the parted surface of her lips, leaving it moist. She waited for him to finally claim her mouth, but he continued to play, nibbling at the bottom lip and the corners.

Desire began to take hold of her, even while she felt herself still stiff in his hold. Cord's mouth left a trail of scorching kisses over her cheek and down the column of her neck. The hand on her waist moved to her hip and pulled her pelvis closer to his. She was instantly aware of his taut maleness, and his need. His other hand easily worked its way under the shirt, gently caressing her breast and she heard herself moan.

Some memory then came back to Monica and she suddenly fought against this exquisite feeling, to try and pull herself away from Cord's magic hold on her.

"No..." she breathed brokenly. But Cord's hand moved from her hip to grab her chin and turn her face back to his.

"Yes," he whispered, as finally he completely closed the distance to capture her mouth and kiss her as though she were some source of nourishment he badly craved.

A burning fire was created between the two of them, locked in each other's arms. For blissful moments while her mind spun in dreamy colors, Monica enjoyed the sensual ravishing of her mouth. Cord's tongue slowly explored the sweet recesses until she felt she would faint. She was molded against the lean length of him and one of his hands still cupped her breast.

But again with tremendous effort she pulled her mouth away from Cord's.

"Cord, please...don't do this..." she pleaded, her hands nevertheless clutching at his shoulders.

"Why not?" he mumbled in a husky voice against the pulse in her neck. She could barely think, could barely talk coherently.

"You don't have to anymore. Now that I'm—"

"I want to make love to you, Monica," he said urgently, trying to recapture her mouth.

"No..."

"You want me to, don't you?" He crushed her to him, brushing kisses over her mouth to quell her resistance.

"Tell me you don't enjoy it."

Monica groaned and suddenly, violently, twisted out

of his arms. But it had affected her so, she was unsteady on her feet trying to catch her breath.

"No!" she lied. "It's more than the bargain we made!"

"What do you mean?" he asked roughly.

"I mean I am not your *wife*! This is no marriage. It's a business arrangement. There's even a contract, remember?"

Cord could not deny her statement, but right now it didn't matter. For the time being, for better or worse, all they had was each other. He'd spent weeks denying his desire for her. She was beautiful and she was here... and he wanted her badly. He wanted to think she was not totally indifferent to him; after all, she had proven to be susceptible to his touch. But to want to touch her, hold her, was that taking advantage? Or was that just simple need?

"All marriages are business arrangements," Cord answered her softly. But Monica only frowned. She felt instinctively that it was not just that.

"No. There—there should be caring, and tenderness and respect. How can we respect each other? We don't even know each other!" She knew nothing of married life. But something inside her said that even as an arrangement, a contract, an agreement, between two people, there was or should also be love.

Cord stared at Monica. His desire began to ebb as he saw that she was serious. He had never in his life forced himself on any woman. He was not going to begin now. "Let's not kid ourselves about what we're doing or why."

"Let's not," Monica agreed. "In six months I'll be gone from your life, and you won't remember a thing about me except... this." She put her hand over her stomach. "But there's more to me than this!"

"Are you telling me that you don't want me to touch you... come near you?"

No, this wasn't what she was saying at all. She wanted very much to feel his arms protectively around her, and to abandon herself to the delicious sensations he was capable of administering to her. But she also needed something else. "I—I—" she fumbled, unable to put it into words. Cord looked at her another instant, and she could see the stiffening take place in him.

"Get out of those wet things and put some clothes on!" he said harshly, treating her like a disobedient child. He stepped aside and waited for her to leave his room. She hadn't gotten through to him at all. She straightened her back and lifted her chin. Without looking again at him, she left.

Cord closed the door to his room and let out a deep sigh. He ran his hands restlessly through his damp hair and began to strip his own wet things. He tossed his shirt angrily into a corner.

*What the hell does she expect from me?* he asked himself. But the question was also, What did he want from her? Cord had never denied to himself that she was attractive, for some reason, more so now than at anytime since he'd met her. And having her so near each day was taking a toll on him. Her presence was everywhere. He had accepted and begun to take for granted the odd comfort and peace of just having someone else there in the house, other movements and sounds and warmth.

Cord walked over to the window and absently watched the torrents of falling rain drenching the already lush green hillsides. He was now glad he had to leave in a few days for a week in Boston. He had to separate himself from Monica for a while.

Monica felt exhausted. It was as though she was drained of all her energy in doing the simplest chore. She didn't complain, but Cord noticed. She was looking pale again, and had circles under her eyes as though she was not getting enough sleep. Cord did not reason that he might at least be partially to blame. He began to watch her more closely, and then one morning came to a decision.

"I think we'll go out to dinner tonight," he said smoothly, casually. Monica looked at him blankly. He grabbed a jacket and began to move to the door. "Montpelier, the capital, is only an hour's drive from here. It has one or two good restaurants." Still, she said nothing, looking at him wide eyed and disbelieving. "Would you like that?" he asked, a bit impatient at her stunned expression. Had he been ignoring her so badly?

"Yes! Yes, I would."

"Fine. We'll leave at six o'clock. Be ready." And he left.

A smile curved the corner of Monica's mouth as she digested the reality of his offer. She called Olivia Gavener, frantic with the problem of what to wear for an evening out, now that all of her city clothes no longer fit. Livy suggested a day of shopping. They drove to Bethel, which was south of Randolph, and explored the main street shops. Monica found a pair of royal blue velvet evening pants and a soft lilac tunic overblouse that was long and loose. Monica also found a floor length dress for more casual wear of soft cotton voile in shades of green that went well with her amber eyes and burnished hair. She didn't know where she'd wear it, but it was beautiful. Olivia also suggested fabric for more caftans and Monica indulged herself in some white wool and some black knit jersey.

They stopped for lunch and Monica was glad for a chance to sit down. She was already beginning to feel ungainly and said so.

Olivia chuckled. "You don't show at all, really. But I

guess a dancer is only used to a flat stomach! Wait until your seventh or eighth month and you can't bend or get up by yourself, and no matter how you position yourself you can't get comfortable at night.''

Monica wrinkled her nose. "It doesn't sound like something to look forward to."

"Well, maybe not, but it's worth it. When you look at that incredible tiny baby shivering against the cold air, even wrinkled and red as it is, and know that you've brought life into the world, you know then it was worth it.''

Monica watched as Livy got a faraway look in her eyes as though she were viewing a movie of the past.

"Were you married, Livy?" she asked now.

Livy's eyes cleared and she turned her head to focus on Monica. "Oh, yes!" she answered as though it were a foregone conclusion. "My husband, Jim, is dead now. Almost eight years...of cancer."

"Oh, I'm sorry!"

"Don't be. It seems so long ago. I'm used to it now."

"Did you...did you have any children?" Livy's face grew very pensive and she sat looking, suddenly, every one of her sixty-odd years.

"Yes, we had a litte girl."

"Had?"

Livy chuckled. "I shouldn't refer to her as a little girl. She was almost twenty when she died. Congenital heart disease."

"Oh, Livy..."

"Now, now, don't go on so! Jim and I always knew that it could happen. We were just very thankful to have her as long as we did."

"And you never had other children?"

Livy shook her head. "We wanted to, very badly. But I was never able to have any more, so..." She shrugged and smiled softly at Monica, her eyes a little misty.

Monica felt like a fraud. She had no particular feelings about the child she carried, had conceived quickly and easily. Why had it been made so hard and sad for Livy who should have had all the children she wanted?

She lowered her head and twisted her hands in her lap.

"Are you okay, dear?" Livy asked gently, which just made it worse.

"I don't know what's the matter with me. I seem to feel like crying all the time!"

Livy laughed. "Some women do when they're pregnant."

"Did you?"

"No. I was too excited and pleased to be having a baby. Jim and I absolutely gloated! And he was so kind and understanding."

Monica sighed. Perhaps that also was the difference. She really had no one to share this experience with. She felt all alone in it. As though she were reading her thoughts, Livy reached over for Monica's hand squeezing it between her own.

"I don't doubt that Cord's a hard man to live with. Being gentle won't come easy to a man like him. The baby coming could make a difference," she said mysteriously. "Just be patient and calm. Everything else will work itself out."

Monica felt encouraged by Olivia's words. She was able to enjoy the rest of the afternoon before they piled their packages into the Rover and headed back to Randolph.

Monica was waiting nervously in her room, completely dressed and ready when Cord came back to the house at five thirty. She heard his footsteps outside her door, and he tapped lightly.

"Monica?"

"Yes?"

"I'll just take a quick shower and change."

Monica went into the sitting room, anticipating the evening ahead, wanting to enjoy it. She tugged at her tunic hoping she didn't look too fat and touched her hand to her carefully curled, upswept hair. She heard Cord's voice twenty minutes later as he entered the room.

"I think we should go if we don't want to—" He stopped talking and walking at the same time as he caught sight of her. Monica watched him anxiously as he looked her slowly up and down.

"Do—do I look all right?"

Cord's eyes came up to her own, and she fancied that they were warm and sparkling as he regarded her.

"I think you'll do." He smiled at her and held out his hand.

Monica came toward him, her eyes locked with his, and put her hand timidly into his. His strong lean fingers closed firmly over her hand.

"You'd better put something over that," he said, touching a sleeve, his voice a little husky. "It will be cold out now."

Monica nodded and walked past him to get her now cleaned black wool cape. She had to admit that she was more than a little giddy at the prospect of an evening out with Cord. She sincerely hoped it meant a more cordial relationship between them.

Cord had not tried to approach her sexually again, and despite her convictions she was disappointed at his acquiescence to her wishes.

They talked comfortably and generally on the ride to the capital and were both relaxed and in good humor when they arrived.

"What do you feel like eating?" he asked her as he

helped her out of the car. "There's Italian, French, and a reasonably good Japanese restaurant."

"Japanese? In Vermont?" she asked, incredulous.

Cord raised a brow. "Civilization arrived some time ago, I believe."

"I didn't mean it that way." Monica grimaced and held her stomach. "I just don't think raw fish and seaweed is a good idea right now!"

Cord grinned widely at her, taking years off his face. "I thought pregnant women had a penchant for odd foods?"

She shook her head, sending some of the curls into motion. "Not this woman! I want to enjoy myself this evening, not get sick!"

"How about French, then? If you don't mind the rich sauces."

"I doubt if it's the rich sauces that's going to make me fat!" Monica said ruefully. Cord laughed briefly and she joined in.

Dinner was a great success. Neither had ever been so at ease in the other's company. There was no sparring or tug of war over wills. Lulled into a comfortable state by the evening, Monica felt bold enough to look at Cord over coffee and ask a question. But she first hesitated until Cord spoke softly.

"What is it?" he asked, watching the candlelight on her face.

"Cord, tell me about . . . the orphanage. How did you get there?"

Something closed down behind Cord's eyes, and he stiffened. "Leave it alone, Monica."

"Please, Cord!"

"It's no longer important," he said tightly.

"It is to me."

"Why?" he asked. "Why do you care?"

"Because I'd like to know more about you. I'd like to

understand you," she said in a low urgent voice, holding his gaze. Monica reached over to touch his arm. "Please!"

Cord swirled the remaining wine in his glass and swallowed it in a gulp. "I was found abandoned when I was about eighteen months old."

Monica felt a gasp rise to her throat, but she stopped it escaping and was quiet, not wanting to do anything that would prevent Cord from going on.

"It was at a bus terminal in San Antonio, Texas," he spoke in a monotone, as if he knew all this information by rote, had been over and over it again and again, but which gave him no comfort at all, and answered no questions.

"I was left asleep in a blanket with a canvas bag containing baby clothes and things. There was a piece of paper pinned to my blanket with the word Cortland, and a date, January ninth. The authorities assumed the date to be when I was born, and Cortland to be my name, but they didn't know if it was a first name or last. It could have been a city, a town!" he ground this out in some bitterness. He suddenly laughed harshly. "Oh, yes, there was also a line, 'Please take care of him.'" He finally let out a deep sigh.

"A name written on the inside of the canvas tote read Temple. Again, no one knew if it was someone's name or not." Monica knew the pain he was feeling as he restated the story. "A year-long search to firmly establish my identity was useless. They could have checked every town in Texas forever! So, I became Cortland Temple of the Children's Foundling Center in San Antonio. When they closed the center there, I was transferred to another smaller town. I was there until I was almost eighteen years old."

There followed a long silence at their table. Monica was at once assailed with her own memories as she

learned of Cord's origins. How horrible a thing it was
for him not to be sure who he was, or who his parents
might have been.

"Perhaps it was a blessing in disguise," Monica said
softly.

"What are you saying?" Cord asked roughly, his
eyes burrowing into hers.

"I mean, if your folks didn't want you or couldn't
keep you, then maybe it was better for someone else to
raise you. Maybe they were sick, or poor or too young.
Maybe just afraid. Having a family doesn't always mean
that you will be loved."

"I would have liked to have found out for myself,"
Cord said bitterly.

"And I wish that I hadn't," Monica quickly added.

He looked at her quizzically.

"My mother died when I was four. I have no memory of her at all. My father was so overcome by his loss
that he had no time or attention to give me. He remar-
ried when I was seven. My stepmother, who was a
dancer, made it perfectly clear that I was a nuisance. As
soon as she could she sent me off to dance classes to
keep me away from home and out of her hair."

Cord was listening now and was as surprised to learn
of her past as Monica had been about his.

"My father died four years ago. During my whole
life he never once told me he loved me. Dance class
was home for me. Dance is all I've ever had to love."

They looked at one another, both somewhat raw
from so much sudden exposure. Monica's eyes glis-
tened with tears and Cord's expression of pain seemed
permanently fixed. For once they knew what the other
was feeling. Cord reached out to take her hand and
squeezed it, running a thumb softly over the back.

"I thought all families were like mine. That you married because it was done. And then you have children

because it was done. And after they were here there was nothing else to be done. They simply grew up somehow."

"But you must have felt that something was wrong?"

"How would I know it was wrong? Or right? I only knew I wanted my father to hold me, and to tell me I was important to him." Monica's voice dropped to a whisper and she pulled her hand away. "I didn't want to be given dance classes. I wanted to be given love. I'm not sure it exists to be given to anyone. I'm not sure people really know how."

"And marriage?" Cord asked. "What do you think of marriage now?"

Monica went pale. She looked intently at Cord and knew she couldn't tell anything other than what she really felt. "It's—it's not all that I think it can be. I still believe there's something deeper."

Cord couldn't accuse her of being cynical. It would have been too much like speaking of himself. "Do you suppose we'll ever find out?" he asked her evenly.

"I don't know" was all she could answer.

It was a silent and pensive couple that entered the house almost an hour later. Cord walked Monica to her bedroom door, his hand lightly on her back. He turned the doorknob and the door swung open into a dark pit. He looked down into her upturned face.

Monica knew that if he asked to come in, made any move to, she'd let him. But Cord only unfastened the heavy cape from her shoulders and threw it over his arm. The ends of his fingers just touched her cheek as he bent forward slowly and gave her a brief warm kiss. It was the first gentle thing they'd ever shared. His eyes lingered on her softly parted lips.

"You looked lovely tonight."

"Thank you," she responded a bit breathlessly. "And I had an absolutely wonderful evening."

Cord quirked a brow and smiled. "That good?"

"Yes, that good."

Monica looked expectantly at him, but he dropped his hands and stood back from her.

"Good night, Monica." Monica only continued to look at him.

"I'm leaving very early in the morning. I'll try not to wake you." Monica was pleased by that consideration, but perversely she was disappointed that he didn't ask her to have breakfast with him. Looking at him another moment, she crossed into her room and closed the door.

## Chapter Seven

It was cold in Boston. Summer was over, and the early September fall stepped in to take its place.

The conference room was warm and brightly lit so that displays and charts and blueprints could be read comfortably. It was an odd contrast to the strange weather outside.

There were two small groups of men clustered in shirt sleeves relaxing and drinking coffee. Matt Bell, hands braced on the oak table, leaned across to the two men opposite him and gave the punch line to his joke as they burst into uproarious laughter.

Cord watched the occupants of the room absently, not really registering their presence or actions. He swung his chair around and looked out the window at the blustering day. He wondered if it was windy in Randolph. He wondered if Monica—

"Hey, old buddy. Why so quiet?" Matt asked cheerfully, taking a seat next to Cord, a half-filled coffee cup in his hand. Cord pulled his thoughtful gaze back to Matt and focused on him.

"What? Oh, sorry, Matt."

"You haven't had more than two words to say outside of the meetings since we got here!" Cord smiled grimly at his stocky friend and said nothing. It was not like him to be fanciful and to daydream. But lately . . .

"I know, you're thinking of Monica. Are you worried about her? Do you miss her? Well, can't say that I blame you. You lucky bastard!" His smile slowly faded and he regarded Cord seriously. "Tell me, Cord. When did it finally end? Was it when you met Monica?"

"When did what finally end?"

"You know. Natalie. When did you finally give up the ghost?"

"What makes you think I have?"

"Why, there's Monica, so you must have. How could you marry her unless you loved her, or—" He stopped as he realized the direction of his thoughts.

"Or what?" Cord asked tersely.

"Oh, nothing, old buddy. I'm just running off as usual. But still, Monica was a real find."

"Yes, she was," Cord quietly agreed.

"Then it's true. You have forgotten Natalie."

Cord looked at his friend and had a memory flash through him of a rainy summer Saturday almost fifteen years ago. Every muscle in his body went taut and his mouth was an uncompromising straight line.

"I will never forget Natalie," he said, every word spoken an indication the subject was closed to further discussion. Cord got up and walked to the coffeemaker, keeping his back to Matt. Matt, for his part, was puzzled. He didn't understand why Cord continued to torture himself with an incident so far in the past. Sure, we all take a kick in the teeth sometimes, but you pull yourself together. You go on. You have to.

Cord had done that, but something important had been left out... or forgotten. It did seem that one only got so close to Cord, and then there was a wall. It protected him, perhaps locked him in, invincible and hard.

It let nothing in that could possibly ever do him harm again.

But Matt knew that wasn't enough. Sooner or later the guard would have to come down if his friend was ever to be whole again. He had to care about someone else besides himself. Matthew thought that someone was Monica, but certainly he had to admit that Cord in no way acted the loving bridegroom toward her. Nor was he the indulgent, malleable way he would have been with Natalie.

This all required more thought, Matt analyzed. He was suddenly more than just a little interested in Cord's affairs.

Cord would never forget Natalie because her actions, more than the woman herself, were indelibly stamped on his memory. She'd abandoned him as his unknown mother had. She had declared him no longer wanted or needed, and had simply let him go. If someone hates you, or loves you, you always know where you stand. But when they are suddenly indifferent, then nothing is clear. It is never really finished because it was never really begun, like being in a state of suspended animation. That two people in his lifetime could do this so freely to him was more than Cord could bear.

Cord took a deep breath and gulped at the coffee, finishing it and instantly refilling the cup. He didn't have time for the pain. He forced the past to the back of his mind and walked back to the window to look outside.

He thought he'd like a fire. There was a fireplace in the kitchen, one in the sitting room, and his room in Randolph. He wondered if Monica was cold. Did she know how to start a fire and to check the flue, how to discard the ashes? He wondered if she was careful in the Rover, if she knew what to do if she got a flat. What if she slid on the sitting room floor? "Damn!" Cord muttered under his breath.

When he'd walked into the sitting room that night and saw the speed with which she could move, and the arching of her foot as she spun on pointe, he couldn't see how she would not badly hurt herself and yes, the baby. He wondered abstractedly when she'd begin to show.

Maybe she was and he just hadn't noticed. He had noticed, however, that it was probably hard on her not being as active as she was used to, and spending every day alone in a house and in a town she didn't know. She'd looked so withdrawn and depressed, not provoking him or arguing like he knew she was capable, that he felt something was wrong. Remembering Molly's instructions to try and be understanding, he had suggested the dinner.

Cord had been surprised at how eager she was, and even more surprised when he'd seen her dressed for a night out. Matt was right. Monica was lovely and he had enjoyed the evening. When she forced the information out of him about his background Cord felt them bond together. Something similar and familiar. And yes, he'd very much wanted to make love to her. He wanted to hold her close and make her respond to him the way she had before.

But he remembered her feelings on being used in that way. She needed more, but for the moment, he didn't.

The meeting was called to attention and Cord shook his head to clear it, raking an unsteady hand through his hair. *Why the hell should I concern myself with her?* he thought. *She's going to get what she wants, and so am I!* But he was concerned nonetheless.

Monica had not expected to hear from Cord. But she'd hoped. She'd hoped that something more tangible—

like friendship and trust—had been started the night of the dinner. It had been a turning point for both of them but it was not yet either friendship or trust. It was more recognition, a mutual seeing on each part that the other was complex, their separate pasts not to be casually shrugged off.

The charming country house was suddenly too large and too quiet, and she spent much of her time at the center in town, or with Livy. As if the sudden realization that she wanted to know Cortland Temple better weren't enough to think about, three days after he'd gone the baby started to kick and move.

She'd been helping Livy to change the linens, Monica insisting on doing the large front room that was Cord's. Her arms were raised in the air, throwing the sheet out ahead of her to cover the gigantic mattress. She was daydreaming about Cord in this large bed when she felt a thud against her stomach wall.

Monica gasped, dropped the sheet, and clutched her stomach wide eyed with fright. She stood perfectly still for a moment, and it happened again. She turned and ran for the sitting room, calling out Livy's name.

"What's the matter, dear?" Livy asked anxiously, stopping her dusting to turn to Monica.

Monica, pale and breathless, said in a tight voice, "Something's wrong! Oh, Livy, something's wrong!"

"What's wrong?"

"Something is happening inside. Here!" she said, placing her hand over her stomach.

"Are you in pain? Do you have cramps?" Livy asked, suddenly alert and concerned.

"No!"

"Monica, describe it to me!" She gently pushed Monica into a chair and held her cold hands.

"It—it feels like—like something moving around!"

The worried frown cleared from Livy's face. "Oh,

you scared me! I thought maybe you were having a miscarriage!''

"A miscarriage? What is it, then?"

"Oh, Monica," Livy said in real amusement now,
"I'm convinced you know nothing about babies! Or
anything about having them!"

"I don't. After all, I've never had one before!"

"But haven't you read anything? Or talked to friends
who've had children? Haven't you talked to your doctor at all?"

Monica sighed. No, to all of the above. And she hadn't
spoken to a doctor. The doctor had spoken to her. Besides, she hadn't realized there was anything to know.

Livy looked at Monica's bewilderment and touched
her cheek.

"You silly child," she admonished. "Your baby is
letting you know it's alive and well."

"Then you mean—"

"Yes, this is supposed to happen. Every woman
looks for this moment. Suddenly she knows for sure
she's going to have a child!"

Monica felt stunned. Why had no one ever told her
about this? Suddenly she was very embarrassed at her
lack of knowledge.

Livy thought she was too excited and insisted she lie
down. As Monica rested on the bed and held her stomach, she felt the peculiar movements inside. She closed
her eyes and tried to imagine what it was like, but she
could only guess. Yet, it was beyond words, this touching from the inside.

She lay for hours, fascinated over this experience.
Feeling elated that everything was happening as it
should, Monica's first reaction was to tell Cord immediately about this. But she made no move to call him in
Boston, as much as she wished she could.

It began to seem to Monica that she'd always been in Vermont. What she was now and what was happening to her had nothing to do with her life in New York. For the time being she belonged here.

Monica had come to accept the situation as not being real, but just a space in time that had a start and an end, after which she would go back to what she'd known before. She had settled into her illusion of being part of this rural life, of keeping house and keeping busy waiting for someone to come home. And she enjoyed it. But it was just an illusion and she was not allowed to see it as anything else.

One morning she received a bank notice that ten thousand dollars had been deposited into her account. She could not ever forget what it was she was doing, or for that matter why. But suddenly she very much wished she could.

It was almost six o'clock on a Wednesday when Monica heard a car on the gravel road and knew that Cord was home. She went to the front door and was there when the car came to a complete stop. She was surprised when the passenger door opened and the stocky form of Matthew Bell appeared. Her eyes sought out Cord, as his taller, much leaner body came around to face her. She was glad he was back. But it was Matthew who reached her first and enveloped her in a bear hug like some long lost relative.

"Hiya, gorgeous!" Matt chuckled, planting a firm kiss on her cheek as he held her. But then he quickly released her, and stood back looking at her in surprise. His blue eyes were wide and traveled the length of her body, from her face to her feet and back again. There was speculation in his expression.

"Did I miss something the last time I was here?" By

this time Cord had removed his luggage from the wagon and was putting it inside the door.

"I don't know what you mean," Monica said, moving out of Matt's reach.

"Cord, I don't know if I can take another surprise from you. Tell me, are you and Monica... I mean, is Monica—"

Cord spoke for the first time. "Yes. Monica is going to have a baby."

"Well, I'll be damned!"

"You probably will be!" Cord said caustically. He turned his head to look down at Monica, and she looked up at him. Cord thought with some surprise that there was something different about her, something very much alive and soft and appealing.

Monica was aware too of the softening look in his eye, and as if by mutual need or agreement they took a step closer, Cord bending forward to kiss her, as a husband would kiss his wife after an absence. When Cord backed away from Monica, her eyes were sparkling and bright and her lips parted. Monica gently touched his arm.

"Come on inside. I—I wasn't sure when you'd arrive but there's something for dinner."

Cord followed her with Matthew right behind him. As they sat down to dinner Matthew told her he had to leave in the morning for Montpelier. She politely expressed disappointment that he couldn't stay longer. But Matt only laughed heartily, shaking his head. "I'm like a leech. A lovable leech, mind you, but, nonetheless, hard to get rid of."

"I don't understand," Monica said.

"Well, Cord and I are working together on some of his building contracts. So you'll be seeing me off and on all winter."

"I'm afraid he'll turn out to be a permanent fixture.

But just say if he gets to be a nuisance," Cord advised.

Monica looked at Cord in surprise. Matthew was his friend. And this was his house. What could it matter what she felt or thought?

"So you're going to have a baby," Matt said thoughtfully, looking at her intently. His gaze held more than just curiosity or surprise. Monica stole a quick glance at Cord, but he was idly fingering the stem of his water goblet, seemingly deep in thought at the moment.

"Yes, I am," Monica finally responded to Matt's question. He leaned toward her, his elbows resting on the table.

"Well, old buddy, looks like you'll get the son you've always wanted."

He raised his brows at his friend and shrugged. "Monica assures me it will be a girl," Cord said.

"Would you prefer a girl?" Matt asked her seriously.

"No! I mean—"

"She means she doesn't care what it is," Cord filled in smoothly, his voice lacking warmth.

"I just want it to be healthy," Monica added tightly and gave Cord an angry look. But it was also one of hurt, and Cord looked away from her back to Matt.

"You seem to be suddenly very interested in marriage and children. When will you settle down?"

"Who, me?" Matt asked surprised, apparently not having thought of this himself. He looked at Monica again for a long moment. "I might give it some thought," he answered, "if it was the right person. Maybe someone like Monica."

Monica's chair grated suddenly on the floor of the kitchen as she pushed back her chair and stood up. She suddenly felt very hot and closed in.

"If you'll excuse me..."

"Are you okay?" Matt asked, reaching out to cup her elbow while Cord merely watched.

"Yes, yes. I'm fine. I'll just get the coffee."

"Not for me, thanks," Cord said, finally standing. "I just want to put away some papers and I think I'll call it a night." He walked away into the sitting room, and Monica's puzzled eyes followed him.

"I don't want coffee, either, so don't bother," Matt added. Monica accepted this and began to clear the table. "Do you want some help?" Matt asked so eagerly that Monica smiled at him.

"No, thanks. I'm just going to leave them in the sink until the morning."

"Well..." Matt looked at her retreating back as she carried dishes to the sink, and at the doorway through which Cord disappeared. He shrugged. "Well, I guess I'll turn in."

"Oh!" Monica looked over her shoulder at him. "I'm sorry! Is there anything else you need, Matt?"

He stopped in his movements toward the stairwell to contemplate her once again, his look almost soft and caressing. "Yes, but I'll take care of it myself," he said, his voice low.

Monica watched as he climbed the stairs, not understanding at all. A moment later she heard a voice behind her.

"You still insist on doing all of this?"

She swung around sharply to see Cord leaning in the door frame, arms folded across his chest. Monica, now completely aware of his presence, felt a response to his masculinity deep within her. He seemed so dark and threatening standing quietly there in the door.

Her eyes were drawn to the close-fitting slacks over his taut thighs, and it evoked a memory of his body naked and hard against her own. Annoyed with her thoughts she turned back to the sink and took a deep breath.

"I don't mind. Really. It gives me something to do."

She continued to rinse and stack dishes, keeping her back to Cord.

"Did you … have a good trip?" There followed a silence and for a second Monica thought he might have gone back to the sitting room.

"It was tiring. I don't really enjoy these lengthy trips. If I had an office or studio here I could bring the clients to me."

"I thought you liked being an architect," Monica responded. Cord came to stand almost directly behind her, watching as she worked.

"I didn't say I didn't like it. I said the traveling was tiring. Do you want some help?" he asked so unexpectedly Monica jumped.

"No, I can manage."

But Cord pulled open the dishwasher and started to put the silverware in. "You pass them to me as you rinse," he ordered, and Monica did as she was told, too stunned to think of doing otherwise. In a few minutes they were finished and she was drying her hands on a towel.

"Thank you." She smiled uncertainly at him, not sure how to take these quick changes in his temperament.

"I don't think you should be doing so much work," Cord said.

Monica laughed a little. "It's good exercise. Livy says it won't hurt." He raised his brows and grunted.

They stood there in the kitchen looking at one another. She was mesmerized by his gray eyes, for once not steely or cold, and she felt riveted in place by their look. They seemed a little eerie and bright under the subtle indirect lighting of the kitchen, reminding her of a cat.

Cord satisfied his previous curiosity by looking down at her. She was beginning to show. He looked back to her face, and slowly reached out to brush a strand of red-brown hair from her temple back across her head. It was a gentle movement, and Monica found herself softening toward him because of it. Suddenly he turned away from her, quickly putting his hands in his pockets. He moved back toward the sitting room.

"I—I guess I'll say good-night," Monica murmured.

"No, not yet."

"What?"

"I want to show you something." He disappeared in the direction of the door and Monica heard it open and a rush of cold night air suddenly blowing a chill across the room. Puzzled, Monica walked into the room in time to see Cord return carrying a piece of furniture. Monica stood aside as he brought it over to the fireplace and sat it down. It was a rocking chair. A high-backed Windsor with a tight cane seat.

"Well," he began impatiently, "do you like it?"

"Why, yes. It's a lovely chair."

"Good. Come closer and look at it. Here, sit down." Monica moved slowly forward and gingerly sat in the chair.

"It's very comfortable."

"I was assured it would be. I hope you enjoy it." Cord went back to his own chair and sat down, propping his feet on the edge of the coffee table.

"You mean this is for me?" Monica asked surprised.

"Yes," he answered shortly. "It's for you."

Monica was confused. She was used to a Cord who was abrupt, cold, and indifferent. This other Cord she wasn't sure how to handle. He had been so clear in the beginning what their relationship should be and what the limitations were. But there had been the dinner and now this gift. Monica frowned deeply, trying hard to understand what it might mean.

Cord's voice cut into her thoughts. "What's wrong? Is the seat too low?"

"Oh, no, it's perfect!"

"But—"

"It's just that I—I'm not accustomed to..."

Cord quirked a brow, waiting. Monica laughed nervously. "Thank you, Cord. It was thoughtful of you. And I do love it."

She sat back and put the chair into a gentle rocking back and forth. She closed her eyes, enjoying the soothing motion. Cord watched her silently, experiencing a strange sensation of comfort and familiarity.

Monica's head turned to the side, and her dark lashes rested against round rosy cheeks. A feathering of loose curls covered her temples and over her ears. Her mouth curved in a satisfied, restful smile. Cord's hands squeezed the arm of his own chair as he watched. He swallowed hard as he recognized a sudden desire to hold her, stroke her, be gentle with her. He wanted to have her lie in his arms, willingly, in warmth and affection.

"Cord?" came her voice quietly.

Cord expelled a ragged breath. "Yes?"

"Where is your home? I mean, when you're not here, where do you live?"

He was glad for the interruptions on his thoughts. "I guess I don't really live anywhere. I have an apartment in San Antonio and this house."

"But isn't there one place special where you'd really like to be?"

A memory racked him. "There used to be."

Monica opened her eyes to look at him. "What happened?"

The lassitude he'd begun to feel slipped away, and a need to protect himself returned. "Things just didn't work out the way I'd planned. And my jobs keep me moving around."

"But everyone should have a home somewhere."

"You're being too romantic. I've never really had a home. And from what you've told me, yours wasn't much either."

Monica sighed. "But still, to be in one place—"

"Monica," he said in a way that warned her she was pushing. He got up and strode nervously around the room, hands deep in his pockets. He shrugged. "It's not a place, a house, that makes it special. It's the people with it. Family, friends..."

"Children," Monica softly supplied. Cord stopped moving and looked bleakly at her.

"Yes, children," he agreed harshly and turned away from her to stare out the window into the night. He felt her leave the chair to move close beside him and he momentarily stiffened.

Monica felt an overwhelming need and desire to comfort him, but his stiff body seemed to reject her very nearness. She thought, ironically, he wanted to sleep with her out of desire and a physical need, but he didn't want her company and softness out of emotional need. Well, maybe he didn't need or want her, but he did want and need the baby she would provide.

"A child would give you the basis for a home, wouldn't it? Your own child you could love and protect and give a life to that you never had. Is that why you want a son?"

"Yes," he said simply, never looking at her.

"Then I will give you that son," Monica said very softly to him, as though it was suddenly her decision and solely within her power. As though there'd never been any other kind of arrangement beforehand. It changed the way she looked at her relationship to Cord, because she was now realizing a desire for tenderness toward him. Monica was coming to know him, and to see in him a loneliness that was painful and seemingly permanent. He had made himself sufficient unto himself. Except for this need for his own child, and there-fore the need for love.

"You told me it would be a girl," Cord responded softly.

Monica grimaced. "I was angry when I said that. All men want sons. You should have sons."

"Sons?" he queried, raising a brow. Monica blushed.

"I—I mean, your child will be a boy."

"Is that a guarantee?" he asked in a teasing voice.

She looked at her curved stomach and touched it gently. "Well, I'll do my best," she sighed.

"I appreciate that," Cord said dryly, but his look was filled with amusement. Smiling, Monica went back to her chair and began to rock again.

An hour later he stretched his long frame and rubbed the muscles on his shoulders and the back of his neck. He'd almost forgotten Monica's presence un-til he saw she'd fallen asleep in the rocker, her feet tucked under her long dress on the seat. Cord stared at her for a long moment. He reached down and slid one arm under her legs and the other behind her back and gently lifted her from the chair. One of her arms fell limply, but the other pressed to his shoulder for sup-port.

Monica came half awake and protested weakly. "Put me down. I can walk." But Cord made no move to set her on her feet. He was surprised at how light she still was, and he cradled her protectively against his chest. Monica's head dropped to his shoulder and she went back to sleep.

Cord slowly walked with her to her room. He laid her down, and she curled onto her side, her knees drawn up to her chest like a child. A feeling he'd had earlier in the evening came back to him and he hesitated. Finally he pulled the cover over her and quietly left the room

Cord felt confused, and he wasn't used to being confused. He was used to always knowing for sure exactly what he was doing and where he was going. His life had never revolved around anyone else...and it had been many years since he'd needed anyone else. What the hell was happening anyway? What was she doing to him? He couldn't seem to get away from her, even when he was away on business. Why wasn't she tough and hard and singular, like himself so he'd be sure what kind of person she was? But she wasn't any of those things, despite her determination, and it made him wonder. He only knew that the thought of her having his baby for money and then giving it up angered him beyond reason. When he'd entered this arrangement months ago he hadn't cared beyond his own purpose why the woman was doing it. And maybe if he had never gotten this close to Monica he could go on not caring. Yet he did.

A comfortable truce existed between Cord and Monica for the next few weeks, sparked perhaps by the gift of the chair. Monica was not sure yet that it brought them any closer or laid a bridge for understanding, but at least they were no farther apart. This was important to her.

She was aware, the morning after his arrival back home, that he'd carried her to bed and covered her in her sleep. It had seemed like such an intimate thing to do. Yet, nothing else much happened. He went back to his schedule of rising early and being gone all day at one building site or another. Mostly they would eat in the evening together and they'd talk comfortably about what he was doing, Monica asking questions in an attempt to understand him better. Then he'd struggle in his chair with masses of papers and blueprints all around him. Monica would rock in her chair by the fireplace.

She looked forward to those evenings when it was just the two of them. She thought, ruefully, it was almost like being a family. The idea was not unpleasant. Monica waited expectantly as though something else should happen, as if there should be more. Her thoughts would be on Cord during the day when he was away, and at night when she was in her room alone. She wondered if he ever saw her as anything else but the carrier and bearer of a baby he would have in a few months.

The leaves changed colors and were swept to the ground by fall winds, and the weather got cold. Monica continued to drive the Rover into the center three days a week, bundled up against the cold, arriving with rosy cheeks and windblown hair. Lynn Martin persuaded her to help choreograph a routine for the intermediate dance class for a Thanksgiving festival. Monica was excited by the idea, wanting very much to use the boys who stuck with the classes in a way that would keep them interested about dance and still make them feel their budding masculinity was not threatened.

She began to listen to all the records in the sitting room and formed an idea in her head to a section of a soundtrack from a James Bond movie. Monica began to visualize the staging and the routine and put together steps. She'd walk through it herself and refine it, and each class would teach another section. The boys saw they were to be like Agent 007 who had to rescue the girls from an enemy, and they insisted on calling the number "Spies."

She worked hard on it, often going to bed at night exhausted. Cord noticed she seemed to be sleeping more and more, but thought it was all part of the physical change she was going through. He never questioned what she did during the day. He was too busy these days trying to finish the first two phases of construction on the library before the weather made it impossible to work at all.

Matt Bell slipped in and out of the house during October and November, and Monica was glad of his company. With him she could relax completely and even laugh and feel totally lighthearted. But the more she enjoyed herself during these times, the more withdrawn Cord became from her and Matt.

He could be so pleasant with her, but also cold and remote. She finally decided that what he needed was a room he could be comfortable in, escape to, where he could roll out his blueprints or read his contracts without the distraction of her or Matthew. She went upstairs one afternoon to look at the other empty rooms.

She was imagining a drafting table and a stool, a comfortable chair and lamps. She heard a door close below her.

"Hello, Monica! Are you here?"

"Yes, Matt. I'm upstairs!" she called out and heard his hard heavy footsteps making their way to her.

"What are you doing up here?" he asked, taking off his gloves and opening his coat as he looked around the near empty room. "Are you deserting the bridal suite?" he teased and was surprised to see her blush and turn away from him.

"Don't be silly," she snapped. "I—I thought I'd convert this room into an office for Cord.

"It's a good idea. Did he suggest you use this room?"

"He doesn't know I'm doing it. I want to surprise him."

Matt raised his brows ruefully at her and walked around the room examining the space. "Cortland is not big on surprises, Monica," he said carefully.

"Why not?"

Matt hesitated. "They have a way of backfiring on him." He saw Monica's confusion and laughed softly. "This is different, I guess. What could it hurt to have a room to work in, right?"

"Surely nothing has been that bad. I mean, I know there's the whole thing about his background, but—"

"And don't forget there was Natalie."

Monica's eyes flew open wide.

*Who is Natalie?* Monica felt a certain hollowness develop inside her.

"That was a surprise to end all surprises. And naturally when he found out—" Matt stopped talking as he saw Monica go pale, with her eyes riveted to his face. "Monica," he asked anxiously, going to take her hands in his, "are you all right? Here, sit down." He pushed her down into a wooden chair that was against the wall. Matt knelt by the chair and began to chaff her hands.

Monica closed her eyes against the awful feeling that had filled her and laughed nervously. "I'm fine, Matt. I—I just felt a bit dizzy."

Matthew noticed she was beginning to shake. "Do you want me to get you something?"

"No, no, I'll be okay."

"Look, let me get you downstairs where you can stretch out." Matt put a strong arm around her waist and, holding her arm, helped her down the stairs to the sitting room. He put her legs up and threw an afghan over her lap. He pulled a chair up next to her and sat frowning at her still ashen features.

"You didn't know, did you?"

"Know what?" she asked faintly.

"Cord never told you about Natalie?"

Monica couldn't bring herself to answer.

"Jesus!" Matt groaned, clenching his fist.

"There was no reason to tell me. What happened in the past is his own business," she murmured.

"It's your business now. It's the reason for him being as he is."

"And what way is that?"

"Difficult to reach, a cold bastard at times. That's why when I found out he'd married I thought—"

"What had you thought, Matt?"

He shrugged. "I don't know. Maybe that he'd changed. That you were responsible for it. After all, he must love you to finally decide to—"

Monica twisted away from Matt, and away from the pain settling over her like a cloud.

"Monica? I'm sorry! Did I say something— I don't understand this!" As Matt looked at her bowed head, another thought occurred to him. "He—he didn't marry you because he had to, did he?" he asked in a tight voice.

Monica chuckled without any humor. "Can you imagine anyone making Cord do anything? Cord and I have an understanding in our marriage," Monica answered.

"And is the baby part of that understanding?"

"Please don't ask me any more about it, Matt!" she said in great agitation. "Tell me about Natalie."

"Monica, I think it's better if Cord—"

"No! I won't ask him. I can't. I want you to tell me."

Matthew hesitated and then leaned forward with his elbows on his knees. He began to talk.

Monica listened, staring all the while with blank eyes into space. Many things started to become clear to her now. When Matt was finished, a strained silence filled the room. He reached out and took one of her hands and squeezed it comfortingly.

"I'm sorry, Monica. Believe me, you're worth ten Natalies!"

Monica smiled at his exaggeration.

"In any case it's all in the past. He has you now."

Monica slowly shook her head and whispered. "It's all in the past. But it's not all over."

The door suddenly opened and Cord came into the room. He stopped and looked from a pale, wide-eyed Monica, to Matt, who was blushing in embarrassment, to their hands locked together. Matt released Monica's hands and stood up.

"Monica felt a little dizzy. I was just trying to comfort her." Matt felt compelled to explain, but Monica was still too stunned to say anything.

She continued to stare at Cord as though he were a stranger. His face was hard and closed and indifferent as he looked at her. She couldn't begin to guess what he was thinking.

"No doubt you've succeeded," Cord answered smoothly, turning away to take off his coat. "I hope you're feeling better," he threw offhandedly to Monica.

Monica felt numb. He didn't care at all how she felt.

"I'll be all right," she said softly.

"Well," Matt began, heading toward the door, "I came to pick up my bag. I'm off to Boston again." He hesitated in the doorway while Monica prayed he wouldn't say any more. "Are you sure you're okay, Monica?"

"Yes, fine, Matthew," she answered in a toneless voice. She heard him climb the stairs. Monica wondered in confusion what had happened now to make Cord so distant. What did he have to be angry about? "I didn't expect you home so early."

"Apparently not," he said blankly. Monica frowned. "I'll begin to fix—"

"Never mind dinner. I think I'll drive into town. I'll get something there."

"Very well," she replied softly, much too drained to be further hurt. Matthew came back down and said good-bye to Monica. He said he'd be in touch in a few days. He had a few quiet words to Cord, presumably about business, and he was gone.

Cord looked finally at Monica briefly, his eyes as icy as she'd ever seen them. "I'll just change my clothes," he said unnecessarily and went to his room. Monica remained where she was, feeling as though a hugh wave had washed over her, splashing her suddenly with cold water. She shivered almost violently. It was getting cold in the room. Or maybe it was just her. She went to the fireplace and began to start a fire. She heard a sound and turned around. Cord was in the doorway, hands in his pockets, watching her. Monica hoped he'd say something; instead, it was she who called his name.

"Cord, I—"

"I don't know when I'll be in. Don't wait up for me," he interrupted her. He put on his heavy outer coat, and then he too was gone, leaving her once more alone.

A wave of depression enveloped Monica for days, and she seemed to be constantly cold. Cord avoided her company, and she'd never felt more alone. She missed the evenings with him and the talks. She'd been sure he was beginning to really like her, was feeling warm and even affectionate toward her.

But Cord had pulled away from her once again leaving Monica uncertain as to her place. She couldn't help feeling now that each time he looked at her he was really seeing Natalie, the face of the one woman he'd ever really loved and couldn't forget. It was hopeless. There was no way she could compete with a memory.

Monica's appetite fell off and she actually lost several pounds. She continued to grow round and to feel the kicking within her, but it meant nothing. Her mind felt empty suddenly of any thought beyond what was happening between her and Cord. She grew pale and gaunt in the face, and suffered many sleepless nights. But Cord was never around long enough now to notice.

Then, one afternoon she sat with Livy holding a cup of tea that had long since grown cold. Livy had been shocked by her appearance, and asked immediately if anything was wrong. But Monica had merely shrugged saying she'd been feeling tired lately, and she passed a shaky hand over her brow. But Livy was sharp enough to see it was much more than that.

"Has something happened, Monica? Is it Cord?"

Monica laughed a bit hysterically. "Nothing's ever wrong with Cord. He'll always be fine because he doesn't care about anything."

"Monica, what are you talking about?"

"No, that's not true. I think he cares about his baby."

"And of course he cares about you too!"

Monica laughed again. Livy, really alarmed now, got up and touched a hand to Monica's forehead. It was very hot. "No, he doesn't. I thought...I was hoping..."

"What have you been doing to yourself? You're burning up with fever. How could Cord let you come out like this?"

"He doesn't know!" Monica giggled. "I'm hiding from him." The cup she was holding slipped from her fingers and shattered on the floor.

"Come on, my dear. You lie down. I'm going to call the doctor."

"Oh, Livy, what am I going to do?" Monica moaned. She lay on the edge of the sofa and began to shiver. Livy dialed the doctor's office.

"He loves her, he loves me not. He loves her, he

loves me not..." Monica murmured incoherently. Livy came back and stroked Monica's forehead.

"The doctor will be here soon, dear," she said sooth- ingly.

"I don't want a doctor. I want him...but he wants her."

Livy frowned, not understanding what Monica was saying.

The doctor came and diagnosed a severe chill and fever, and a mild anemia. Livy tried reaching Cord, but it was Matt who answered the phone. Livy suggested he locate Cord at once.

The doctor and Livy got Monica to a bed in the guest room. She was delirious and unclear, but the doctor was unconcerned.

"She'll be uncomfortable for a few days until the fever breaks. But it's nothing serious. Just see that she takes this medicine and drinks a lot of liquids. And sleep, Livy. She hasn't been getting enough sleep."

It was a grim and somber Cord who showed up later. Livy pointed to the room Monica was in, and hesitating for a moment, Cord went in.

Monica was restlessly moving her head on a pillow. She moaned softly and her brow was furrowed. Cord stood looking at her, a half dozen different emotions assailing him. He set his mouth firmly and sat gently on the edge of the bed. Her face was damp and hot when he pressed the back of his large hand to her cheek. Something quivered inside him.

Fitfully Monica pushed back the blankets and Cord could see she had no clothes on under the pile of covers. With unsteady hands he pulled them back into place under her chin. He took a cloth and dampened it in a bowl near the bed and bathed her face gently.

"He's so cold..." she mumbled and again pushed the blankets away. Cord did not understand her words.

He redampened the cloth and wiped her neck and shoulders, and across her breasts. Monica suddenly groaned and turned onto her side. The sheet was wet under her. Cord wiped her back and pulled the covers up again. He waited until she slept peacefully and then quietly left the room.

Livy was nowhere around. He sat on the edge of a chair and put his face in his hands. Something awful had ripped through him when he'd seen her lying there, weak and fretful. Something had broken inside and fallen to the pit of his stomach. He recognized it at once. It had been a long time since it had happened to him, but it was nonetheless familiar.

It was fear. It was the kind of fear that comes with caring, with being exposed and reaching out and touching, and most of all that comes with need. God help him, he did care about Monica. But he didn't have it in him to risk a second time everything that went with it. He remembered coming in that afternoon to find her and Matt together. He'd wanted to break Matt's arm in his anger and that had frightened him. He couldn't be indifferent if he was angry.

Cord moved his hands to find a glass of something dark being held out to him.

"Drink this," Olivia said bluntly. Cord took the glass.

"The baby?" he asked in a dead voice. Livy regarded him for silent moment. "The baby's fine. You might ask how your wife is!"

Cord stiffened and his head jerked up at that.

"Cord Temple, what is the matter with you? You treat that woman as though she were a stranger! My goodness, man, she's going to have your child. Doesn't that count for something?"

"I don't need instructions, Livy, on how to treat my wife!"

"Oh, yes, you do. You're behaving like you're punishing her for something."

"Am I supposed to be ashamed and repentant?" he asked angrily.

"You should be. But you won't," Livy said sadly. "And more's the pity. She cares so much for you it's just about to break my heart. She needs you to love her...to tell her!"

"I doubt that, Livy."

"Then you would be wrong! And you don't know women as well as you think you do. And you don't know your wife at all. How could you marry her, Cord, if you didn't really care?" She didn't give Cord a chance to answer but turned away to the room where Monica lay. She entered quietly and took some medication from a vial next to the bed. She poured out some water and, coaxing Monica to sit up a little, tried to get her to take it.

"Cord?" Monica asked in a vague voice.

"It's Olivia, dear."

"Where's Cord?"

"He's just outside the door. Do you want me to get him?"

Monica shook her head and turned on her side again and cried. Livy wasn't sure what to do. She finally got up and headed to the door. She thought she heard Monica say something, but wasn't sure with her moaning. And it was only after the door had closed that Monica repeated over and over in her delirium, "I love you, Cord. I love you...I love you..."

# Chapter Eight

There were so many things that Monica had not known. Slowly she came to recognize the changes that were rounding her out like the physical transformation that was taking place as well.

Monica was first of all to see that the love she felt for her stepsister was not at all like the feelings she had for Cord. This newer feeling was overwhelming in its magnitude. Yet Monica felt hopeless that he could ever feel that way for her. She saw clearly that he was a man much in need of tenderness and understanding, and she wanted very much to be the one to give it to him.

She saw Cord as the man who had awakened her physical senses and she wanted only him to let her have that again and again. She wanted to touch him, feel his arms around her. She wanted his full kiss, which left her drugged and dizzy. She wanted the hardness of him against her, on her, through her, releasing the ecstasy he alone could bring. Monica wanted to smooth out with her hands the grim lines around his wonderful mouth and make it soft and sensuous for her. Monica wanted to love him, give to him everything she was so that he'd be whole and, in turn, so would she.

It was bizarre in a sense that she would fall in love with the man to whom she was married, but who was not at all her husband.

Monica would not know for a long time that in her illness it was Cord who was constantly at her side, who fought to understand her disconnected, incoherent words and pleadings, who, against the objections of Livy Gavener, bathed and cooled her and forced liquids into her body. Cord cradled her gently as damp bed linens were changed and held her hand in his own when she wept in her sleep.

But when she finally woke up on the third day, she found herself alone. She cried again, feeling sorry for herself, believing Cord hadn't cared enough to stay and find out how she was.

During her recovery, Monica had the chance to reflect on her pregnancy. She was the bearer of new life. She had not connected being pregnant with any sense of creation. She was awed. She'd been like this inside of her mother, and Lee Ann inside of Eileen. The movement of the fetus and the realization of life inside her was a stunning shock. Her body was not her own. She shared it, and what happened to her in turn happened to this baby. And when it was all done, the growing and developing, it would come forth into the world a child in need of care and attention. The love she gave Lee Ann as an infant had been out of need and loneliness. It was not the same as what a mother gives a child. She had only now come to see that both she and Cord together had made the child growing in her. It was part of both of them. It was this sudden insight also that made her feel closer to him than she ever had before.

And then Monica felt horror for herself. In less than six months she would give up the life she carried into someone else's care. She would turn away and ignore its existence as she had been ignored by her father and stepmother. She would, God help her, abandon it as Cord had been.

She'd cried a heart torn, body wrenching torment of tears for the utter confusion she felt. What was to happen now? The story that Matt Bell had related had been further proof of the strangers she and Cord were to each other. She'd begun to hope that all their time together would have been enough to infiltrate the barriers and facades and reach each other's vulnerability. But that hope had been dashed with the realization that for all those years Cord had carried the memory and love for only one woman. Monica could never hope to inspire that kind of devotion. How foolish of her to harbor the hope that she could be everything to him. But she loved him nonetheless.

She could never go back and retract the love she felt, the awakening she had in her body, and the frustration and pain that came with both. Cord must not know how she felt. The one thing she did not want to see in his eyes was pity for her.

Cord had slept around the clock.

He had been so exhausted he'd fallen to sleep across his bed fully clothed. When he opened his eyes he sat up quickly wondering where he was, and it took him a moment to realize he was on his own bed at home and that Monica was at Mrs. Gavener's.

He groaned as he sat up on the edge of the bed, rubbing the back of his neck and ruffling his hair. He remembered the fever had finally broken and Monica had fallen into a deep peaceful sleep. Cord had never felt so helpless in his life as he had sitting there for three days and nights not knowing what to do to make her more comfortable.

Cord whispered to Monica, called her name softly, soothed her. Sometimes she'd open her eyes and look right at him and murmur his name, but he didn't know for sure if she really knew he was there. Once she said a name he'd never heard before and he bleakly wondered who this person was and what part they played in her life.

Cord staggered up and headed for the bathroom. He would shower and shave and change clothes. Then he would get back to Olivia's house. If Monica felt up to it, he would bring her back with him.

She was sitting up drinking tea when Cord came back in. He looked tired and pale to her, his mouth hard and tight. She must have been a terrible nuisance to him.

"Oh, good! Cord's here," Livy said, getting up from her chair. Cord moved slowly into the room, watching Monica's face. Her hair had been combed and she was wearing one of her own blouses and a shawl. Her cheeks and eyes still looked hollow and he frowned.

"I'll just go make some soup for Monica. You know you've eaten almost nothing for days." Livy left the room closing the door behind her.

Cord came forward and sat in the vacated chair. "How are you feeling?" he asked in his deep voice, searching her face with his gray eyes.

"Much, much better. Thank you. But I still feel so weak..."

"Like Olivia said, you haven't eaten anything for days."

She looked down at her fingers pleating the material of the bedspread. "I'm sorry I was so much trouble."

"I'm sure you didn't plan on getting sick," Cord said somewhat impatiently.

"Of course not!" Monica responded. "But I guess I could have taken better care of myself. Isn't that what you were going to say?"

A muscle tightened in Cord's neck. "No, it wasn't. But you're right nevertheless. I was going to say—"

Whatever it was was lost in the opening of the door as Livy entered with a soup bowl on a round wicker tray. She set it across Monica's lap. "There, this should help fill you up a little."

Monica slowly lifted the spoon and began to eat, but

after a few mouthfuls had to stop. She felt almost too weak to lift the spoon. Cord clenched his hands resting on his thigh, wanting to help her, but not wanting to treat her like an invalid.

"You'll feel much better in a few days," Livy was saying. Monica looked apprehensive first at Livy and then at Cord. He understood her appeal. "I think if Monica's up to it, I'll take her back to the house this afternoon, Livy."

"Oh, Cord, not so soon. Why, she could catch another chill. And who'd take care of her?"

"I would!" Cord said caustically.

"Don't be foolish, Cortland Temple. You can't do everything—"

"Livy!" Monica interrupted pleadingly. "I—I know I must have been inconvenient—"

"Nonsense!"

"But if you don't mind, I . . . I'd really like to go back."

Cord watched her. Olivia turned away and forced a low voice. "Well, if you feel that way!"

"Oh, Livy. I don't mean to sound ungrateful," Monica said contritely.

"Oh, I understand you'd rather be with your husband!" She shot a wicked gleam at Cord. "You just finish your soup and I'll get the rest of your clothes."

After she'd gone Cord sat back in his chair and silently watched Monica as she finished eating.

"How is your work going?" she ventured.

He shrugged. "I wouldn't know. I sent Matt to cover for me."

"Oh, Cord, I'm sorry!"

"It'll keep him out of trouble. He sends his regards, by the way."

"That was nice of him," she murmured and stole a glance at him sideways. "You look tired. Haven't you been getting any sleep?"

"I haven't gotten much rest in the last few days," he said, more roughly than he'd meant to.

Monica looked at him stricken and opened her mouth to speak.

"And for goodness' sakes please don't apologize again! Finish your soup," he said in a more gentle voice and smiled at her. Monica nodded, swallowing a knot in her throat and once again lifted the spoon.

She was speechless with joy at being back in the white house. Cord moved to carry her into her room, but she protested. She'd had enough of lying in bed. He put her instead in the rocking chair by the fireplace and started a fire to keep her warm. Monica secretly gloried in the attention he silently gave her.

Monica became cozy and comfortable and the heat of the fire made her sleepy. She protested weakly when Cord at last carried her to her bed.

"You need to rest!" he countered. "Besides, you're too weak to fight me." That made her smile and she tightened her hold around his neck.

Cord put her to bed under a pile of quilts and she fell instantly to sleep. When she woke again, it was dark. Cord brought her juice, toast, and more soup, which she ate without complaint. Much to her chagrin, however, she again felt tired and went back to sleep almost immediately. It was almost ten the next morning when she opened her eyes.

Monica slowly sat up and wobbled to the closet to get a fresh set of clothes. She combed her hair and straightened the bed and felt utterly exhausted when she finished. The brush she'd used slid off the nightstand to the floor with a thud. She bent to pick it up and a second later there was a light knock on her door and someone called her name.

"Yes? Come in."

It was Matthew Bell's boyish face that peeped around the edge of the door. "Hello, gorgeous!" he said cheerfully, stepping into the room.

"Good morning, Matt." He came over and planted a firm kiss on her mouth.

"Where's Cord?" she asked quickly to hide her confusion.

"Oh, he decided he'd lost enough time at the site."

"Oh."

"He went over this morning. They're predicting snow in a few days and he wants a certain amount of work done by then."

"I see." But she felt very let down. Well, what did she expect? That he'd stay around and wait on her hand and foot? That would not have been like Cord at all. Yesterday was one thing. It had been her first day up. Today, it was life as usual. She was on her own.

"Won't I do as a substitute?" Matt asked, feigning sadness. Monica had to laugh.

"I'm sorry. Of course you will."

Matt sat next to her on the bed. "I came to say hello last night but you were asleep. Cord threatened to break my legs if I woke you."

"I doubt that!" Monica laughed.

"Oh, you don't know Cord very well yet. He has the devil of a temper at times!"

"Now, that I do know!"

"I'm really glad to see you up. You know, you had us worried?"

Monica smiled at him, but something in his eyes made her nervous.

"You're going to have to put up with my cooking today. What would you like for breakfast?"

"Oh, don't bother. I don't feel very hungry."

"How about some tea and a couple of slices of toast?"

"I—I guess I can manage that."

Matthew got up and touched her cheek affectionately. "Good. I'll get started. Oh, by the way, Cord said you were to have some eggs as well."

Immediately Monica's hackles were up. "He did, did he?"

"Absolutely!" Matt grinned wickedly.

"Well, I don't want any eggs."

"Right! Two eggs over light." Throwing her another grin, he walked to the door ignoring her frustration.

"And suppose I refuse to eat them?"

"Then you'll have to answer to Cord!"

Monica sighed and gave in, ungracefully.

"Oh, there's some mail for you this morning." He left and returned a moment later with several envelopes held out to her.

"Breakfast will be ready in twenty minutes." And he walked out again.

There were three envelopes. One from Donna, one from Lawrence Gordon's law firm, and one from Lee Ann. Monica tore open that one first. It was postmarked Paris, and she chewed her bottom lip wondering what Lee Ann was doing in Paris.

Lee Ann was in love. Or so that was how the letter read. Monica groaned. The letter went on to say they'd had a five-day field trip to Paris for performances. Lee Ann explained how magnificent Paris was. The city, the people, the churches...and there she had met Jean Paul. He spoke no English, she spoke no French but he was wonderful! An older man...nineteen. Monica groaned again. He thought she was beautiful and the best dancer he'd ever seen...so on and so on.

Monica put the letter down in frantic despair, feeling very much like a parent with a wayward child. She wondered if Lee Ann had...if she'd thought of...

Monica shook her head against the thoughts she had

as to the relationship between her sister and this Jean Paul. She got up and paced the room wondering what to do. She forced herself to sit and finish the letter.

> I know I complain a lot about school, but honestly it's the greatest place in the world. We attend performances constantly and we've seen all the great Royal Ballet dancers dance. I know someday I'll be up there in front of an audience dancing *Coppélia* or *Sleeping Beauty*, and I'll remember that none of it would have been possible except for you. I love you. You're the best sister in the whole world!
>
>       Love,
>       Lee Ann

Monica let out a sigh, and tears rolled unchecked down her face. She had very real doubts now about what she was doing. But the letter from her sister also served to make her feel that if she had to do it over, it would be worth it.

The letter from Donna was a cheerful account of all that was happening in New York. It was fun and cheered her a little.

The letter from Lawrence Gordon was only a record of the interest accumulated to date on the money Cord had given her. She felt suddenly ill at this reminder. She closed her eyes tightly and unconsciously stroked her stomach gently. Damn the money!

She sat and quickly wrote a note to him asking that he authorize a bank draft to be sent to the following account in London.

Monica was sealing the letter when Matthew called her to have breakfast.

Cord had threatened to lock Monica in her room unless she did as she was told. She was not to cook, or dust, or clean. He snapped at her, growled at her. Monica snapped and growled back, but Cord was satisfied. If she could spit fire at him as she used to before she got sick, she was herself again.

But the idleness left Monica bored and restless. She did floor exercises in her room to help keep her muscles toned. If she lifted so much as a towel to fold, it was pulled from her hands and she was shooed into the sitting room to her rocking chair. There, she rocked back and forth in furious frustration thinking that if she didn't find something to do she'd tear her hair out strand by strand.

Livy Gavener came to the rescue by patiently teaching Monica to do needlepoint. She did one simple project after another until she got an idea for a larger piece, and with Livy's help set to work on it. But she couldn't needlepoint all the time, and she got tired of reading.

Olivia humored her and tried to smooth her ruffled feathers, but Monica was livid.

"I'm going to go mad! He won't let me do anything!"

"Now, Monica, getting excited isn't going to do you and the baby any good at all! Besides, Cord is just concerned that you'll overtire yourself. You should be glad he's worried."

Monica started to retort that he was not the least worried about her, but stopped herself. If she could be sure that he was indeed concerned, she'd cheerfully do as he asked. In her mind it would have been a confirmation of his real feelings.

"You just sit in that chair and let out a deep breath. Expectant mothers are supposed to be tranquil, serene, and joyous!" Livy said.

Monica sighed. She sat back in her rocker and ruefully passed a hand over her pregnant form. The baby was getting bigger—and moving around in there. She wondered abstractedly if he was trying to get comfortable. Maybe he was unhappy with the accommodations. More and more Monica was thinking and feeling the baby a real person, a tiny person waiting to be born. The baby moved around under her full breasts, as though hugging himself to her for warmth and comfort. Monica felt curiosity toward it, and protectiveness. Perhaps it was the same protectiveness that Cord felt.

She could begin to see that Cord might also feel the responsibility by way of being careful of her. She just wished he was more loving. It was so easy to indulge in a fantasy of her and Cord belonging together and waiting together for their child to be born. The thought sent devastating shock waves through her. Monica wanted to believe now that her feelings for him were really the reasons she was round and heavy with his child. That it was out of love—in mutual love that she'd conceived.

Ever since she'd been ill almost two weeks ago, Cord seemed not to want to be in her company, not to want to talk to her. She'd resisted the need to touch him in the most innocent way, of smiling at him in her joy of just being with him. She deliberately matched his indifference and then later, alone in her own room, she'd cry out of loneliness and need.

But the truth was Cord didn't trust himself around her. She was too appealing and he was feeling more susceptible with each passing day. She moved with the most phenomenal grace and ease he couldn't help staring at her from time to time. He wanted to touch her, to share in this experience of her body changing. But their relationship had never allowed for the real intimacy that was possible between a man and wife in marriage. Yet, he felt something pulling him to her that was both awesome in its attraction and fascinating in its power. He saw Monica fully as a woman in the midst of one of life's marvelous adventures, and he had been a part of it. He had not considered her existence before but he could not ignore it now. She was no longer someone who would just bear his child: she was the mother of that child. Cord's lack of knowing how to handle this feeling made him brusque and short with her. When he showed strength, he was on safer ground.

One afternoon Livy offhandedly left an old hat box at Monica's feet.

"I thought you'd like to have some of this," she said by way of explanation. Monica looked curiously at the box and then to Livy.

"Well, I'm long past it doing me any good. I'd almost forgotten I had them all these years."

Monica lifted the cover of the round green box and carefully folded back tissue paper to reveal a stack of baby garments, all handmade and skillfully crafted. Monica lifted the first item. It was a minute sweater of blue and green wool with ribbons to tie it closed. She knew for certain that Olivia had in no way forgotten about these things. These were heirlooms, treasures that one coveted and protected. They must have been very precious to her for many years. Tears of pleasure and sorrow filled Monica's eyes as she lifted them to those of her friend.

"I made them for my daughter," Livy said, "and I saved them thinking, hoping, that someday—" She stopped, her chin quivering.

Monica was overwhelmed that Livy would make such a sacrifice of her precious things. She would have been honored to have used these lovely things for her baby. But this was not her baby, and the joy of the gift was lost. She replaced the sweater and hat and folded down the tissue.

"I couldn't possibly accept such a gift. A lot of time and love and hope went into making each piece."

"In all these years, even after our daughter passed away, Jim and I never thought of parting with that box." Olivia looked at Monica. "You're the first person I've ever wanted to give them to. Freely and gladly. They should be used. Please take them."

Monica sat in indecision.

"I was very careful in the colors," Livy said. "A boy or girl could wear them." She smiled coaxingly.

"It—it's a lovely gift. And I will use them."

"Good!" Livy responded getting up from her seat. She went on to the kitchen leaving Monica to sit pensively in her rocker. She opened the box once again. Everything was so tiny, so small. It was like having a box filled with doll clothing. But a warm flush filled Monica's cheeks as a memory of the newborn Lee Ann came to mind. She had been this tiny, wiggly little life that had been so wonderful to hold and care for. Whenever Monica thought of Lee Ann she came closer to the realization that the baby she carried would be like that. The difference was she would have given this child life.

She sat with a lap full of baby clothes suddenly thinking of Cord and wishing desperately to be held and loved by him. It was not going to happen. But there was the baby.

Monica awoke late one morning to a snow-covered paradise. It was breathtakingly beautiful, the Green Mountains and the treetops heavy with the powdery stuff. Monica had never known snow as white and clean as this.

She dressed quickly and stepped out of the house, all alone, into the clear crisp frosty air that momentarily stripped her lungs of breath. She wished that Cord was there to share this with, to go for a walk through the back woods.

Monica started out gingerly by herself. She walked for quite a long time, unmindful of the cold, and was only brought back to earth when she developed an ache in her lower back and began to feel tired.

When she walked past the sugar mill she saw Matthew Bell's blue sports car parked at the side of the house. Monica entered letting the door close sharply behind her. Her cheeks and nose were red from the brisk air and her eyes clear and sparkling when Matt came from the kitchen, a mug of something hot in his hands.

"Hey, gorgeous!" He smiled at her warmly. "I wondered where you were." He stepped forward and Monica allowed him to kiss her hello. Her eyes widened when his firm mouth brushed gently over her own.

"H-hello, Matt," she said a bit nervously. "I didn't know you were expected." He grinned sheepishly at her, a brow quirking on his boyish face.

"I wasn't. But I was in Montpelier and thought I'd stop by once more before heading home."

"Home?" Monica asked blankly, starting to remove her cape and gloves and depositing them on the back of Cord's chair. She hadn't given any thought to the fact that Matt must live somewhere, have family somewhere.

"Yes. Home."

"Where's that?"

"Washington," he said, watching her intently.

"There's nothing more that I can do with Cord's contracts until after the next phase is finished. That won't happen until February when the worst of the cold weather is over. Will you miss me?"

His last comment was so unexpected that Monica jumped. "Of course we'll miss you, Matt," she answered softly, taking safety behind the plural. Monica looked apprehensively into his eyes. What she thought she saw there left her holding her breath.

"But will *you* miss me, Monica?"

She quickly stepped around him, heading for the kitchen. "Don't be silly, Matt. You'll be back. I—I won't have time to miss you." She busied herself in the kitchen making a cup of tea with shaky hands.

"You're very jumpy. Is anything wrong? Do you feel okay?" Monica looked at him and saw genuine puzzlement in his face. Maybe she'd just overreacted.

"I—I guess I've been stuck indoors too long. I'm sorry."

"I tell you what. You fix me lunch and put up with me for one more night, and I'll take you out this afternoon. Okay?"

His smile was so infectious. She laughed and shook her head. "That sounds suspiciously like blackmail, but okay."

Monica prepared soup and sandwiches, then sliced carrot cake that Livy had made the day before. "You have to promise not to tell Cord that I did this. I have strict orders not to do any work," she said ruefully.

Matt lit a fire in the sitting room, and they sat for a while over tea. He got up and walked around. He picked up a piece of needlepoint she'd started and examined it.

"Is this your work?" he asked.

"Yes."

"Very nice. What is it going to be?"

Monica lowered her head in embarrassment. "I'm making a cover for a footstool."

Matt came to stand in front of her, hands in his pockets. Some emotion went quickly over his face.

"Is it for Cord?"

Monica nodded. Matt turned away and a sigh, long and tired, left him. "Why don't you go bundle up and we'll go for that walk," he said evenly and went to put on his coat.

Matthew walked through the deep snow in his heavy boots and left a narrow trail for Monica to follow. Being outdoors again lifted her spirits and she exclaimed and chatted gaily, kicking at the snow and sending drifts of it floating in the air. Matt looked back at her in amusement.

He led the way up to the pond on the other side of the house and they watched as a small doe darted across the frozen ice and into the woods. Monica was enchanted. They completely circled the pond and headed toward the sugar mill in a wide circle. Matt stopped suddenly when he felt a soft thud againt his back. He turned around to find Monica poised with a snowball in hand, ready to throw at him. She let it go and it landed on Matt's arm as he raised it to shield his head.

"Hey!" he exclaimed, laughing. "Is this any way to treat your guide?"

Monica laughed and threw another softly packed snowball.

Matt turned and ran into the doorway of the sugar mill for protection. He could still hear Monica's merry laugh.

"Chicken!" she yelled. "Afraid of a little snow!"

But Matt only laughed as he shook the snow from his collar and arm while he walked to the other end of the mill house and came out again into the cold sunny air. He smiled, looking around the corner expecting to see Monica. But his eyes grew puzzled as he scanned the landscape with no sign of her.

"Monica?" Matt called but there was no answer. He began to walk back to the main door of the mill, his frown deepening. "Monica?" he called again, louder. Matt began to trot now, very worried. He got back to the door and swung around looking in all directions.

"Monica! Where are you?" he shouted. There was a sound of some kind beyond a little rise, to his left. Feeling real panic, he ran until he cleared the top. He stopped dead in his tracks as he saw her stretched out on her back in the snow in front of him. Her arms were out from her body and her eyes were closed.

"Oh, my God!" Matt groaned and ran to her.

Her arms began to move above her shoulders and down again. Matt reached her, dropping to his knees in the snow by her side, grabbing her shoulders to pull her up.

"My God, Monica..."

At that moment she opened her eyes to look at him and giggled girlishly. "Matt, you're spoiling my angel!"

He looked at her dumbly. "What?"

"My angel!" She struggled to stand up. She turned and pointed to the impression her body had left in the snow. "See! It's an angel. Haven't you ever made angels when you were—"

The next instant Monica found herself crushed suddenly against the solid stocky body of Matt Bell.

"Dammit, Monica. I thought—"

"What's the matter?" she asked in confusion. Matt looked at her, and there was that look that she'd seen several times before that had disturbed her. Matt groaned, bending his head to kiss her full on the mouth. Monica stood still for a moment under the surprise of this contact. Matt's mouth became demanding and searching on her own unprepared parted lips. Then she realized what was happening and struggled to pull away.

"No, Matt!" she gasped, pushing against his chest.

"Monica, I love you!" he said huskily, trying to pull her back to him.

"No, Matt. No! Please stop." Monica jerked her arm away, freeing herself. They stood staring wide eyed at each other, panting.

"Oh, Matthew...why?"

"Monica," he breathed in a low unsteady voice, "I'm in love with you! I have been since the moment I first saw you!"

"That's crazy!" she said, bewildered, shaking her head. "You can't be. I never said...I never led you to—"

"I know. I know. You didn't have to. It was just— just you!"

A frightened cry escaped her and she turned away from him, a pain spreading through her heart. "Matt, please! Please don't do this! Don't say any more."

He gently put his hands on her upper arms and touched his lips to her thick wool hat. Monica, in horror, felt herself succumbing to his gentleness. She resisted being pulled back against his chest.

"It's too late. It was too late from the beginning. If I'd had any sense then, I'd have turned around and gone back to Washington. But I didn't. And I'm crazy about you!" Matt suddenly came to stand in front of her. "Monica, come with me!" he pleaded, caution thrown to the wind.

"Oh, Matt, you're crazy. I'm married to your best friend, remember?"

"No, you're not!" he gritted urgently through his teeth. "I don't understand what's going on between you two, but it's not a marriage! Cord barely acknowledges you! He doesn't love you!"

"It doesn't matter!"

"You're in love with him, aren't you?"

Monica only looked at him feeling helpless. "Yes. I'm in love with him. And I'm going to have his child!"

"And that may be all you have of him. Monica, Cord

gives you nothing of himself. Nothing! He treats you like—like a stranger. Is that what you want?"

"I don't know! I only know I love him... and I have to stay!"

"Monica," he said softly, still pleading, "I'd be a good father to the child. I wouldn't care that—"

"I believe you," she interrupted. "But I won't do that to him. Cord wants his child. We have an arrangement."

"Forget the arrangement! What do you want?"

"Time... to wait until February when the baby comes and then see what happens. You're supposed to be his best friend, Matthew. Don't do this to him... or to me!" Matt watched her, knowing he'd never change her mind, never have her.

"Monica," he said softly as she turned away from him, "let me hold you."

"No!" She shook her head sharply from side to side.

"Look, I promise—"

"No, Matt." She was firm. But Monica was also afraid of letting him come near her. He would just hold her. And he would be gentle. She needed that—but not from Matthew.

Monica turned and slowly trekked through the late afternoon light to the house. A tall, graceful, rounded figure, a little pathetic against the brilliant background.

## Chapter Nine

It would be a very long time before Monica would remember exactly how the rest of that interminable day went. She closed herself away in her room, sitting by a window in a numb stupor. Matt's declaration had only served to awaken all her senses, and every nerve in her body to her love for Cord. She felt such despair at the futility of it all, that the feelings threatened to burst out of her. In a moment of panic she wondered if she could last until February when the baby was born and she could leave. But even the thought of leaving had the power to make her heart feel as though it were squeezed into a tight space in her chest.

She came out of her room sometime later when she heard Cord's wagon in the drive. He came into the sitting room and didn't see her immediately as he leaned wearily against the door. Monica watched him and saw how terribly tired he looked, and almost gaunt.

Cord sensed her presence and turned to look right into her soft amber eyes. "Monica?" he began, pushing himself away from the door and walking in her direction. "I didn't realize you were standing there. Are you okay?" he asked, searching her face.

But Monica was mesmerized by his features, and the drawn look around his full mouth. Unconsciously she raised her hand to stroke over the rough surface of his cheek where a growth of beard bristled.

"You look tired," she said in a vague voice, ignoring his question. Cord was so surprised by this show of concern that he just stared at her and let her soft delicate hand move over his skin. He suppressed a shudder of feeling and abruptly turned his head away and said in a strange voice, "I'm fine. Don't worry about me."

Monica felt hurt.

"How are you feeling? What did you do all day?"

She moved to sit in her rocker, only now wondering where Matthew was. She had not seen him since their encounter by the sugar mill. She hoped he wouldn't be foolish enough to make mention of it in front of Cord.

"Oh, not much. I went for a walk in the snow and had some lunch—"

"You what?"

"I went for a walk."

"Jesus, Monica! The ground is uneven and slippery in spots. What if you'd tripped or fallen—"

"It was okay," she interrupted, every nerve on edge. "Matthew was with me."

At first Cord was silent. "Was he?" he then asked speculatively. "And where is Matt now?"

"I don't know. I came inside to rest for a while. I haven't seen him for the last few—"

"Here I am!"

They both turned around to see Matt standing near the doorway. "I was upstairs packing my belongings," he supplied in his usual Matthew Bell manner, except that his normally bright blue eyes were dark with emotion and guarded.

"Matt's leaving in the morning, Cord. He said we won't see him until after the holidays."

"I see," Cord responded in a noncommittal way.

"Yeah, old buddy, time for me to vacate for a while."

"You don't have to, Matt..." Cord began.

"Yes, I do. I don't want to overstep my welcome. I may really need it someday!" He sent Monica a rueful grin, causing her to blush. Cord did not insist again.

"Look, since this is my last night, why don't I take you guys out for dinner? Are there any decent restaurants in Randolph?"

Cord quirked a brow at him. "As long as you don't expect haute cuisine or four-star service." Matt laughed in a hearty way that finally allowed Monica to unclench her hands. Cord turned to regard Monica. "Do you feel up to it? We could just stay in—"

"Oh, no, not on my account. And it will be good to get out for a while." Cord frowned at the implication fully realizing that he'd not offered to take her to dinner again since their first outing.

"Great!" Matt said, clapping his hands together.

"I guess I should change," Monica offered, getting up from her chair.

Cord's eye ran over the green caftan Monica wore, the one he liked so much. "No, don't change. You look fine just as you are." It was said so quietly, so smoothly, that Monica continued to look in surprise at him.

"Well," Cord said, breaking his gaze first, "why don't I call and make reservations." He moved into the kitchen, where the phone hung on the wall.

Monica once more found herself alone with Matt. She was unaware of her body stiffening in alarm and her eyes widening in apprehension.

"Don't, love," he whispered, smiling sadly at her. "Believe me, I'd never do anything to hurt you."

Monica let out a tight sigh. "I—I'm sorry..."

"There's nothing for you to be sorry about, either."

Somehow Matt managed to carry the evening. Even Cord was in good humor, smiling often and sending soft looks to Monica, making her blush in confusion. He bantered with Matt while Monica listened in relative silence. She watched the two men on either side of her. How different they were! Matt, so open and uncomplicated, so full of life and good humor. She felt a sudden strong affection for Matt. She liked him. In a way, she was sorry it couldn't have been Matt she was in love with. But her eyes softened as they swept over Cord, and she knew there was no help for it. She was terribly in love with him. His very presence had the power to make her weak. Monica knew that no matter what, she'd never again be able to love someone this way.

She realized she must have been staring. She blinked quickly at Cord's questioning look. "What? Did you say something?" she asked, horrified at being caught so exposed.

"I asked if you were okay," Cord repeated, searching her face with concern.

"Oh, yes." She laughed nervously. "I guess I was daydreaming."

"I think you're more tired than you realize. Come on, it's time to go home."

"Oh, really, just because I—"

"You're overruled on this one, gorgeous!" Matt laughed, signaling the waiter for the check.

"We'll wait for you in the car, Matt." Cord stood up and reached for Monica's hand. She reveled in his strong grip over her fingers as he helped her to her feet.

Matt kept up a constant chatter on the way back to the house, but Monica realized that she was very tired. She had a slight headache and there was that ache again in her back.

At the house, Cord suggested she might want to go to bed, and she didn't argue. She never questioned the brief kiss Cord left on her mouth.

"You should sleep in tomorrow," Matt suggested. [1] "You need lots of rest."

Monica was curious. "How do you know rest is what I need?"

"Two sisters with five kids between them?"

Monica smiled at him. "Okay, you win. Good night. I'll see you in the morning." She stifled a yawn and walked to her room.

Cord turned to Matt. "You know there's no reason for you to leave, Matt."

Matt answered bleakly, "I have to, Cord."

"Why?" Cord asked softly, his voice even.

"Because you two need time together. I've imposed long enough. Two's company; three is trouble." Matt headed for the stairwell leading up to his room. Cord finally looked up at him, and the two friends regarded each other. They knew one another very well. They had been through much together and the friendship was sure. There was no misunderstanding now as they were about to part.

"Take care of her, Cord," Matt said seriously. He put out his hand and Cord gripped it in farewell.

"We'll see you in a few months" was Cord's grim response.

Cord didn't understand why Olivia Gavener was so insistent, but he found himself promising that he and Monica would attend the Thanksgiving Festival at the Randolph Recreation Center. Livy also invited Cord and Monica to have Thanksgiving dinner with her after the activities.

It snowed again on Thanksgiving day. Monica began to worry that Cord would never be able to get them to the center through the storm, and indeed he even suggested that perhaps it would be better to stay home. She coaxed him saying they couldn't disappoint Livy for dinner, and Cord gave in.

The center was ablaze with light and color and children running around in the excitement of performing in front of family and friends. Cord sat Monica on a side aisle seat so that she had the most room and could get up if she had to without disturbing anyone. The events began, starting with the younger groups and progressing to the preteens.

Cord paid attention and didn't seem impatient as Monica thought he would be. When at last her dance group was announced she began to fidget in her chair. Cord looked at her curiously once or twice and she fought to sit still.

The lights went down and the music began. It was mostly horns and string instruments with a jazzy upbeat. The dancers, ages twelve to fifteen, were all wearing black eye masks. The girls wore French berets, black tights, and miniskirts over long sleeved red leotards; the boys wore black turtleneck sweaters and black jeans, having refused outright to be seen on stage in tights. But still, with the lights, the effect was the one Monica wanted. The choreography was fast paced and crisp, giving the five boys in the set the full opportunity to leap, turn, kick, and slide across the floor in vigorous exercise. When the number ended six minutes later, Monica felt very proud. The curtain came down and there was wild applause and whistling.

"That was very good!" Cord said in surprise. At that point the lights came up and tiny Olivia Gavener came on stage demanding silence.

"We are very pleased that you enjoyed the program this year. We think it's one of the best ever. How about a hand for all our hardworking and very talented boys and girls!" And she led the applause that followed, then she again signaled for silence.

"I also think we owe a very special hand to Monica Temple who is responsible for that exciting dance routine by our teen corp. We recruited her in September and she worked very hard with the kids for tonight's performance. Also, anyone who can get thirteen-year-old boys to dance on stage is pretty special in my eyes!'' There was laughter at Livy's last remark, but there was again applause, loud and continuous. There was a cheer from Monica's group who waved at her from behind the curtain on stage.

Cord listened bewildered to the clapping and it finally registered that it was indeed for his wife. He stood up suddenly taking Monica's hand and gently pulled her to her feet. He then joined in the applause, a smile playing around his usually stern mouth.

Cord held her hand as they later made their way to the car for the drive to Livy's for dinner. He was patient, and only stood silently observing as many people approached Monica to congratulate her on the fine dance routine, and to thank her for getting their sons and daughters interested in something else besides disco and television.

Finally they got to the car.

"You're full of surprises," Cord said evenly. "Why didn't you tell me what you were up to?"

Monica turned her head to look out at the cold clear night. "I didn't think you cared what I was doing," she answered simply without emotion. Cord grimaced. It was true. Until a month or so ago he didn't care. But now he didn't know how to reverse the path he'd taken in their relationship, and he wasn't sure she wanted him to. He let her answer go, feeling a little empty.

"It was a very good piece. You should be pleased."

"I am."

"Have you done much of that sort of thing?"

"No. It was my first attempt at choreography. I like doing it." She turned to him shyly, watching his profile as he concentrated on the snowy road.

"If it means anything to you, I was very impressed."

"It means a lot," Monica answered truthfully. Cord turned his head briefly to smile at her. He felt a certain relief all at once. And he was hopeful.

With the work stopped on construction because of the cold, Cord found himself more often at the white house with Monica. He did not allow himself yet to fully admit the time with her was important, nor would he admit that when they were apart he missed her. With her here it felt like home. But to openly admit to any of this would mean to realize deeper feelings. Living with so many past hurts and disappointments still would not allow him to see that he was his own oracle.

What Cord did see and could admit was that Natalie would never have been happy here. She would have despaired at the lack of social life and the lethargic pace of the people.

Cord did not realize right away that thoughts of Natalie no longer sent stabbing pains through his chest. He was finally healing, but he was too close to the cure to recognize it for what it was.

Monica was having a devastating effect on Cord. He found her more physically appealing every day. Seeing her swollen body as she moved through the house had the power to weaken him, make him feel helpless before her. What would it be like without her? How could he stay here afterward with the memory of her presence everywhere? She had gotten past a barrier and he was vulnerable enough for all the walls to come tumbling down.

But Monica was blissfully ignorant of the power she wielded and would not have known how to use it in any case. She was just very grateful for the weather, which made it possible for her to be constantly near him.

She woke one morning well into her seventh month
to hear her name being called.

"Monica, wake up!" came Cord's voice through her
door. He knocked sharply. "Are you awake yet?"

"Yes . . . yes," Monica managed.

"Well, hurry and get dressed. We're going out!"

His use of "we" was enough to spur her to action.
When she emerged fifteen minutes later, Cord was
drinking coffee in the kitchen.

"Where are we going?" she asked. Cord looked at
her protruding stomach and felt oddly complacent. His
eyes traveled up to her pretty face, the surface skin soft
and rosy from recent sleep.

"We're going for a sleigh ride," he said casually.

"Really? Oh, Cord!" She came to stand right in
front of him expectantly.

"We need firewood. So I thought we'd take the old
sleigh from the mill up into the mountains. I borrowed
a horse from the farm down the road. I don't want to
keep him standing so go get your coat." He headed
toward the door.

"I'll be out in twenty minutes," she yelled excitedly
after him.

"Fifteen!" Cord countered.

"Okay . . . fifteen!" Monica went to the kitchen and
quickly filled a thermos with the remaining hot coffee
from the pot. She found some cheese and rolls and
apples. After putting her treasure into a tote, she put on
her cape, hat and gloves and went to meet Cord.

"What kept you?" Cord asked.

"Lunch!" She smiled appealingly. He helped her
into the high seat and, taking the reins into his hand,
started the sleigh across the back of the house and onto
the trail running into the hills.

She was delirious with joy. How perfect to share this
with someone she loved. They were gradually climbing

into the hills when Cord finally stopped the sleigh at a spot obviously used before to fell trees.

"This is still your land?" Monica asked.

"Yep," Cord answered, looking around at the available material. He didn't want to cut down a perfectly healthy tree if there was dead wood around. Monica struggled down from her seat as Cord proceeded to chop. She wandered off a ways into the forest looking at the bird and animal tracks in the snow. There was a movement in the corner of her eye and she turned her head scanning the snow drifts. Suddenly there was a hop and then another as a furry animal bounded skittishly across the path in front of her and into the woods. It was a snowshoe hare.

She continued her walk but began to feel tired, her feet feeling heavy as lead as she trudged through the thick snow. She came to an almost flat smooth boulder and sat to catch her breath. After a while she rose and started back in the direction she'd come. She was almost back to the clearing when Cord's large frame appeared before her. She was surprised at the thunderous expression on his face, his eyes hard and icy again. Monica's heart sank.

"Where the hell have you been?" he shouted.

"I only went for a walk."

"I had no idea where you'd disappeared to or where to begin to look for you!"

"I wasn't lost. I merely went for a walk. I got a little tired and I stopped to rest." Cord's face went completely ashen. Muttering an oath violently, he scooped her into his arms and began to walk back to the sleigh.

"Cord, put me down! I'm okay."

"You can get into more mischief," he ground out as he put her on the seat. Monica pulled back from him and stared into his face. Tears of humiliation threatened to roll down her cheeks.

Cord cursed himself for overreacting. Couldn't she see he was only concerned about her? "Monica?" He touched her arm; she pulled away. "I'm sorry I shouted," he said contritely.

"I know you'll be glad to be rid of me. Well, February is almost here!"

Cord paled even more and frowned. "Are you so anxious to leave in February?" he asked tersely.

"It will be best," she cried, not looking at him. "The sooner I leave, the better."

Cord felt miserable. And he felt defeated. If she wanted to leave there was nothing he could do. Cord climbed up next to her and Monica served their lunch. They ate in silence.

The fire crackled with a life of its own, shooting up flames in a crazy dance. Cord poked at the two logs, sending sparks up the chimney. One foot rested on the elevated edge to the hearth. He frowned in concentration, an image of Monica at dinner coming to mind. They'd been eating in relative silence recently, each left miserably to his own thoughts. Once or twice Cord thought she fought down tears. He wondered if she was in pain or felt ill. He remembered the last time she was sick and how badly it had affected him. But when the silent meal was over Monica excused herself and went to her room.

He'd come very close once during the week to asking her to stay past February. Perhaps until April or longer. But the thought of her saying no, of telling him she had to get back to New York and her career had stopped him. Suddenly there didn't seem to be enough time to have her here with him, for the feelings in him to grow and be understood or to stand unafraid of the future. When Monica left he would have gained a child but he would have lost her.

In that moment there was the sound of an exclamation followed by a number of things hitting the floor in the kitchen. Cord's head came up.

"Monica?" he called out. She did not answer. Putting down the poker, Cord walked quickly into the kitchen. There he found Monica standing, her face buried in her hands, sobbing. On the floor at her feet was a fork, a towel, and a leftover roll from dinner. Cord frowned, not understanding what had happened.

"Monica? What's the matter? Are you okay?" She only cried harder.

"Monica?" Cord said urgently, touching her shoulder. He was surprised when she pulled away from him.

"No! I'm not okay!" she wailed. "I'm awful!"

She looked up, her face flushed and streaked with tears. Her hair was fallen partially loose from its usual knot. She wore a white wool caftan, which accented the red of her hair.

"What's the matter?" Cord asked a bit afraid.

"Everything! I can't sleep. I can't move. I can't do anything without bumping against something else." She cried and hiccuped and shook her head. "I knock things off tables and then...and then I can't even bend to pick them up!" She stopped talking as a wave of wrenching sobs shook her. Cord again reached out to touch her, and again she pushed his hand away.

"Monica..." he tried softly.

"Nothing fits me. I don't look nice in anything anymore. I—I've grown so fat and ugly. I—I feel like...a cow!" she ended on a cry, remembering painfully her stepmother's description.

Cord didn't wait for her to say another word. He lifted her into his arms and quickly walked with her into her room. She tried to still the anguish enveloping her, but it seemed beyond her control.

For the moment Cord sat on her bed with Monica across his lap. She lay back against his strong arm, her head against his shoulder. Cord's free hand stroked her mussed hair and he could say nothing. She continued to cry, shaking in his hold. Through her teary deluge Monica was aware of the overwhelming male scent of him. She snuggled further into his shoulder.

"Oh, Cord!" she moaned. "I'll never look pretty again. And I can't even see my toes!"

Cord was himself shaken with the depth of her feelings. But a rueful smile curved his mouth and he chuckled. "Your toes are still there," he assured her in his deep voice. "And still the prettiest dancer's feet I've ever seen!"

"Really?" she asked, very much like a dispirited child who needed reassurance.

"Really," Cord responded. He tightened his arms around her. Her stomach, high and round, rested oddly against his chest and the feeling was indescribable. Protected inside was his baby, and this woman whom he held so carefully nurtured it and continuously gave it life.

He wanted so desperately to tell her she gave *him* life. But still he held back.

Cord stood up suddenly but he only turned around to gently lay her full upon the bed, and then he sat on the edge facing her. Monica's eyes were wide and sparkling with unshed tears. Cord reached up his hands and began to pull the pins from her disheveled hair. And when the last one was removed the burnished strands fell in silken glory to her shoulders and below. He had never seen her hair down before, though he had often imagined it. It was beautiful.

Monica watched his face, mesmerized by the soft look in his gray eyes, as he stroked and smoothed her hair with both hands. Monica reached up with tentative fingers to gently touch his lips. They parted in surprise as her soft cool hand moved and came back to lie in her lap again.

"I've always wanted to do that," she murmured honestly.

"Why?" he asked in a low voice.

"To smooth away the tension. So it wouldn't seem so hard," she replied simply, moving her eyes from watching his mouth to meeting his gaze.

"Do I appear so hard?" he asked tightly.

"Sometimes. I know I've been a lot of trouble, and you haven't been very pleased with me. And now that I've grown so—" Her voice faltered. A tear slipped down her cheek and Cord slowly bent forward to kiss it away.

Cord was suddenly aware of desire burning in his loins, but it wasn't all sexual. It was also a need to hold her against him to stroke and caress her. To kiss her gently. He wanted to be tender to her. He gently put both hands to cradle her face.

"Monica, you could never be ugly. You're more desirable and beautiful now than ever before." Her large amber eyes searched his face for the truth and her lips parted as she found it. Cord slowly bent forward again and softly rolled his lips across hers before settling on them in a kiss of infinite tenderness. Gradually he deepened the kiss until his tongue leisurely explored her mouth.

How could she bear to live without him? What was life, dance, without him to love her this way? Cord's hand slid down to caress the sides of her neck, and then continued down her back as he pulled her against his body. He continued to kiss her sensuously, one hand moving into her hair, loving the feel. She was suddenly so overcome with a need for him that she started to tremble and feel dizzy with desire.

"Cord..." Monica whispered pleadingly against his mouth. He teased her before pulling back.

He knew he was not mistaken in reading her look. She wanted him to make love to her as much as he wanted to. He brushed her open mouth again with his and slowly shook his head.

"I'm afraid I'll hurt you...or the baby," he said huskily. Monica lowered her eyes, embarrassed that she'd been so obvious. Cord lifted her chin to see into her face. "Don't be ashamed of wanting me," he told her seriously. "I feel the same way."

Cord's arm braced against the bed pressed against her side. He felt something move. He looked up startled and found Monica grinning at him. Cord's heart turned over. Monica took his hand and laid it flat against her stomach. Nothing could have brought into focus more poignantly than this contact the reality of his baby. For a moment he couldn't speak.

"He's very active!" Monica mused, all her tears finally spent and gone.

"Does it hurt?" Cord asked curiously.

"Unh-unh." She smiled gently at him. "It feels... odd. He is awfully strong though. Last week he kicked a book out of my lap!"

"Really?" Cord murmured, amazed. Monica laughed merrily. Cord reached up and gently pushed her hair back from her face.

"It doesn't have to be a boy, you know. I'd love a girl just as well."

"It's a boy. Only a football player would kick this hard!" Monica said sagely.

"Or a dancer!" Cord smiled, his face suddenly years younger. Monica wondered abstractedly what he'd been like ten or fifteen years ago. Had he laughed often with Natalie? She sobered quickly.

"What's the matter?" Cord asked, noting her withdrawal suddenly.

"I—I'm sorry. I didn't mean to create such a scene!"

"You didn't. Besides, I understand crying is a symptom of the condition. Do you have any others?" he teased.

"Well, I do sometimes have a craving for strawberry ice cream!"

"Are you serious?" he asked suspiciously.

"You have to admit it's better than pickles!"

"Not by much," he said ruefully. Cord stood up and looked around the room. Seeing her nightgown over the back of a chair, he reached for it.

"Turn around," he ordered, and when she'd turned her back to him he bent and pulled the zipper of her dress down. It seemed the most natural thing in the world all at once as silently he helped her out of the caftan and into her silk gown, dropping it over her head and uplifted arms. Then he made her lean back comfortably against the pillows and drew the blanket up around her chin. Monica lay under her quilt looking at Cord appealingly.

"I'll be back in a minute." He left, and shortly Monica could hear movements in the kitchen and the sitting room. After about fifteen minutes Cord came back into her room with a mug in his hand. He walked over to the bed and handed it to her.

"It's not strawberry ice cream, but it's probably better for you." She looked to find the cup filled with hot cocoa. She relaxed and began to sip. Over the top of the mug she watched as Cord unbuttoned his shirt and removed it. He hesitated again, and then removed the rest of his clothes.

Monica watched the hard firm body, the sinew stretching and moving in his thighs, arms, and back as he undressed. He was really magnificent, she thought with some pride. She finished her cocoa and Cord took the empty cup from her hands, placing it on her night-stand. He turned out the light.

Monica was aware of his weight on the bed as he climbed in beside her. There was only one position possible. She turned on her side her back to him. Cord closed the distance until Monica felt his middle and chest right against her back. She felt his hand stroke her hair, could feel his warm breath stir the strands over the top of her head. The hand then gently crossed over her hip and once more settled on her stomach in the dark.

She was delirious. An unseen smile shaped her mouth and a comfortable drowsiness assailed her.

"Go to sleep," Cord whispered. Monica felt that if she died tomorrow, she couldn't have been happier or have known more joy than she did in this instant with Cord beside her.

Monica's arm swung out from her body, falling heavily, but the space next to her was unoccupied. Her eyes flew open and she struggled into a sitting position. Had she dreamed it all? Had Cord really been here holding her the entire night?

She wasn't sure.

She got up and dressed in one of her roomy caftans. She braided her hair, and warmly remembering Cord's reaction to it the night before, she made one braid to hang down her back.

It seemed very quiet in the house as she left her room, but then she heard a noise and peeked around the edge of the marble counter to find Cord sweeping ashes from the hearth onto a tin. Monica smiled to herself at the sight of him. He was dressed in corduroy slacks and a heavy black turtleneck sweater. As she watched, Cord turned his head, smiling as he looked directly at her.

"Good morning. Did you sleep well?" He stood up dusting his hands against each other and walked to stand right in front of her.

"Very well," she answered. "And you? Were you very uncomfortable?"

Cord took the time to look over her face and the changed hairstyle. "Yes," he said ruefully, a quiver of amusement in his voice. "But not for the reasons you imagine." Monica flushed.

"Would you like some breakfast?" she questioned.

"That would be nice."

Monica turned to the counter, Cord's eyes on her as she moved. She began to prepare the makings for French toast and to section a grapefruit. Cord reached over her shoulder to get mugs from a cabinet, giving a gentle tug on her long braid. He poured the coffee and to Monica's surprise set out plates and cutlery on the table. It made her feel normal, standing there fixing breakfast for her husband. The word *husband* now had a magical sound to it, and she rolled it around her tongue, and through her mind. Together they served each other breakfast and sat down to eat at the kitchen table.

"That's the best French toast I've ever eaten," he admitted.

"Thank you." She smiled. "Surely someone else must have come close!"

He shrugged. "Maybe the orphanage. But you have to try and imagine French toast for one hundred kids. Somewhere around the twentieth batch they begin to lose something." His eyes closed down.

"What are you thinking?" Monica gently asked, not wanting him to slip away from her.

"Just that all things considered, they did very well by

me. They gave me a home, clothed, and fed me, sent me to school."

"What made you decide to be an architect?"

"One of the trustees was an architect. He designed and built his own house. When I was fourteen, maybe fifteen, he recruited some of the boys from the home to help with the building. Well, we thought it was great! He had a huge pool, and his wife used to feed us all day long until we were rolling on the ground in agony!"

Monica laughed.

"I used to think it was really something to be smart enough to build a house. I wanted to be able to do that. Also—" He stopped, ran a hand through his hair making the curls spring. "There really wasn't enough room for all of us at the home. They'd never turn anyone away but it was tight. I used to sit and think up ways to create more room. I finally decided that I'd just have to become an architect and build a new orphanage."

Monica listened, fascinated and grateful that he could at last talk freely to her of those early years.

"And did you?"

"Yes," he said sadly. "It was everything I'd imagined. Lots of space and windows and rooms, but I can't help thinking, I'm sorry it ever had to be built."

Monica knew that once again a never-to-be-answered question of his own parentage was echoing inside of him. It contained a kind of pain he'd have with him all the days of his life. Unconsciously Monica reached over to touch his hand. He moved his hand to grab her fingers and idly play with them.

"I have to go to New York for a few days," he stated without preamble. When she would have drawn her hand away, he tightened his hold. "Would you like to come with me?"

The relief Monica felt at knowing he wouldn't leave

her alone made her glow. She relaxed and when he looked up at last, her dimples were showing as she smiled winningly at him.

"I would like very much to come with you. If you don't think I'll bother you."

"You always bother me, in one way or another!" he said bluntly, startling Monica. "But I'll take you with me anyway."

"When?"

"We'll leave day after tomorrow. Take a plane out of Lebanon. I don't think a five-hour car ride would do you any good." She was pleased with his concern.

"Monica, are you sure it will be okay? I mean, if you'll be more comfortable here..."

"I'll be fine! And if it will make you feel better, I'll go see Molly Kaplan as soon as we reach Manhattan and I promise not to get into any mischief!"

"How can I refuse an offer like that?" he said, raising his brows in amusement.

"Then it's okay?"

His grin was slow in going from his mouth to his gray eyes.

"Yes, sweetheart," he said in a husky voice. "You can come."

Monica stared. He had used the endearment as though he did so all the time.


"Oh, Monica! It's so good to hear your voice! I can't believe you're really here in New York!"

Monica laughed. "I can't either. I've been away so long, everything looks odd and out of place...and the snow! My goodness, Donna, was it always so dirty?"

"Of course! Isn't it everywhere?"

"Not in Vermont! It's white and crystalline for weeks, and then it snows all over again on top of it."

"It sounds a bit unreal."

"I suppose it is."

"And you are obviously spoiled by it all."

"Yes, I suppose that's true too. But I am glad to be back."

"For how long?"

"I think about a week."

"When do I get to see you?"

"Oh, anytime, I guess. Cord has business to attend and I have to see my doctor, but I'm dying to see you and hear how things have been. And I have to thank you for letting Cord and me stay in the apartment. I feel so guilty that you have to stay somewhere else!"

"Well, don't be, you goose. It is still half your apartment, you know."

"But still—"

"And besides, it was a perfect excuse to spend a week with Paul!"

"Paul? Who's Paul?"

"Oh, just someone I met last autumn. We, er, we've been seeing each other pretty regularly."

"Oh" was all Monica could think to say. Suddenly she felt there were months and months of things that had happened that she knew nothing about. Despite the emotional strain of being with Cord constantly in Vermont, she had also been isolated, cut off effectively from everything and everyone she was familiar with.

"Don't worry, hon. I'll tell you all about him when I see you. So, when will I see you?" Donna asked, coming back to the original question. Monica laughed.

"Can't you come here? It's home and it's comfortable."

"Ummm. I have a better idea. Why don't we meet for lunch? When do you see your doctor?"

"Tomorrow morning."

"Fine. Meet me at O'Neal's, say, one o'clock?"

"That sounds good. I should be finished by then."

"Good! You won't mind if I bring someone else, will you?"

Monica was curious. "Like whom?"

"Well, Mama for one. She's been asking about you for months!"

"Oh, yes! I'd love to see her. Anyone else?"

"Well..." Donna hesitated. "We'll see. You just make sure you're there!"

"Oh, I'll be there! Without my dancing shoes, but—"

Donna laughed. "Okay. See you tomorrow, then."

Monica hung up the phone and sighed. She hadn't realized how much she'd missed talking with Donna, and the companionship of similar interests.

She shifted positions, easing the ache in her back. It was five o'clock and she wasn't sure when Cord would get back. He'd been so busy the two days since they'd arrived, and somewhat preoccupied, so they'd spent no time together.

Also, Cord had become aloof again, and Monica didn't know why. She was sure that there'd been a turning point in their relationship the night of her emotional outburst. The next two days Cord had been very gentle and solicitous of her, but there had been no repeat of his staying with her through the night. He expressed concern for her and asked after her welfare, but he did so from a distance again, leaving her confused as to where she stood with him. She agonized over what he could be thinking, believing in her own mind that Natalie somehow lurked in the background.

Monica was filled with anxiety as to what to do next, or for that matter, what to expect from Cord. Under the circumstances, she could not bring herself to tell him of her love. She would have to try to work it all out. And she would have to do so very soon.

Dr. Molly Kaplan greeted her the next morning in

the same cheerful manner she'd used the first time they'd met.

Molly examined Monica, all the time keeping up an unending chatter that Monica found soothing. Molly wanted to know what plans she had for the baby. This last question caused Monica's heart to leap to her throat.

"What—what do you mean, what plans do I have?"

"Only whether or not you, Cord, and the baby will stay in Vermont or New York. For that matter, where you intend to have the baby."

Monica went limp with relief. "Oh...I—I don't know. Cord and I...we haven't really given it any thought." The mere mention of these considerations was enough to depress her.

"Well," Molly sighed, smiling at Monica, "physically, everything is fine. But I want you to promise me to relax and get more rest. You seem anxious. That's not good for you." A thought occurred to Molly. "You're not concerned about labor, are you?"

Monica hadn't thought of that either. "No," she answered blankly.

"Well, then, you just take it easy. Believe me, everything will be fine!"

Monica groaned. How she wanted to believe that.

Monica caught a cab to keep her luncheon date with Donna. Any unsure thoughts were temporarily dispelled when she saw her friend, and they threw themselves, somewhat awkwardly, into each other's arms.

"My goodness!" Donna exclaimed, holding Monica at arm's length and searching her up and down. A brilliant smile lit up her pretty brown face. "Monica, you look wonderful! Radiant, to put it frankly."

Monica blushed as Donna launched into a set of adjectives to describe her. Then there was greeting Mama Connors, and to Monica's surprise and pleasure, it became obvious that what she'd been invited to was no mere lunch, but a baby shower.

They were seated in a private corner of the restaurant, and since it was after the normal lunch hour, the restaurant was half deserted. There was much laughter and talk and gossip and fun. One by one the women presented Monica with gifts. They were all entirely practical things meant for use by the baby. Things quieted down and they had lunch, the talk becoming more general. But Donna, sitting next to Monica, took the opportunity to speak low to her.

"So, how are things going?"

"Okay, I guess."

Donna raised her brows. "You guess! Don't you know?"

Monica couldn't answer. She nervously pushed the leftover food around on her plate. "I'm fine, Donna."

"I don't mean just with you. How's everything?"

Monica laughed. "I suppose you want a blow-by-blow description in twenty-five words or less?"

Donna looked pointedly at her. "One would do fine, if it's the right one!"

Monica paused trying to think of something to say that would satisfy Donna.

"Okay," Donna sighed. "Let me make a number of observations." Monica looked apprehensively at her. "First of all, you look absolutely beautiful. Being pregnant agrees with you. Second of all, it must be Vermont, or Cord—or both!" Monica moved to interrupt, but Donna continued over her gestures. "Third, I think it's Cord. I think...No! I *believe* you're very much in love with him!"

The look on Monica's face made Donna catch her breath.

"I'm right, aren't I?" she probed quietly.

Donna could see also that while her friend was obviously in love with her husband it was equally apparent that all was not well.

"Monica, I think that's super! It changes everything!"

"No, it doesn't!" Monica responded miserably.

"But why not?"

"Because he doesn't know I'm in love with him."

"Why not?" Donna repeated, persisting.

"I haven't been able to tell him. The timing never seems quite right. You see, there was someone else in his past. He was very much in love with her. I think he still is."

Donna moaned, running a hand through her tight curls. Men were such imbeciles! She stole a glance at Monica and studied the changed person there. Despite the unrest she might be feeling Donna still had to admit that Monica looked vibrant. She knew that when you find something or someone capable of doing that for you, you hold on to it.

"What are you going to do?" Donna asked.

Monica shrugged. "What can I do? The baby is due in less than two months."

"But what if he has feelings for you too? I mean, you two were together in fairly secluded surroundings for months! Wasn't there any sign that he might feel the same toward you?"

In her mind Monica went over all the wonderful gentle moments, the comfortable moments, with Cord. The times of laughter or of quiet talk. But Monica also remembered the arguments and the conflict of wills, and they seemed to cancel out everything else. Still, what if Donna was right?

"Maybe," Monica answered with uncertainty.

"Well, it seems to me you should tell him how you feel. What have you got to lose?"

"Donna, I couldn't! He might laugh at me."

"Or he might tell you he loves you!"

"I can't. I just can't!"

"But you can't go on like this!"

"I know, but maybe something will happen in the next month." As she talked, Monica gently rested a hand on her stomach and stroked over the shape of it. Donna noticed and frowned.

"But enough of me and my problems. Tell me all about Paul! How did you meet him?"

Donna was instantly diverted. "Oh, what's to tell? He's this handsome man I met at an audition for an off-Broadway show. He's directing it. Very sophisticated, calm, and mature."

"And you're crazy about him!"

"I think he's pretty terrific!" Donna corrected.

"I'm so happy for you!"

"So's Mama," Donna whispered in a low voice. "You know what's on her mind!"

They laughed over that. Monica began to repackage all the baby boxes, smoothing gentle hands over the soft items. A smile curved her mouth as she recalled the things that Olivia Gavener had given her. This baby would certainly come into the world well prepared for!

Monica kissed all of her friends good-bye, thanking them for the surprise.

"I hope I'll see you before we head back to Vermont," Monica said.

"Oh you can count on it," Donna chuckled. She then leaned closer to Monica and whispered for her ears alone.

"Monica, I have just one other observation to make." She hesitated and Monica looked at her puzzled.

"What's that?"

"I don't think you'll ever be able to give up that baby," she said.

Monica went ashen. Not because Donna had been so

bold, but because Monica herself fully realized the truth in what she'd said.

Cord settled back into his chair and casually stretched out his long legs in front of him. Lawrence Gordon pulled on his mustache and raised his brows in surprise. A smile played around his mouth as he dared to speculate.

"I was surprised when you said you wanted to see me, Cord. Wouldn't a phone call have served?"

"I didn't want to talk to you from the apartment. I'd prefer if Monica didn't know about this visit."

"How is the, er, the young lady?" Gordon asked, not sure how to address her.

"Monica is fine," he said evenly.

Gordon was thinking fast. This certainly was a different Cord. "And I suppose everything is working out satisfactorily as planned?"

Cord turned around to face him.

"No, it's not!" He stood up rigidly but then his body relaxed and he raised a rueful brow at Lawrence.

"'The best-laid plans . . .'" he began and stopped.

"Is something wrong? Is it Miss, ah, Mrs., ah—"

"Monica?" Cord supplied, smiling grimly. He sat back down in his chair. "No, nothing is wrong. Everything is just different!"

Lawrence had a pretty good idea that Monica played a very large part in things being different. But it did not speak well that Cord was here and didn't want her to know of it. Of course, he had to admit, six months ago Cord wouldn't have cared one way or the other. Another smile grew on Gordon's face, this time larger.

"Is the difference good or bad?" he asked. Cord looked suspiciously at him.

"Let's just say for the time being it's unexpected," he answered caustically.

"Well, in any case, how can I be of help?"

Cord frowned and chewed the inside of his bottom lip. He leaned forward resting his elbows on his knees and clasped his hands together.

"Lawrence, I want you to find out where Monica has been sending money from her account. More specifically, I want to know who is receiving it."

After Gordon had recovered, he tugged on his mustache and cleared his throat.

"Well, I know that some went last month to California. That could have been family. I know she has a stepmother there. And some was sent to London."

"London?" Cord interrupted, very much surprised.

"Yes. A rather large amount, as a matter of fact."

"Lawrence, I want details. I want names and addresses if you can."

"I can do it but it may take time. Christmas is next week, you know.

"Well as soon as you can," Cord responded a bit impatiently.

"This could go beyond the bounds of the agreement, Cord. I'm sure Miss, er, Monica has very personal reasons for what she's doing."

"And I have very personal reasons for needing to know!" Cord said tightly. He strode in agitation around the office, his steps quieted by a layer of carpeting. He came to stand in front of Gordon's desk and looked intently at him. Gordon watched Cord's features relax as a look of anxiety replaced the sternness.

"Larry, I have to know," Cord whispered urgently.

Lawrence Gordon let go of his mustache and spread his hands in a helpless gesture of surrender.

"Okay, Cord. I'll get started on it right away."

Monica could not contain her joy when Cord said they were going out for the evening, that he had a surprise for her. But after the initial elation came panic. Cord smiled in exasperation. "Don't tell me, I know. You haven't a thing to wear!"

"Cord, don't laugh! It's true!" He laughed nonetheless. He came to her and put his hands on her shoulders.

"Take it easy! Why don't you wear that sexy black jersey thing you made."

"Sexy bla—" Monica flushed. He was teasing her.

"Yes. Now go and put it on. And hurry!"

When the cab pulled up in front of the New York State Theater where the State Ballet Corp was performing, Monica turned tearful eyes to Cord.

"Don't, sweetheart," he whispered as he carefully helped her from the car. "You're supposed to enjoy this."

"Oh, Cord, I will!"

In fact, they both did. It was a little bittersweet for Monica, who knew some of the dancers and had danced the female lead a few seasons back. She was in agony over her fear that she might never be able to perform herself again. Cord spent as much time watching Monica's reaction as he did the stage. For the very first time he saw clearly in her expression how important dance was to her, and was glad of his decision to bring her. If her dancing meant this much, she would not possibly want to give it up. Certainly not before she knew for sure whether she'd ever dance again. Recognizing the sense of this, however, only tightened the muscles in his chest.

During the intermission Monica turned to him, unconsciously grabbing his hand. "Thank you, Cord. It's a wonderful surprise!"

He smiled. "Are you always so easy to please?"

"Yes," she answered honestly, and it softened the look he gave her.

He winked at her, and she was able to relax and enjoy the last two performances. When it was over, Cord suggested they sit until most of the audience had cleared the aisles. So Monica sat, dreamily reliving the performance and humming the music while Cord sat pensively, watching her.

When they at last got up to leave, he took her arm to support her up the aisle.

"Would you like to go for a late supper, or are you tired?"

"If you don't mind, I am a bit tired. My baby is getting so heavy these days." When she realized what she'd said, she paled and drew in her breath.

"Home then," he answered evenly, "so I can put you both to bed."

When Monica could finally turn her head, she saw that his face was calm and open. His generous mouth was soft and curving. His eyes gentle and intent on her own. She smiled at him and dared to believe in that moment that maybe Donna was right.

## Chapter Ten

Monica hummed as she sat at the kitchen table in Vermont, colorful paper, ribbons and tapes a mess in front of her as she finished wrapping a small box. It contained a pair of earrings to be sent to Lee Ann.

"Oh, raspberries!" came the expletive from Livy, sitting next to Monica. "I cut my paper too short!"

"Well, there's plenty more." Monica shrugged.

Livy sighed. "I was never very good at this. Jim used to wrap all of our presents. He really enjoyed it. I did all the baking. It seemed a fair exchange! You can tell Cord I wrapped that one," she offered, and got up to refill their teacups.

Monica lifted her eyes and looked over her shoulders at the brilliantly decorated tree in the sitting room. She had not even considered that they'd have a tree until Cord brought one home two evenings ago. He'd stamped excess snow off his boots and moved to set the tree by the front window. Monica had been speechless watching him.

"Someone gave this to me," he said. "Didn't want to see it go to waste."

But his explanation only made her suspicious. They had then been forced to get a stand for it, and the many bright lights. And since they'd gone so far as this, she did some shopping to help complete the sense of celebration. She had not celebrated a Christmas since leaving home to be on her own. She quickly found herself caught up in the spirit of the holiday.

Livy returned with the tea and sat down. "You look very content these days. I take it the trip to New York was successful?"

Monica took the question literally and nodded.

"I'm glad to hear it. I think you two were due to get away together for a while. It seems to have done you both good."

Monica frowned. "What do you mean?"

"Oh, Cord seems more relaxed. And you are certainly blooming!"

Monica made no comment, but smiled.

"He has changed quite a bit this fall."

"Has he?" Monica asked, trying to keep the blatant curiosity out of her voice.

"Oh, yes! Cord used to be so formidable! You didn't dare cross him in anything!"

Monica had to laugh then. "And what makes you think he's changed? You should have heard him bellowing at me last night!"

"What on earth for?"

Monica recounted the incident to Livy of how Cord had come into the sitting room to find her standing on a kitchen chair leaning forward to place the silver star at the top of the tree. Cord had gone absolutely white finding her thus, but Monica didn't tell this to Livy, because she herself had not known how badly she'd succeeded in scaring him again.

Cord had walked up next to her and lifted her easily off the chair and put her on the floor.

"What the hell do you think you're doing?" he'd yelled, shaking her. "Are you totally demented or are you only this way when you're pregnant?"

"What is the matter with you?" she asked, pulling away from him. "You're hurting me!"

"That's nothing compared to what would have happened if you'd fallen off that chair!"

"I wouldn't have fallen. I knew exactly what I was doing!"

"I doubt that. You could have gotten dizzy."

"Well, I didn't! I was only trying to place the star and—"

"Give me that!" He pulled it from her hand. Cord turned to the tree and Monica sent a baleful look after him.

"You're not concerned about me anyway. It's only the—"

"Let's not start that again," Cord said tightly. "Where do you want this damned thing?"

Monica suddenly felt very intimidated by his anger and said nothing. Cord put the silver star on the protruding uppermost branch and turned to glare at her.

"Bend it forward a little," she said contritely in a small voice. Cord complied, looking again at her. "And a bit to the left." He pulled and tugged on the stubborn limb.

Monica crossed her arms and with her hands absently rubbed the tender spot where he'd grabbed her. When Cord turned back to her, he saw her hurt amber eyes swimming in tears.

"How is it now?" he asked in a more controlled voice.

"Fine," she barely whispered. Monica continued to stare at him but when her tears threatened to spill she turned her back to him. In a second she felt his hands tentatively touch her shoulders.

"Monica..." he began softly.

"You frightened me!" she said on a sob. Cord turned her around to face him, and taking one of her hands, he led her back to the tree. He pointed to an ornament on a level with her brow.

"You see this?"

She nodded sadly.

"Anything above that and I'll put it on the tree. Understand?"

She nodded again and made to move away. Cord held her fast.

"Monica, I'm sorry if I hurt you," he said softly. Monica rather reluctantly looked up at the helpless look on his face. It surprised her when he held her face in his hands and bent to kiss her gently, stroking her cheek with his fingertips. He shook his head and frowned.

"What am I to do with you?" he asked more to himself than to her. But the uttered question nonetheless puzzled her. Then he walked back to what he'd been doing before.

When Monica had finished her slightly edited version, Livy had laughed heartily.

"So, you got under his skin, did you?"

"I do seem to make him angry a lot!" Monica sighed.

"Oh, that just sounds like the actions of a man who very much cares what happens to you! And that's as it should be!"

"I don't see how his yelling at me proves he cares!"

"But that's Cord's way. If he was indifferent, you'd never get a rise out of him. Besides, I saw how he took care of you when you were sick and I know—"

Monica was instantly alert. "When I was sick? What happened?"

"Why, when you caught that chill. Cord took care of you. Wouldn't let anyone else near you. I finally had to put my foot down and tell him there were certain, er, things it was best I handle. But he didn't leave your side for nearly three days."

Livy watched Monica's face. "You mean to say he never told you?"

Monica shook her head dumbly.

Livy sighed. "Well, I guess it's typically Cord. He doesn't like a fuss being made."

Monica suddenly laughed. "You know something, Livy, you know Cord much better than I do."

Livy scoffed. "Don't be silly! I only know Cord loves you. And maybe I see some things that you don't because you're so close to him all the time. You have been very good for Cord, Monica. He needed someone like you in his life."

But Monica felt doubtful. He had said nothing to her to indicate he felt any different now than when they'd met, or that he'd feel any different when she had to leave. A wave of apprehension grabbed at her heart as she realized what a mess she was in. When she left, she wanted her baby with her. She had finally come to seeing it as hers. But there was the money, and the legal agreement. Could Cord really fight her on that? She felt sick with worry.

She had no idea what her effect was other than the ability to get him mad. She did know, however, that his effect on her had been swift, forceful, and complete. She loved him and there was nothing she could do about that.

The troubled pensive mood stayed with Monica, and she couldn't shake it. Her nerves were positively raw and she lived each day now in a state of constant anxiety. Never had her life seemed so complicated and filled with problems to be solved. She wanted her baby perhaps more than ever now because it was Cord's and would give her a part of him to keep forever.

Monica began to experience more frequently an ache in her lower back and sometimes had trouble breathing. Sleeping had also not gotten any easier, and she was more tired than usual. She knew Cord would accuse her of not taking care of herself. She didn't think she could bear censure from him right now when she so wanted his love and affection. She spent more and more time alone in her room pretending to rest. But a state of rest was the last thing she achieved.

They had dinner on Christmas Day with Livy, giving her a few presents in way of thanking her for all her help during the last months. Livy in turn surprised them by handing Monica a hand-knitted afghan for the baby, and to both of them a brocade-covered photo album to be used for baby pictures. Monica became very still, her face draining pale. Only Cord noticed and he evenly told Olivia he thought he should get Monica home because she looked tired. Livy agreed at once.

They were silent when they got into the car, but Monica suddenly couldn't stand the silence.

"It was very thoughtful of Livy to make something for the baby," Monica commented.

"Yes, it was," Cord responded dully.

"It will take you a very long time to fill the album."

For a long painful moment there was silence. "I suppose" was his terse response.

Monica said no more after that.

At the house Monica took off her cape and hung it on a peg. She was about to say good-night and go to her room when Cord spoke.

"Before you go to bed, I have something to give you." He disappeared into his room and returned with two boxes in his hands. She looked into his eyes, which were bright and intent on hers, and followed him into the sitting room, continuing past him to her room and also returning with several boxes. Monica sat in her rocker and Cord in his high-backed chair. She passed him his presents.

"You first," she said softly. Cord hesitated, looking frankly suspicious.

"You shouldn't have bothered," he said to Monica, frowning. "I'm not very good at this." Monica remembered Matthew's comment that Cord didn't like surprises.

"They won't bite, I promise." She smiled encouragingly.

He started with the largest package, peeling away cautiously the ribbons and paper. He found it was a footstool with a needlepoint design on the cushioned top. He ran his hands gently over it, turning it this way and that while Monica chewed nervously on her lower lip.

"Are you trying to tell me that I'm getting old and need to put my feet up to rest at night?"

Monica blanched.

"Oh, no!" she hastened to correct him, mortified that he'd take it that way. "Oh, Cord, you're not old at all! Why, to me you're very—" She stopped realizing what she was about to admit.

"What?" Cord prompted, very curious. "To you I'm very what?"

Monica twisted her hands in her lap. "I—I think your—your gray hair is very . . . attractive," she finished lamely.

"Maybe. But obviously my legs are showing signs of wear and tear!"

Monica finally saw that he was teasing her, and she relaxed and answered his smile.

"Did you do this?" Cord asked. Monica merely nodded.

"It's beautiful work. It must have taken you weeks."

"Not many." She shrugged. "Try it out. I wasn't sure if it would be the right height to be comfortable."

Cord placed the stool in front of his chair and sitting

back, put his feet up. "Perfect!" he announced, quirking a brow at her. "Thank you." Then Cord found himself opening a large brown leather portfolio. It was the perfect size to hold his contracts and preliminary layouts and sketches. Monica was delighted with the surprised look on his face. She'd made the right choice.

Now it was her turn. The first gift was a necklace of evenly matched pearls. "Oh, Cord! You shouldn't have. This must have been so expensive!"

"I wanted you to have pearls. I was sure they'd suit you with your reddish hair." He took the strand from her and stood behind her to clasp it around her throat.

"They're exquisite! Thank you seems not enough to say!"

"Don't say anything. I can see you're pleased," he said softly to her.

Her second gift was a black jersey dress with a gentle scoop in the bodice and with long full sleeves.

"This is beautiful! But I can't wear this. It's fitted, you see, and I'm much too large."

"It's not for now. It's for after you have the baby. The pearl necklace will look very nice with it," he said smoothly.

Monica herself was shaken by his reference to afterward.

"It was very thoughtful of you. Thank you." To hide her confusion, she pulled from the side of her rocker yet another gift and handed it to him. Cord did likewise. For Monica it was a record, but one she thought she already had, of ballet movements to piano music. She looked puzzled at Cord.

"That's to replace the one you told me I ruined, remember?"

She remembered. She didn't need to be reminded of how foolish she'd been that afternoon.

Cord unwrapped the last gift, and Monica sat now

wishing that she hadn't gotten it. She'd agonized over its purchase. It was a book on being a father, a light-hearted view with colorful cartoon drawings.

When Cord finished opening it, he looked at Monica long and steady and she grew warm under his gaze. Monica would never know what really happened next. Whether it was she or Cord who moved first, but suddenly she was standing, clasped in his arms, her high round stomach pressed into him. She could barely breathe he held her so close, but she didn't care.

"I love you! Cord, I love you so!"

"Monica, I don't want you to leave."

Their lines crossed each other in a jumble of words, neither certain they'd heard the other correctly. But it didn't matter as Cord held her face and bent to kiss her. Monica clung to him unashamed. Her parted lips answered his kiss without hesitation. She wanted him to feel the love vibrating from her.

Cord was very gentle, but his mouth moved sensuously and deeply over hers, exploring the sweetness, and seeming to draw her very soul from her. A shudder went through Cord and with an effort he pulled his mouth from Monica's. A small cry escaped her throat. He pressed his lips to her forehead while his other hand moved to rest on her stomach. He moved his hand gently over the surface and down the side. Monica closed her eyes and drew in a breath, finding the experience totally erotic and disturbing to her senses.

"I want you so much," he murmured in a strained voice, beginning to press scorching kisses down one side of her face until he could again ply one from her mouth. Monica was beginning to tremble. Suddenly Cord took her by the arms and forced her away from him. He swallowed hard, all the muscles in his arms and jaw tensing for control.

"I want you to go to bed now," he said in a quivering husky voice.

"I want to stay with you." She tried to come back into his arms.

"Not tonight, Monica," he said firmly, but gently. "We'll talk in the morning."

Monica looked with appeal to him. She put her hand to his cheek to stroke it and Cord turned his head until his lips kissed her palm.

"Cord, couldn't we—"

"God, Monica!" he breathed, and against his will once more had her in his arms. The kiss this time was persistent, probing and passionate. Monica pressed to get closer to him, feeling his rapid heartbeat on her breast. Cord cupped her face.

"Sweetheart, one of us has to keep a clear head."

She started to speak.

"No," he said in interruption. "Please, Monica." And she gave in knowing his control would outlast her own. He brushed his thumb across her lips and then replaced it with a last quick sweet kiss.

"We'll talk it all out tomorrow."

Cord turned her and walked her to her room. She whispered a reluctant good-night, but Cord's only response was to close the door firmly on her. Monica went to bed. To her surprise she fell into an instant peaceful sleep, the first in many weeks.

When Monica finally woke up she scrambled to get dressed, anxious to be with Cord and have him repeat his words of last night. Dear heaven, it was going to be okay. She wouldn't have to leave. She wouldn't have to give up the baby. She would be free to love Cord and they would be a real family. More than anything, Monica wanted them both to have that. Gone for the moment were all thoughts of New York, of the apartment with Donna, of Lee Ann, of even her own dance career. Her new relationship to Cord was the most important thing in her life.

Monica dressed in her green caftan, the one Cord liked, and her pearls. She swept out of her room and into the sitting room and then she continued on into the kitchen calling out his name. There was no answer. The coffee had been started, but there was no fire in the fireplace. One look at his bedroom door standing open and she knew Cord wouldn't be there either. Monica frowned in confusion wondering where he was.

Letting out a disappointed sigh she knelt awkwardly in front of the kitchen hearth and got a fire going. Struggling to her feet, she went to plug in the coffeemaker. It was then she found Cord's note resting on the top. There had been an early morning phone call from the site of the new library. Sometime during the night vandals had broken into the protective barriers of the construction site. Cord didn't go into details, but explained he had to go and see what damage had been done.

Monica didn't remember the phone ringing, but then she'd slept so deeply the whole night. The kitchen clock read eleven fifteen, and she wondered how long Cord had been gone. The answer came twenty minutes later when the phone rang. It was Cord calling her to tell her what was happening.

"Is everything all right?"

"No, but not as bad as I thought it would be."

"How much damage is there?"

"So far just stolen supplies and equipment. We haven't finished checking the construction to see if there's any damage to the work done."

He sounded very tired.

"I've been here since seven thirty. I'm not sure when I'll finish. There's the authorities to contact, and a list of damages to make for the insurance company."

"I don't suppose you've had anything to eat?" she asked, concerned.

"No," Cord admitted, "but I've had about a dozen cups of coffee."

"I'll have a meal waiting for you."

"That sounds nice," Cord said in a low voice. "Look, I've got to get back. I just wanted to—to—"

"Yes?" she prompted.

"Last night wasn't a dream, was it?"

Monica smiled and laughed softly. "If it was, we both had the same dream! I'll be here waiting."

"I'll see you when I can," Cord said now. "Bye." And the call ended.

She hoped it wouldn't take too long. There was still so much to be said, and she needed the security of his arms about her. Suddenly with Cord not there, last night did take on dreamlike qualities. She wished that he'd not been called away so suddenly.

Monica spent time cleaning the sitting room, burning the torn scraps of paper and placing the open boxes under the tree. She planned a cozy dinner for the two of them that she hoped would reestablish the atmosphere of the night before. She found a drop-leaf table in the pantry and set it up in the sitting room complete with candles.

Livy called once to see how she was feeling and to thank her and Cord for her presents. She promised to come and see Monica soon. The call inspired Monica, and dialing the overseas operator, she placed a call to London and Lee Ann. After a few detours and some waiting, the distant excited voice belonging to her sister was on the other end.

"Hello, Chicken! Merry Christmas!"

"Niki! It's so good to hear you!"

"It's good to hear you too! How's the holiday there?"

"There's a lot less celebrating here than home. But seeing Mother was the real surprise. You know something, Niki? I really missed her!"

"I was sure you would. After all, you've never been away from home for so long a time before."

"She told me you sent the money."

"Don't worry about it."

"But how? There's my room and board and tuition—"

"Don't forget you have a scholarship for part of it."

"Yes, but—"

"I robbed a bank!"

Lee Ann laughed merrily. "Oh, Niki."

"Look, don't you worry about the money. That's my department. When I'm old and gray and you're famous, you can support me! So, have you been showing Mother all of London?"

"Oh, yes. We've been having great fun."

"And what about Jean Paul?"

"Well, he was okay. But he decided he liked Mariette better. She's another dance student, who's French."

Monica was relieved, but also felt sympathy for her sister. "Well, maybe they have more in common. Besides, it's not the end of the world."

"I suppose," Lee Ann sighed. "Being in love is exhausting and takes so much time. And I don't understand why something that feels so good can hurt so much!"

"I don't know, darling," Monica said sighing, recognizing the validity of her sister's comment. "But if you ever find the answer, there are a lot of people who would like to know about it! How's dance?"

"A lot of work. I come back to the dorm each day thinking my feet are going to fall right off. But I love it."

Monica laughed. "I know the feeling!"

"I miss you, Monica. I can't wait to see you! You won't recognize me, you know. I'm all grown up now."

"I bet you are, and I miss you too, Lee. Very, very much."

"Can you come to London and visit?"

"No, I can't get to London right now, but soon, love. I promise."

Lee Ann sighed.

"Look, Lee, I've got to go now. There's a check on the way to you, and I'll write soon."

"Okay, Niki. Happy New Year. And I love you."

"Happy New Year, Lee. I love you too. Bye."

Monica sat deep in thought, a smile playing on her lips, and she absently rubbed at a small pain in her stomach. Monica missed Lee Ann, missed not being there to answer her questions and fuss over her. But there would soon be her own baby to take care of.

She looked up to find Cord leaning in the door frame of the kitchen. "Oh, Cord! You frightened me!" She smiled broadly getting up from her chair.

"How long have you been standing there?" A sudden twist of apprehension grabbed at Monica as she looked into the tight, cold countenance of Cord's face.

"Long enough" came his answer.

"Are—are you okay? Is it the library?"

"The library is fine," he said impatiently.

"Then what is it? You look so—"

"What? How do I look?"

Monica tried hard to understand what could have happened. "You seem angry. Something must have happened."

Cord moved almost threateningly toward her. "Something did. I just realized what a complete fool I've been."

Monica frowned. "Why?"

"For thinking that you were different. For believing that you could make a difference. But I was wrong.

You're just as I'd first thought you to be. Hard and calculating!''

Monica's mouth dropped open and she stared in total disbelief at him.

"What are you saying!"

"Come off it, Monica!" He laughed mirthlessly. "Cut out the act! I don't know how you managed to do it for so long, but you sure did fool me!"

Monica suddenly stiffened under his scathing tone and the look of hate on his face. Her voice trembled. "I don't understand you! And I don't know what you're talking about!"

"You seemed so soft and vulnerable. Yet, so strong and determined. I wanted so much to—" His face contorted into anger again. "I'm no longer even sure the baby is mine!" he exploded at her. "Whose is it, Monica? Is it your lover's? Who's Lee? Is that why you're doing this—so you two can have enough money to do what you want? And Matthew...I was beginning to wonder. Was he your lover too?"

Monica's eyes grew steadily wider and she went white with shock. God! What was he saying? Tears filled her eyes but she refused to let them spill. Cord never had a chance to say another word. Before she realized fully what she was doing her right hand landed with all the power she could gather across Cord's face. He grabbed her wrist and she jerked it violently away from his grasp.

"How dare you!" she gritted through her teeth, every part of her body trembling in rage and hurt. "Matthew Bell is not my lover. Nor has he ever been! And Lee—Lee Ann Hamlin—is my sister!"

Cord went still with disbelief. A dawning expression of horror slowly filled his face. He mouthed something Monica did not hear, but neither did she care. She grabbed at her stomach as a pain shot through her. She bit down hard on her lip. Cord made a move toward her and she quickly moved back out of his reach.

"You're right about the baby, however," she whispered in a voice tinged with pain. "It's not yours. It's mine! And I'll never, *never* give it up to you!"

Monica rushed past him to her room, sobs finally escaping her. She slammed the door so hard a plate tipped over on the kitchen hutch and smashed on the floor.

"Oh, no!" Cord groaned. He closed his eyes in pain, realizing his awful mistake. He'd never be able to tell her how sorry he was, or that it had been said out of fear and jealousy. She was not going to let him come close enough to explain now, and he couldn't blame her. Cord ran shaky hands through his hair and he could hear Monica crying in her room.

The door to Monica's room was locked, and he could still hear her crying. He softly called her name several times, but she didn't acknowledge him. It was not Cord's nature to plead and after the first try he gave up remorsefully. He could easily have forced the door open, but what would that have proved? Sooner or later she'd have to come out and, hopefully, he would repair the damage he'd done.

Why didn't he remember that she had a younger sister. Hadn't Lawrence Gordon told him so, last spring when she'd come for the interview? But then he hadn't cared anything at all about her, and he didn't remember for the same reason.

Cord sat in anguish in the sitting room, staring bleakly at the table set romantically for two. Every now and then a muted cry would come from Monica's room. The sound tore at Cord's insides. He would do anything to take back the hurt. But he couldn't do it through a locked door.

He listened to her crying well into the night, until finally it stopped and he knew she'd fallen asleep. But it would be almost dawn before he took himself off to his own bed to sleep fully clothed across the top.

Cord woke up at noon and only then because the phone was ringing. The call was from the town council, asking about the incident of the previous day. Cord forced himself to talk calmly, at the moment not in the least interested in that problem. They wanted him to come into town and make a report so that an immediate claim could be filed with the insurance company. Cord ran a hand through his tousled curls and looked down at his rumpled condition. He'd have to shower and change quickly. He walked to Monica's door but there was no sound on the other side. He raised his hand to knock but didn't. He still didn't know what he could say to her yet. He walked to his room, stripping off his shirt as he moved. Twenty minutes later he was struggling into his heavy coat, but Cord felt suddenly confident that he and Monica would straighten this mess out when he got back. It was beginning to snow heavily outside, and he knew she'd be forced to stay inside. As an opening gesture, Cord took a sheet of note paper and scrawled "I'm sorry" on it hastily and left it on the counter.

Monica had not heard the phone ring again. But she had heard Cord leaving. The sound of the door closing behind him put a finality to her feelings of despair and hurt, and she collapsed in fresh tears after she thought there were no tears left. She felt limp, weak and sore all over. She hoped she had done no harm to her baby. Not Cord's anymore, but hers. Monica knew suddenly she could no longer stay. He'd accused her of terrible things last night, and he couldn't care for her if he believed them. How could he think that this baby might not be his?

Even Monica's heart hurt. The pain that seared through it was continuous. She loved Cord as she'd never believed it possible to love anyone. And she knew with every fiber of her being that it would always be so. But he did not trust or love her. That left her with only her dreams, and with the baby.

She listlessly found one of her suitcases and began to pile in her clothing. Her agitation was reflected in the thoughtless shamble of items she threw into the open case. But she was very meticulous in packing the baby things given her by Olivia and her friends in New York. Everything else, including her wool cape and the pearls Cord gave her, she left behind.

A frightening rigidity settled on Monica, as methodically all of her actions fell into place with a purpose—to get her as far away from Vermont as possible. She made one final phone call and began to load her bag into the station wagon, not stopping to consider she'd never driven it. But it didn't matter. She never saw Cord's note on the counter. She only knew the pressing need to get away.

Although it was twice as large, the station wagon was not all that much different than the Rover. She managed well enough, despite skidding several times in the fast freezing snow on the ground.

Twice cars honked at her as she carelessly wandered over the center line, but she continued on in grim determination.

The wind began to whip the icy snow against her windshield and she couldn't see clearly. Only then did she begin to regret her impulsive actions, suddenly afraid that she couldn't reach her destination. More and more she found she had to struggle to keep the car on her side of the road. Without warning, the tires slid over a slick portion of the road and the car went into a complete spin. In fright Monica began to turn the wheel every which way fighting for control. But it did no good, and she watched helplessly as the car slid off the shoulder into a snow drift on a lopsided angle.

Monica sat for a breathless moment before struggling to get her door opened to climb out. It was bitter cold and the wind went right through her. She huddled against the side of the wagon wondering what she was going to do now when a pickup came ambling along. It stopped, and a middle-aged farmer poked his head out the window and shouted at her.

"You in trouble, lady?"

"Y-yes! My car went off the road."

"Well, you'll have to leave it. It's stormin' too bad to try and pull her out now. Where you headed?"

"I'm trying to get to Lebanon."

"I'm headed a little west of there, but I can take you."

"Oh, yes! Please!"

The man helped Monica into the passenger side, saying a bit sternly when he saw her condition that she was crazy to be out here anyway. She didn't argue the point, just said there was an emergency and she had to get to Lebanon. He got her bag and soon they were back on the road. She was exhausted now, physically, emotionally, and mentally, but she had to plan what she would do once out of Lebanon.

It took almost two hours to cross the Vermont border into New Hampshire, and soon the pickup was pulling up into a parking lot. The driver got out and went into the small modern structure, returning less than ten minutes later.

"Well," he shouted over the rising wind to Monica as he helped her from his truck, "it looks like you just made it! They'll have to close down after this one leaves."

"I can't thank you enough for all your help," Monica said.

"Not to worry," he responded quaintly, walking Monica with her bag into the airport for her flight to New York.

## Chapter Eleven

Cord did not reach the house until almost seven in the evening. The work had taken longer than anyone had anticipated. The muscles and nerves in his arms and back were tight with the tension of the last hour's drive from Randolph center.

There were no lights on in the house when he arrived, and it felt cold, as though no one was there. A sudden fear grabbed at Cord's chest and he ran to Monica's room to find it empty. Then he noticed her closet door open, and knew what he'd find if he looked inside.

Cord closed his eyes in anguish and he slumped against the door. A number of different things happened to him. First was the feeling of having been left again, even though he recognized at once that he was responsible for Monica's flight. And second was the overwhelming feeling of tremendous loss, leaving a large open void.

Cord sprung into action at once. He called Olivia Gavener. There was no answer, and after letting it ring a dozen times, he slammed the phone down in frustration. He lit a fire to warm the room. His note was still on the counter and he had no way of knowing if Monica had seen it or not. Cord went to her room again and stood in the center looking around. He saw one suitcase gone from the closet, and some but not all of her clothes. He noticed her cape still on a peg behind the door and wondered suddenly in real concern what she had on to keep warm. As he was leaving the room he saw the pearl necklace carefully laid on the dresser top. Cord walked quickly to the phone and once again tried calling Livy. She finally answered the phone.

"Olivia, this is Cord. I—I wondered if Monica was there with you."

"Why, no, Cord. Don't tell me she's out in this horrible weather?"

"I've been gone all day in town. When I got back the wagon was gone."

"Didn't she leave a note? Cord, did something happen between you two?"

"I can't talk about it now. If you hear from her, will you—"

"Of course I will. But, Cord—"

"Thanks, Livy." He hung up and began to pace the room. If she wasn't with Livy he had no idea where she could have got to in the storm. A fear such as he had never known before shook him. What if she'd had an accident in the wagon? What if she was lost somewhere in the snow? Oh, God, what if she was hurt?

Cord was beside himself. He didn't know if he could take it if anything happened to her. She was out there in a storm, even at the risk of harming herself, just to get away from him.

The phone rang at almost nine thirty and Cord ran for it. But it was the highway authorities asking what he wanted to do about his car. They explained that they'd found his station wagon off the road in a snow drift, about three miles north of Woodstock.

"Look," Cord began, trying to speak calmly. "My wife was driving the wagon. She's more than seven months pregnant and I'm worried that something might have happened to her."

The man on the other end let out a low whistle. "Any chance she was trying to get to a hospital, or to a friend?"

"Not in that direction," Cord answered, "Look, are you sure you checked around the car?"

"That's the first thing we did. Believe me, sir, if she was anywhere within one hundred yards in any direction we would have seen her. But don't worry. Someone probably gave her a lift. No one would leave a pregnant woman out in this weather! She's probably trying to call you right now!"

But his assurance did nothing for Cord. Someone might very well have given her a lift. The question was, to where? Cord thanked the man and said he'd make arrangements to have the car towed when the snow let up. Then he sat down to think.

Woodstock was southeast of Randolph, near the New Hampshire border. If she was driving east, she was very likely headed for the airport. Cord picked up the phone and tried dialing the airport in Lebanon. He got a recording stating that his call could not be completed at this time. Damn! There must be lines down somewhere. He knew the futility of trying again this late at night. They wouldn't be able to restore the lines until early the next morning, and the thought of wasting all that time ate away at him.

He had never felt so completely helpless in his life. When Natalie had left him, there had never been any question of going after her and bringing her back.

But Cord knew now with a dismal certainty that there was no other man Monica would run to. He had thought for a while that maybe it could be Matt, and he winced when he remembered accusing her of that.

He had to find her and make things right. He had to

bring her back home. A second chance had been waiting, offered him all these months, and he'd ignored it in an effort to keep himself immune and therefore safe. But what good was being immune and safe if you were alone and empty inside?

He fell into an exhausted sleep around midnight, sitting upright in his chair. But he slept badly, still hoping the phone would ring and it would be her. But all through that long night the only sound was the wind whistling eerily outside.

The very first thing he did the next morning was to call Lebanon Airport. Their records did not show a passenger named Monica Temple. Did they show a listing for Hamlin? Yes, there was an M. Hamlin on the last flight out before the airport was shut down. The clerk told him it would be another twelve hours before the airport was functioning normally again.

Next Cord called the Central Park West apartment in New York. A very surprised Donna answered the phone. She had not seen or heard from Monica since the trip down almost two weeks ago. She also had no idea where else Cord could check in New York. Donna was very concerned and Cord assured her there was nothing to worry about. He hoped secretly he was right.

There was just one other number Cord had to call. It would be seven in the morning in San Francisco, but if she were there, it was the best time to catch her off guard. There was no answer. He tried calling every hour until almost two in the morning, each time with the same result.

Cord had not eaten or slept completely for two days, and he wondered if he ever would again. He sat listlessly in his chair in the sitting room, staring at Monica's rocker, almost seeing her there with that green flowing dress she wore, and the firelight making the red color dance in her hair. Her dimples suddenly appearing when she laughed, her cheeks flushing when she was angry. He groaned in anguish knowing that he had indeed been a fool, and not being able to stand the thought that maybe he'd lost her.

Cord had no cause to celebrate the New Year, sitting silently in the big house as he had for nearly a week, hoping to hear from Monica or anyone who knew where she was. He kept Livy at bay, but she openly accused Cord of having done something to upset Monica. He continued to call California and continued to get no answer.

On January sixth Matthew showed up, struggling past a silent Cord with a large awkward package in his arms. Cord was actually glad to see him, his presence eliminating yet another question. Matt shook off the snow and cold from his body and turned his smiling face to his friend. He was shocked at what he saw.

Matthew raised a questioning brow and grinned, but his eyes were filled with concern as he regarded Cord.

"I don't mind telling you, old buddy, you look like hell! But I don't want to see you anyway. Where's your gorgeous wife?"

Cord just stared at him. Matt grew cold inside, remembering now that bewildered look only one other time in Cord's life.

"Where is she, Cord?" he asked in a low voice.

"I don't know."

"What do you mean, you don't know?" Matt asked in disbelief.

"I mean Monica's gone, and I don't know where to. I—I've been calling all over, but—"

"What happened? What did you do to her?"

Cord's eyes narrowed as he looked at Matt. He had been right. He'd known Matt too long not to be able to recognize that look on his face. It was real concern...and love.

"What did you do to her?" Matt almost shouted again. "So help me, Cord, if you've hurt her, I'll—"

"You'll what?"

Matt stared stonily at him.

"I think you forget Monica is my wife!"

"Only because a piece of paper says so. You've never treated her like a wife. I don't understand you! She's probably the best thing that ever happened to you in your life. And you—you ignore her, take her for granted. Why can't you forget Natalie?"

"To hell with Natalie!" Cord ground out, swinging out an arm violently in a gesture of dismissal. "I don't give a damn about Natalie. She no longer exists!"

"You don't give a damn about Monica either! I should have made her come away with me when I left. I could see then it wasn't working with you two."

The next thing Matt knew was an explosion against his jaw rattling all his teeth and sending a shock of pain to his head. He wheeled back against the mantel under the force of Cord's fist, stunned and breathing hard. He reached out a hand to steady himself. Matt wiped the back of his hand across his mouth and smeared the blood trickling there. His fists clenched and unclenched as he regarded Cord.

Slowly Matt let his tense body relax. A deep sigh escaped him. "I probably deserved that," Matt breathed, wiping the blood off his hands onto his jeans. "But that doesn't change a thing! I'll tell you this: Monica would never want me. And she'd never do anything to hurt you."

"You asked her to go with you?" Cord exploded, moving toward Matt, his fist already poised. Matt never moved. He was very precise and very quiet in his response.

"I would have taken care of her."

Cord stared at him as his hand came down. "And I suppose I didn't?"

"I think you were afraid to. And I believe that Natalie still stood between you."

"Dammit! Natalie is like a recurring nightmare!"

"But you allowed it. Natalie is a dead dream, Cord. Monica is real...and she's here. At least, she used to be!" Matt ended roughly.

Cord seemed not to have heard. "She's my wife, Matt."

"You say that as if you're only just finding out!" Matt said impatiently. "Monica loves you, Cord. Heaven only knows why! But she said you had an arrangement. What did she mean?"

Cord stiffened. "I know you mean well, Matt, but let it go. Don't ever ask me again about my marriage to Monica."

Matt saw that he meant it. He shrugged and backed away. He walked over to a chair and sat down heavily.

"What happened?" Matt asked quietly.

Cord tensed muscles all over his body. "I said some things...I accused her of—" He stopped.

"Good God!" Matt groaned, perfectly capable of filling in the details. "You treated her like she was all the women you've ever met. Couldn't you see from living here with her that she was different?"

Cord rubbed at his temples. "I only know that I want her...and it may be too late."

Matt shook his head. "Would it have been so hard to tell her that? Monica is so much in love with you."

Matt got up and paced heavily on the floor. He started shouting questions at Cord, organized and more clear headed as he listened to what Cord had done so far in his efforts to locate Monica. Together they planned another line of action.

It was Matt who fixed something for them to eat.

"Taking care of you in a crisis is getting to be my life's work!" he quipped to Cord.

"I appreciate your help, Matt."

Matt brushed that roughly aside. "Save your breath. Just find Monica, tell her you're sorry. Better still, tell her you love her."

Cord looked very long and steady at Matthew as he realized how true a friend he'd been.

"Do you love her so much yourself?"

Matt's head jerked up sharply and his eyes looked hollow with feeling for the merest second. But quickly a lopsided grin took over and he forced a sheepish laugh.

"Hell, Cord, Monica is a special lady. Who wouldn't love her?"

Cord stared a moment longer, still uncertain, and Matt sat in brooding silence.

The weariness had finally caught up to Cord. After eating, Matt insisted he go get some rest. Cord tripped over the package Matt came with, still sitting in the middle of the floor.

"What is that?" he asked, tapping it with his toe.

"Go on and open it," Matt advised. "It's your Christmas present."

Cord pulled away the paper and sat looking at the wooden structure in front of him. He looked up bleakly at Matt.

"I picked it up in West Virginia. It's all handmade," Matt said softly.

It was a cradle.

# Chapter Twelve

Two phone calls the next morning finally gave Cord all the information he needed to find Monica. The first was a call from Lawrence Gordon. He'd found out that the money going to London was for one Lee Ann Hamlin, Monica's younger stepsister, enrolled as a talented prospect at the highly regarded Royal Academy of Ballet in London. Lawrence broke down all the information for Cord as to amounts and dates. None of the money had been personally used by Monica. He thanked Lawrence Gordon for getting the information. But if Cord had known all of this weeks ago, Monica would be with him now.

As Cord would have said good-bye, Gordon had one other bit of puzzling information for him. He'd received in the mail Monica's account book, canceled, along with a check for the complete balance of the money in the account to date.

"This greatly changes the arrangement," Gordon said anxiously.

"Don't worry about it," Cord said more confidently than he felt. "I'll get back to you later about the contract."

Cord and Matt were just about to leave the house when the second call came in from Molly Kaplan. She wasted no time getting to the point.

"Look, I don't know what's been going on up there, and right now I don't care. But I have Monica here with me, and I believe she's going to go into labor anytime now."

"Monica... with you?" Cord asked.

"Yes. She's been here for more than a week. I have to admit she arrived in a pretty bad state. She's been somewhat hysterical."

"No..."

"I haven't been able to get much out of her except she made me promise not to tell you where she was."

"How could you keep a promise like that, Molly? I've been out of my mind with worry! I didn't know where she'd disappeared to!"

"Cord, my first concern is for Monica and the baby. It was very obvious that she was upset over something to do with you. I'm her doctor and I felt at the time I had to comply. I couldn't risk her getting any more worked up."

"How—how is she, Molly?"

Molly let out a deep sigh. "I don't know. She's still emotionally wound up and that could present problems during labor. She's not relaxing enough to let her body do what it's supposed to. I don't want to do a C-section, but I may have to if she doesn't calm down!"

"Oh, God."

"Now, take it easy... we're not in trouble yet. But I think you'd better get down here as fast as you can. She's at Lenox Hill Hospital. I'll talk to you then."

At five thirty Cord walked briskly through the doors of the hospital and over to the information desk. He was given the direction to maternity and Molly Kaplan's office. Cord turned away and began moving down the corridor in search of Molly and his wife.

"Cord!" he heard behind him. He whirled to find Molly walking quickly toward him.

"Monica?"

"There's been no change."

"Where is she? How is she?"

"I have her prepped and she's in a private room. She's in first-stage labor but she's still having a bad time. She's holding herself in. That's the only way I can describe it!"

Fear finally made him explode. "For God's sake, Molly! Is she going to be okay?"

Molly sighed. "Yes, but labor could be long...and difficult. I told her I'd called you, and..."

"And?"

"She got very agitated. Not angry, but upset. I told her you were very concerned and had been looking for her."

"What did she say?" Cord asked, somewhat afraid to know the answer.

"She said something about only having the baby, and then she cried."

Cord felt defeated. But he straightened up and spoke with determination. "I want to see her."

"Of course."

Cord followed Molly a bit down the hallway.

"See if you can calm her down, Cord. We need her cooperation. And be gentle with her." The door swung closed behind him. The room was small, just enough room for the bed and one chair. It was very well lit and Monica was immediately visible.

She lay on the bed in a partial sitting position, her eyes closed and she appeared to be sleeping. But her face was damp with perspiration. Her breathing was ragged, and he watched as her stomach rose and fell with the effort. Her face suddenly contorted into pain and she grabbed the metal side of the bed. Cord went quickly to her side, placing a hand over hers as a moan escaped her. Cord softly called her name.

Monica turned her head slowly to him and opened her eyes. The were slightly glazed with pain and unfocused.

"The...baby doesn't want to be born," she whispered hoarsely.

"Maybe it needs help." Cord tensed his jaw.

"You can't take him if I don't have him," she said tersely. She slid her hand out from under his.

"Monica...Monica, I'm sorry. I'll never be able to tell you how much—"

"It doesn't matter. You can't have the baby! It's my baby." She turned her head away again, crying silently. "It's all I have."

"I want you, Monica. I need you. I—I don't know what I'd do if anything happens to you!"

"You'll just go back to being Cord." She suddenly arched her back, grimacing, then she slumped back, panting and breathing hard.

"You'll never need anyone," she finished in a moan.

Cord leaned over her. "That's not true. I need you more than anything else in my life. I want you and the baby. Please try to forgive me. I've been such a fool."

There was real anguish in his voice and Monica turned her head and tried to focus on him. "You never say please." Her eyes closed tight again in pain.

Cord brushed a shaky hand over her wet cheek. She seemed to be in such pain. He tried to distract her. "Listen. Matt says hello. He expects to see our son anytime now. And he's expecting to be a godparent."

"Matt? Matthew loves me!" she said vaguely.

Cord paled. "Yes, Matt does love you."

Monica laughed weakly. "But I love you. Isn't that funny? I can only love you and it doesn't matter!"

"Monica, listen to me! I do love you. I should have told you when I realized."

She looked at him not quite believing him, but desperately wanting to. "W-when? Why didn't you tell me?"

"When? The week you got sick at Olivia's. It scared me so badly to see you ill. I didn't know what to do . . . and I thought I'd lose you. But I don't think I was willing to admit even then how much you'd come to mean to me."

"Instead, you accuse me . . . Matt, of all those awful things!"

"I was beside myself with jealousy. I thought you preferred him to me. Don't you see, if I didn't love you it never would have mattered what you did or said."

Monica blinked up at him.

Cord looked at her with tenderness. "You're my wife. I love you, Monica. I want another chance to prove it to you. You'll never know how crazy I was without you!"

Monica breathed a shaky laugh. "You'll never know how crazy I was with you! Oh, Cord, I don't know if we can do it. There was so much said."

"Trust me! Believe me, I'll make it all right!"

She looked again at him. She loved him so much she wanted to take all the worry lines from his face. She reached up a hand to touch his cheek, and once again she twisted in pain, this time letting out a cry. Cord grabbed her hand and her fingers closed tightly, convulsively, over his.

"Monica!"

"I—I think you'd better get Molly," she whispered in a barely audible voice.


At 12:17 A.M. on January 9 Cortland Temple became forty-one years old, and the father of a little girl. She demanded instant gratification upon her entry into the world, and after having been washed and wrapped, was placed in Monica's arms for a well-deserved meal.

She soon fell asleep and was taken to the nursery.

Cord came cautiously into the room to find a glowing but exhausted Monica. She looked beautiful. He'd forever remember this sight of his wife minutes after their baby had been born. Cord took Monica's hand and bent to kiss her gently.

"Are you okay?"

"Ummmm. Just a little tired. Have you seen your daughter?"

"Not yet. I wanted to see her mother first. Monica, was it very difficult?" he asked with concern.

"It was long." Her voice was fading, but a smile curved her mouth. "But Livy was right. She was worth every minute. And she's beautiful. She looks just like you."

"Then she can't be beautiful! But maybe she'll grow out of it."

Monica smiled wanly, her eyes struggling to stay open. "I'm very happy with her. She's perfect. But I wanted so much...to give you a boy. I'm sorry." Her eyes closed.

"I'm not," Cord whispered, bending to kiss her again. "Next time it will be a son."

A very faint smile lifted Monica's mouth. But she was already asleep.

She was five weeks premature and weighed two pounds less than she should, but she was healthy, beautiful, and perfect, as Monica had said. They named her Erin Bridget Temple, and the nurses took to calling her Brig.

Cord called Donna to tell her the news and Donna insisted he come to the apartment to rest. But he was up again at eight in the morning and on his way back to the hospital. He'd shaved and looked much better for a few hours' sleep. But Monica complained that he'd been taking poor care of himself.

"That's because you weren't around," he teased affectionately. "I admit you do a better job."

Monica searched his face. The mouth was generous and curved, the eyes softly gray and watchful. All the hardness, the protective shield, was gone for the moment. She took her hand and slowly wove it into the curls over his ear. "Do you suppose Erin will develop gray hair early?" she asked in an abstract voice.

"I hope not. Although I have it on the best authority that it's very attractive!"

Monica's mouth dropped open.

"Why don't we just wait and see?" Cord suggested, smiling at her.

"What are you suggesting, Cord?" she asked in a whisper.

"That you let me take you and our daughter, home. That we love each other and try to forget the past. I love you so much, Monica. I love you and I don't want to lose you again."

"And—and Natalie?" she asked now. Cord stiffened, but his expression never changed. "Matt told me all about her," Monica said.

"I loved Natalie very much. At least I thought I did at the time. It took me years to realize I was in love with a dream. It was...this crazy fantasy I had, that with her I could make my own family, begin my own history. But that's all it was...just a fantasy. It's been many, many years since I've loved her, Monica. And it was different from what I feel for you. Natalie...was an obsession, a madness I let get out of hand."

"And with me?" Monica asked softly.

Cord smiled gently and ran the back of his long fingers along her chin and jaw. "With you I feel protective. I want to be gentle with you. I want to hold you tenderly in love, not possess you.

"When you were pregnant with Brig, I was so afraid

something would happen to you. Not just for the sake of the baby, but for just you!''

Realizing that Cord had come a long way to be able to make such a declaration, made Monica smile at him. She reached up to put her arms around her husband's neck, bringing his face close to her own.

"You make me sound...precious."

"To me you are."

"Don't treat me as though I were fragile. I won't break, you know." And she boldly pressed her parted mouth to his, giving him free reign to take possession, which he did. It felt very good and secure holding her this way. And Cord knew, kissing her gently but thoroughly, that this was not a dream, that the love he felt for her was more real and lasting than any he'd ever known.

It was almost six in the morning when Erin Bridget Temple started to cry, wanting to be fed. Monica groaned and pushed her body closer to the warmth of Cord's as he lay behind her, arms holding her against him. But it was Cord who disengaged himself gently to quickly get out of the king-size bed to get his daughter from the room that used to be Monica's.

Monica was already sitting up preparing to feed the wiggling fretful baby that Cord laid in her arms. Brig's tiny angel's mouth groped until she located Monica's nipple.

Her minute fingers spread open and pressed to Monica's breast. Her lids fluttered open, and through eyes the color of her mother's she regarded the person feeding her. The sensation of Brig pulling and kneading made Monica feel a combination of warm giving and sensuous needing. When she'd first arrived back in Randolph with Cord and Erin, she was still too much the bemused new mother to do much else than wonder at her responsibility. But soon Monica's eyes would seek out Cord's as she fed the baby, a secret electrifying message passing between them. When Monica was fully able to, it would be Cord who replaced his daughter, kissing and stroking at Monica's breast until she was a limp helpless mass of desire waiting for him to assuage her need.

Monica smiled softly now at Erin, taking a finger to gently smooth an errant unruly curl. Cord watched them both with something akin to adoration on his face.

Brig had been a pure and simple miracle. She was to be the start of his continuity in the world. Wanting a child of his own had been an abstract thought laced with emotions he'd never settled from childhood. But having her here was so real and tangible, that Cord knew it would be years before he fully realized the impact of her existence on his life. For the first time Cord felt real ties and responsibilities, he belonged somewhere. He had a wife and daughter and someday, perhaps, a son. Together they were a real family.

He put a long finger against Brig's hand and her fingers closed around it with a cool sweet touch.

Erin finished her nursing and Monica moved to return her to her cradle. Cord usually did this. He was insistent on lifting the infant when she cried, and laying her down when she slept. For the first month they were home, half a dozen times a night he'd go to make sure she was covered and safe. He insisted on holding her across his shoulder, gently patting the air out of her system after she'd nursed.

Monica remembered once recently softly coming into the baby's room to find Cord's long masculine form seated in the rocker holding Brig as she squirmed and cooed happily for her father. Cord held her, head in the crook of his elbow while his other hand examined her feet and each toe, the small hands, and smaller fingers, the shell of her ear, and the incredible cover of curls on her head. He looked her over intently with the most profound expression of wonder that Monica had ever seen. Cord slowly bent his head and pressed a reverent kiss to Erin's soft cheek. Monica slipped away, leaving him to his moment of private discovery.

As Monica walked long legged and naked to the room to put Brig to sleep, she left Cord admiring her slender back and dealing with the desire rising fiercely in him. He held up the blanket for her to crawl under once more and quickly moved to settle full length on top of her. Cord lowered his head and mouth and began to nuzzle and stroke his tongue over the sensitive skin of her breast. Monica responded beneath him, putting her arms around his shoulders. Cord lifted his head smiling at her.

"I swear I can hear you purring!" he said in a hoarse voice.

"Ummm, it's contentment."

Cord kissed his way up a breast to the erect peak. "Anything else?"

"Love."

"And?" he persisted.

"Need." Monica enjoyed the feel of his chest hair on her softer skin. Cord played with her lips, the probing point of his tongue leaving her mouth moist and open before capturing it to press deeply inside. The kiss started a low flame deep within Monica as she pressed closer to Cord, eliciting a moan from him. The flame leaped higher as she yielded in ecstasy completely to him, to the touch of his fingers along her spine and under her thigh. She raised her hips to his hard middle. Cord pressed gently upon her, eliminating spaces and distances, playing upon her, coaxing an easy response until her rhythm matched his. Straining together, both finally collapsed in exquisite release.

Monica ran her hands through his hair and held his head fast to her chest. "I love you, Cortland Temple," she whispered.

"And I love you, sweetheart." Cord rolled to the side, keeping his hold on Monica, their legs and arms tangled. "I'm looking forward to having you to myself again after next week."

"Tired of your daughter already?" she teased, stroking his bristled cheek.

Cord growled, squeezing her. "You know that isn't true! I'm just wishing everyone else would go away. I want you all to myself," he said huskily, lips against her forehead.

"We have a lifetime for that. We should be able to survive a few days of visitors.

He sighed good-naturedly. "I'm not too sure! While I'm grateful to Olivia for wanting to baby-sit for a few days, I don't really want Brig away from us."

"She'll be fine, Cord, and it will be good for Livy. And it *will* give us a few days before Donna and Lee Ann arrive. Brig will be back before you've missed her."

Cord grunted. Monica laughed.

"I don't know if I can take a house filled with women. Where was all of this when I was young and available?"

"Too late now! You're spoken for!"

"Thank God!" Cord breathed into her mouth before kissing her hard and long.

He got serious while Monica played with the hair on his chest.

"There's so much about you I don't know yet. I know that you're beautiful and loving and sexy"—he accentuated this with brief little kisses to her face—

"but I want to know about your family, about you and Lee Ann. When I think what you were willing to do for her—"

Monica put a hand over his mouth. "I'm a very good dancer, Cord. But Lee is brilliant. She's always showed great potential. She deserved a chance to realize it. I didn't know what else to do at the time and everything was happening so fast. I thought it would be so easy!"

"But the thought of you doing something like this for anyone else makes me—"

"But I didn't! I was lucky. It was you!"

Cord shuddered against her. "Sweetheart."

"I didn't know. I didn't realize the enormity of bringing a new life into the world. I didn't realize a baby, my own baby, could mean so much...that you would mean so much."

Cord kissed her gently, stilling momentarily her flow of words.

"When I knew that I loved you, everything changed," Monica told him with great tenderness.

They were silent for a while and Cord ran his large hand erotically down a thigh and up again, caressing the smooth skin along the inside. She quivered, putting her arms around his neck.

"It didn't take me long to know I really wanted to have the baby for you. I really wanted to give you a son. I still do."

"But not right away, I hope. We need the time together. I'm delighted with my little girl, but I want at least three days to tell you how much I love you, how much I need you."

"Cord."

"And three days isn't going to be enough time." He bent over to kiss her once more, already wanting her again. "I think," he said nibbling at an earlobe, "that you have to find out if you can dance again. Even if you decide you don't want to, you should know if you can."

Cord stroked his hand down the length of her hair.

"I want to see you dance at least once for me."

"And for Erin."

"Then I think I'm going to tear up that damned contract and we'll get married again, the right way!"

"Oh, Cord!"

"And Lee Ann will continue at the academy. She'd better be as good as they say!"

Monica wiggled in delight against him, and Cord grew taut. His hands moved over her buttocks, pressing her sensuously to him.

"Maybe next summer we'll go someplace for a honeymoon, you, me and Brig." He began to kiss her, biting at her bottom lip, rolling his tongue across the parted surface, pressing, probing, until she was breathless in anticipation.

"Maybe Europe, so I can show you those cathedrals." His voice was unsteady as they both began to open up, to give of themselves to the other. Groping, yet gentle. Urgent, yet tender. "And then we'll think about having a son." His mouth became greedy.

"But not now, or tomorrow. We have these three days before the outside world descends upon us."

"Yes," Monica agreed, yielding eagerly to him. "Oh, yes!"

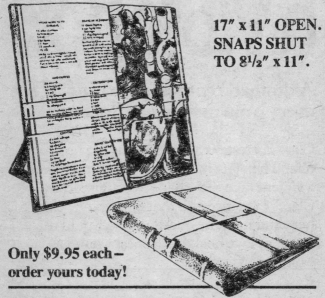